UNMASKING THE DUKE

Pleasure Garden, Book 4

Mary Lancaster

DRAGONBLADE PUBLISHING, INC.

ARE YOU SIGNED UP FOR DRAGONBLADE'S BLOG?

You'll get the latest news and information on exclusive giveaways, exclusive excerpts, coming releases, sales, free books, cover reveals and more.

Check out our complete list of authors, too!

No spam, no junk. That's a promise!

Sign Up Here

www.dragonbladepublishing.com

Dearest Reader;

Thank you for your support of a small press. At Dragonblade Publishing, we strive to bring you the highest quality Historical Romance from some of the best authors in the business. Without your support, there is no 'us', so we sincerely hope you adore these stories and find some new favorite authors along the way.

Happy Reading!

CEO, Dragonblade Publishing

The Wicked Marquis
The Wicked Governess
The Wicked Spy
The Wicked Gypsy
The Wicked Wife
Wicked Christmas (A Novella)
The Wicked Waif
The Wicked Heir
The Wicked Captain
The Wicked Sister

Unmarriageable Series
The Deserted Heart
The Sinister Heart
The Vulgar Heart
The Broken Heart
The Weary Heart
The Secret Heart
Christmas Heart

The Lyon's Den Connected World
Fed to the Lyon

De Wolfe Pack: The Series
The Wicked Wolfe
Vienna Wolfe

Also from Mary Lancaster
Madeleine

PROLOGUE

Seven Dials, London
October 1800

THE RAID CAME out of nowhere, but any fool could see it was not the magistrate's men who barged inside so suddenly. They ran immediately upstairs to the first-floor landing, where three once ornate, crumbling plaster arches gave access to different rooms, most with partially broken doors. Probably, several families lived in each.

Two men bolted out of the biggest room on the left, shouting and ready to fight. Unceremoniously, they were shoved back in.

The sounds of cracking fists and yelps of pain mingled with the rest of the chaos in the building. Children were crying, dogs barking, but curiously, no one came to the aid of their neighbor who was being robbed. A vast array of goods was quickly carried outside from the left-hand rooms—elegant furniture, porcelain vases, ornaments, gilt mirrors, silver cutlery, beautiful decorative boxes that might have contained jewels but were clearly valuable in themselves.

The neighbors who began to gather watched, wide-eyed, as the men carried their plunder out to the cart waiting below.

"He took all that from *you*, Bill?" asked the neighbor across the hall with some awe.

From his place in the middle of the big room, Bill Renwick grinned. He was a fierce-looking young fellow with a handsome if rather hard face and bright, intelligent eyes. "Mostly, Jimmie. I feel he owes me the rest for my trouble in taking it back."

At his feet lay the bully of a man who lived in the rooms and his henchman, both unconscious. The only other occupant of the apartment seemed to be a dirty child, no more than two years old, who sat on a grubby mattress, watching silently and sucking on a filthy blanket. Renwick wondered why it didn't cry.

The whole place stank, mostly of gin and tobacco, but also, more faintly, of human waste.

He scowled at the infant. "Where's its ma, Jimmie?" he asked his friend across the hall.

"Maggie? Dead these last three months or so."

The child was skin and bones, although its father was substantial enough. Worse, beneath the grime, old bruises and swollen bumps showed the unmistakable signs of not just rough handling but blows.

With a muttered curse, Renwick strode the few paces to the mattress and picked the infant up. It did smell. Its little bones felt so close to the skin they would break if he just squeezed. It did not even cry or protest when a stranger seized it, though its lower lip trembled in a way that pierced Renwick's anger with pity.

"Is it his?" he demanded.

Jimmie glanced at his Sal, who said. "She was certainly poor Maggie's." She glanced at Jimmie, then held out her arms as she walked across the landing. "Give her here, Bill. She'll do fine with our Toby and Vera."

Bill seemed about to hand the child over, then frowned again. "He'll just take her back or use it as an excuse against you. I'll take her."

"Don't be daft, Bill. She ain't a cat. What do you know about children? She needs a mother."

"Then I'll get her one. You've enough on your plate." He marched out of the room, the child held somehow incongruously in his muscular arms. He paused on the landing to gaze around the gawkers. "If I was you," he said, jerking his head back into the room he'd just left, "I'd get rid of the vermin before he wakes up. Any problem, send for me. Jimmie knows where to find me."

As he stalked off, the last of his men falling in behind him, he looked at the infant in his arms. "Sal's right," he said ruefully. "You ain't a cat." And the child, no doubt in response to the first non-angry voice to address her in at least three months, smiled at him.

And Renwick was lost.

CHAPTER ONE

October 1818

KITTY RENWICK ADJUSTED her half-face mask, so that she could see out of the eyeholes and pulled the old blue domino cloak around herself. The lady smiling back at her from the looking glass was elegant and mysterious and nothing like her mundane self. Her own uncle would not recognize her.

She hoped.

Just for good measure, she drew the hood over her smooth, auburn hair and left the empty cottage.

Immediately, the faint hum of music and laughter that she was used to hearing at a distance grew louder, and excitement drew her on.

The path leading from the cottage to the main part of the pleasure gardens was quite dark to discourage revelers from straying from the public areas, but night or day, Kitty knew the way as well as her own bedchamber, and in no time, she approached the lantern-lit path. All around the Gardens, lights twinkled on gurgling water and fairytale follies. The trees in their autumn colors looked unworldly and beautiful.

Kitty smiled in delight, for these were her precious, stolen moments when she could be anyone she wanted to be, from princess to wronged lady to fairytale creature, surrounded by beauty and chatter and laughter, and music and merriment. The Gardens were so different at night that she might never have walked these paths before.

Of course, she had, for she had lived here most of her life *and* worked here during the day, too, selling tickets, organizing plays and musicians, jugglers and fire-eaters and clowns to make the children laugh. She served drinks and ices, and meals and generally did whatever her uncle asked of her. And mostly, it was fun. Except she itched to see more.

The Gardens after dark had always been forbidden to her, even when she had grown up, although her male cousins, Rob and Dan, were not only allowed but commanded to be there. And so she was always forced to sneak out here during the public masked balls to satisfy her curiosity and her need of company. Not that she did so often, only when the loneliness grew unbearable.

And in truth, the Gardens at night were another world. Some men would look her up and down as she passed them, snatch at her if she wasn't quick enough. Others would walk beside her, talk, and make her laugh. Sometimes, she would be adopted by a happy, loud group of men and women, and she would feel, briefly, part of their happy lives. Once or twice, she had even danced with the more respectful of the men who asked, and that had been strange, though quite entertaining.

The night was cold and sharp, the black velvet sky twinkling with stars, almost like a reflection of the garden lights below. Fascinated by this idea, Kitty climbed the path toward the lily pond looking upward more than straight ahead. Only when she reached the stone steps off the path toward the pond did she bring her attention back to her feet.

The lily pond was one of her favorite areas. Hidden from the path by boulders and greenery, it felt like a secret garden, almost separate from the rest. A small waterfall tumbled from above into the pond, and from there, a stream trickled downward. In the daytime, Kitty liked to sit here and think. In her occasional evening excursions, she nearly always paused a few moments before joining the busier areas and the ballroom itself.

Tonight, it was probably too cold to linger, and as she reached the top step, her heart lurched in shock, for someone else was already there. Hastily, she dropped her foot to the step below and began to creep back down. Solitary men in under-lit and isolated parts of the Gardens were rarely safe.

This one seemed large and well-dressed, a gentleman in evening clothes wearing no domino cloak—or mask, for he twirled it idly around one finger as he gazed into the pond. He was fair and handsome in profile, and when his head turned suddenly, all the breath seemed to leave her body at once.

It's him.

He smiled, that charming, toe-curling smile that had dazzled her more than a year ago, now seemed to sweep through her like wildfire. He rose fluidly, just as if she were a lady deserving of his courtesy. He even bowed, and she wondered numbly if he ever did anything without that casual, entrancing elegance.

She had envisioned this moment so often, though not much in recent months as she had given up hope of it, and yet all she could do when faced with reality was stare at him like a great, stupid lump.

Quizzical amusement flickered across his face. "Would I be less appalling if I put on my mask? Or just got out of your way?"

"Of course not," she said fervently. "You are not appalling at all."

His lips twitched. "I shall have that inscribed on my tomb."

"You cannot be thinking of death!" she said, alarmed.

"I wasn't until your beautiful eyes shot my self-satisfaction through the heart."

"You talk nonsense," she observed, wary of being mocked. "And you can't even see my eyes in this light."

A teasing smile lurked on his sculpted lips. "I am willing to take a closer look if you would care to join me?" He crouched and held down his hand to help her up the last few steps.

She regarded that hand, smooth, elegant, well-manicured. A gentleman's hand, which only made her conscious of her own rough fingers, which she whipped behind her back. "I expect you came here to be alone."

"I am more than happy to be alone with you," he said gravely.

She frowned. "Are you flirting with me?"

There was that smile again. "Would you mind?"

"No," she admitted. "Though my uncle would."

"Then it's as well I don't want to flirt with him."

A breath of laughter escaped her, and seeing the answering gleam in his eyes, she took a deep breath and sank onto the top step. He resumed his seat on the boulder but leaned forward to face her, asking, "So what brings you to this quiet spot when there is music and dancing below?"

"It's my favorite place in the Gardens. I come here to hide, usually."

"Most people here use a mere mask for that."

"Oh, the balls are different. I shouldn't even be here."

"I am intrigued."

"You shouldn't be. It's not an interesting story. What brought *you* here?"

"I'm looking for someone."

"Oh, dear. Then I am interrupting *your* intrigue."

He smiled. "No, it is not that kind of a search."

"What other kind of search brings you away from all the people in the Gardens?"

"I was just exploring, between searches, you might say." His gaze was steadily on her face. "You know, even masked, you look vaguely familiar. Do we know each other?"

"Don't be silly." It didn't even enter her head that he would remember her from one brief encounter when all she had done was bring food and drink to his table—and plant a playing card up the sleeve of another gentleman. "You and I would never move in the same company."

"And yet here we are."

She could not help smiling at that. Here they were indeed, and in that moment, there was nowhere else in the world she would rather be.

He stretched one foot in front of him. "I am told Maida is the place to meet people of all walks of life."

"Yes, but I can't imagine you need to do so."

"Is it a question of need?" he asked, apparently surprised.

"I believe so. In gentlemen of your class."

A wicked smile crinkled the skin at the corners of his eyes. "Are you accusing me of coming here to seduce women of lower standing and of dubious morals to match my own?"

"I just said I couldn't imagine it. Though I'm not sure what other search might bring you here."

"I'm looking around. Perhaps you know the owner, Mr. Renwick."

She dragged her gaze free, examining the pond lilies instead. "I do, as it happens."

"I'm told he has a daughter."

"No, he has two sons and a niece."

"Perhaps you know the niece?"

"Why would I?" She met his gaze fiercely, knowing she should leave and yet unwilling to walk away from her first real encounter with him. "Because I am clearly of similar station?"

"You are very conscious of station," he observed.

"Aren't you?" she retorted.

"Lord, no, I don't have to be," he said flippantly. "Being so immeasurably above everyone except God and royalty, it never enters my head. Would you care to dance, my nymph? It's a cold evening for sitting still outside." He stood and brushed past her to stand on the step below where she sat.

She glanced at him fleetingly. He seemed a long way up. "I don't dance very well. I'll probably trample all over your feet."

"I might trample all over yours, though I admit mine are a bigger target."

She laughed and took his proffered hand without thought. Neither of them wore gloves, but if he noticed the roughness of her skin, he gave no sign of it, merely drew her to her feet and placed her hand in the crook of his arm as they descended the steps to the path and walked down toward the main pavilion.

Her heart beat with excitement. Was she really about to dance with him? This truly was playing with fire.

It's only a dance.

A waltz. All the dances at the Maida balls were waltzes now, and they were largely an excuse for close embracing. And she did not even know his name.

Well, at the table, the spring before last, most people had addressed him as Johnny. A few of the gentlemen had called him Fish, which she had found odd for he looked nothing like a fish. There had been so many *my lords* being flung among the company that she had never been sure if any had been addressed to him. What she did know was that he was a gentleman, a friend of the Earl and Countess of Wenning, and so far above her social stranding that a secret, masked dance with him was as close as she should get for the sake of wisdom and her own heart. For nothing in their brief encounter so far had even begun to break the nameless fascination of that afternoon last year.

She was at a loss to account for her feeling. It wasn't awe, for he was not the first gentlemen to show her kindness. For example, the Earl of Wenning himself, a tall, handsome nobleman, who had once actually lived in her uncle's barn for several nights, had been kind. He, too, had a charming smile, and yet it had never melted her bones as *his* did. Even when not directed at her, there had been something open and carefree about him, a genuine pleasure in life as well as in his company.

For some reason, this *spoke* to her, caught her attention, and held it. The fact that he had noticed her enough to take a heavy tray from her, to see her as a person and not just a servant there for his convenience… He was an unusual gentleman. She had seen that people liked him, listened to him, and she knew he had been in Lord Wenning's confidence concerning the card trick.

"You have turned very silent," he observed now.

"I was just thinking," she blurted, "wondering who you were." She glanced up to find his gaze on her face.

"Isn't that the point of masked balls? Which reminds me…" He stopped on the path, wrapping the plain, black mask around his face and wrestling with the strings.

She smiled, for somehow, his obvious difficulties with the task made him endearingly human. "Let me." She reached up, taking the silk strings and brushing his hands aside. His hair was thick and unexpectedly soft, and she had to resist the urge to run her fingers through it. Warmth radiated from his broad back. She could not help inhaling his clean, masculine scent of woodland and some subtle spice that seemed to liquify her insides.

"Thank you," he said meekly, turning to face her.

"I expect having regiments of servants to dress you puts you at a disadvantage on occasions."

"I wouldn't say that." A smile lurked in his eyes, a little more than teasing, and butterflies soared through her stomach.

Hastily, she took his arm once more and tugged him down the path. She hoped he didn't hear the breathlessness in her voice. "You still haven't told me your name."

"John Winter," he said easily. "You can call me Johnny if you like."

He was telling her the truth, which mattered in some way she was at a loss to understand, even as she breathed a sigh of relief that there was no grand title involved. It seemed to make him marginally less out of her reach.

"What do I call you?" he asked, his gaze steady, intent, and yet still teasing. It was exhilarating to be the sole center of his attention.

"Kitty," she managed.

"Just Kitty? Like the cat?"

"My uncle gave me the name because everyone thought he was only fit to bring up a cat, and he proved them wrong."

"Then your uncle adopted you?"

"He did."

"I suppose then, he is a wise uncle, trying to keep you from places like this and men like me." There was an odd ruefulness in his tone that made her glance at him again.

"Men like you," she repeated. "Are you a bad man, Johnny?"

"Sometimes. But I don't think you are—er…a bad girl, so that will probably save you."

"Save me from what?" she asked bluntly. "You?"

"I am something of a hedonist," he admitted. "And you are quite delightful."

Heat flooded her body. Even though she knew men said things like that just to get their own way.

"Because I tied your mask?" she scoffed.

He laughed. "No, though it undoubtedly helped."

As the path led them toward the pavilion, she grew ever more conscious of the long, lean body strolling along beside her. He moved with careless, unconscious grace, and yet she could feel the hard muscle of his arm. He was no mere elegant fop. His coat fit him perfectly, the material fine and soft beneath her fingers, but he wore it somehow casually, indifferent to how he was perceived. She liked that, too.

A sudden glimpse of her cousin Rob striding toward the main entrance made her reach up to make sure her hood covered her hair. It didn't, so she hastily dragged it back up.

In truth, it gave her something of an extra thrill to sail past Rob and into the pavilion on the arm of a gentleman who had just admitted, more or less, to being a rake. But mostly, she breathed a sigh of relief that Rob did not notice her, for she could not have borne to be deprived of this dance—wherever it led, and she did not want to think of that.

Besides, the music and the gaiety inside the pavilion brought their own seductive charm. He led her past two screeching women, a bashful couple, and through a throng of noisy people deciding on partners. The anonymity of masks removed many inhibitions, which was, her uncle always said, why the public masquerades were always so popular. And she had to agree. Only a mask had given her the courage to enter the pavilion before on a ball night, to accept dances with strangers.

Johnny paused at the edge of the dance floor and turned to face her. Below the mask, his mouth curved sinfully, and she could not breathe. He gave a slight bow and took her in his arms.

Heat rushed through her, and she forgot to move her feet, stumbling as he swept her into the dance. Dear God, this was not the effect of her other waltz partners, one of whom had held her rather closer than this.

"Look at me, not your feet," he advised, and that helped, for she could not look away and her feet, freed from her conscious attention, followed his from instinct. "You don't dance often enough."

"I don't," she agreed. And she suspected dancing with him would spoil her for other partners forever more. Despite their disparity in height, they seemed to fit together magically, and, somehow, she felt *graceful* in his arms. Gladness seeped through her as she relaxed into the music.

"If you expect me to be good," he said softly, "you will have to stop looking at me like that."

"Like what?"

"As if dancing with me is your sole happiness."

"I like dancing."

Laughter sparkled in his eyes. "Another shot through my self-satisfaction. I like dancing with you."

"Is that what I should have said?" she asked.

"Why no. By most customs, the gentleman makes the compliments."

"Then it's a silly custom because no one need mean anything they say."

"That is very perceptive and lamentably true in most cases. But since we are masked, I feel we might speak the truth to each other."

"You are making fun of me again."

He drew her a fraction closer. "Actually, I'm not. And I could happily dance with you all night."

"You don't feel constant waltzing might get dull or sore on the feet?"

"Not with you," he said, his eyes gleaming beneath the chandelier. "And besides, there are many dances."

Since he drew her almost against his body as he spoke, she wondered wildly if he was making suggestions she didn't understand.

"Not at Maida," she said firmly, and his breath of laughter brushed her cheek, her lips. His thigh almost touched hers as he swept her backward and around in the dance, and nothing in the world had ever been so exciting.

"No. Not at Maida," he agreed.

"And you're still flirting, aren't you?"

"It's easy to flirt with you."

"Why?" she asked, genuinely curious.

An almost arrested look came into his eyes. For an instant, his expressive mouth was quite still, and then curved into an odd half-smile. "I don't know."

It wasn't what she had expected, and she had no idea what to make of it. Perhaps fortunately, the music was coming to an end, but the idea filled her with panic. As the other dancers began to mill around, leaving the floor, exchanging partners, he did not release her.

"Another?" he asked softly.

Oh God, yes… "One more."

There were always spare musicians to spell each other and avoid any need to stop for more than a few seconds, so in no time, the chaos around them resolved into more couples, and another waltz began.

With a sigh, she glided into the dance once more. Somewhere, she knew it was more intimate than it should have been. His hip should not have brushed hers; her breast should not have been so tantalizingly close to his chest that she ached. Nor should his thumb have been caressing her wrist in sweet, seductive circles.

But it all blended into the thrill of the waltz, of being held in his arms, pinioned by his intense, smiling eyes which somehow darkened and warmed at the same time. She grew increasingly fascinated by every tiny movement of his lips as they bantered. She exulted when she brought the laughter into his eyes and thrilled to the heated glow that frequently replaced it.

Everything was so new and wonderful that this time, when the music began to draw to a close, she felt no sense of panic at all. Instead, she let him spin her off the edge of the dance floor and out one of the many doors into the cool night.

He waltzed her off the path and behind a broad elm tree that more or less hid them from view, both from the pavilion and the various paths. Slowly, his arm fell away from her waist. At the same time, he released her hand and, reaching behind her head, drew deliberately on the ribbon of her mask.

She grabbed at the falling wisp of muslin, half-stumbling back against the tree. He stepped closer and rested his palms on the bark at either side of her head. Her heart thundered, not in fear but in some desperate anticipation.

"Are you *still* flirting?" she asked unsteadily.

A smile flickered across his lips as he bent his head nearer hers. "Yes. And perhaps… just a little bit more."

His breath kissed her lips, and she gasped as though she needed to inhale him to survive. He gazed down at her, predatory and overwhelmingly masculine. There was nothing in her head, in her whole being, but *him*. And yet he waited, his gaze fixed to her lips.

"May I kiss you?" he whispered.

She couldn't speak, not with words, and so, suddenly terrified that he would take silence as refusal, she stood on tiptoe, all but closing the last of the distance between them. His lips quirked with what might have been relief, and then his mouth took hers.

CHAPTER TWO

KITTY WAS ONE and twenty years old, sociable, and curious. This was not her first kiss, but it might as well have been, for all she had to compare with it. Toby's wet, smacking kiss had made her laugh and push him away. Another, more timid friend's awkward attempt during a Christmas party at Vera's house.

There was nothing awkward about *this* kiss, nothing to make her laugh. Somewhere, she knew that Johnny was both skillful and practiced, but that didn't stop her from melting at the first touch of his mouth.

It was a silken caress, a soft sealing kiss as though given as a fitting end to their dance. God knew that was astounding enough, but when he released her lips, and she stared up at him, something changed in his eyes, a glint that was both rueful and voraciously hungry. Again, he gave her a moment to avoid it, and then he slanted his mouth across hers and kissed her with far greater abandon.

Nothing had prepared for this, for the surge of hot, heavy desire knotting in the pit of her stomach. She clutched his coat with both hands for fear of falling because he did not hold her, merely kissed with slow, invasive sensuality. In wonder, she pushed her hand up over his chest and shoulder to his cheek, and from sheer instinct, kissed him back.

It was several wild, delicious moments before he slowly

broke the kiss and raised his head.

"Well," he murmured, one hand caressing the lock of hair that had escaped from its pins. "Would you consider..." He paused as something beyond her caught his eye. "What the devil is that?" he asked in some amusement, dropping his hands at last from the tree and stepping back.

Quite naturally, he took her hand, drawing her with him as he gazed up at the vehicles lumbering along the top road toward the barn.

Still stunned by the blinding, astonishing kiss, Kitty blinked at the caravan in the distance, and reality hit her with a thud. *Oh, no...*

"Let's go and see," Johnny said, tugging her with him.

She pulled back. "What's to see in a couple of old carts?"

"At night?" His gaze came back to her, considering. Then he smiled, swung up her hand, and kissed it. "Then wait here for me if you choose. I'll only be a few minutes." He dropped her hand and loped off, his long strides eating up the ground far, far too quickly.

"Oh, the *devil!*" she muttered and hared around by the quicker route.

She did not know for certain what was in the wretched carts, but she had a pretty good idea, and Dan had no business bringing them in before the Gardens were closed. Uncle Bill would be furious when he came home, and rightly so. All she could do now was try to hide the goings-on from Johnny.

Knowing where the carts would be unloaded gave her some advantage, so she bolted through the trees, along the path to the cottage, through the gate, and across the garden to the back of the house where the barn stood.

The inside of the barn was lit by several lanterns, though not so many as to draw too much attention from the Gardens. But there was no sign of the carts or Johnny, and just for a moment, she thought she might be in time to prevent disaster.

Only then, through the sound of her ragged breathing, she

heard voices drifting out through the open doors, along with various bumps and dragging sounds. Of course, the carts were farther inside the barn than she could see, ready for unloading. If she simply closed the doors, Johnny would see nothing.

With this in mind, she hurried forward. The barn was a hive of activity, with crates and barrels being unloaded from the carts and stacked against the walls. The horses were happily munching the hay from the floor. Dan and Cousin Pete were the only men present she recognized. Although she had seen a couple of the others with her uncle from time to time, they had never been introduced to her, which told her a good deal.

She grasped the edge of the door, but before she could move it, she caught sight of Johnny, standing to one side, masked and elegant, lounging casually against one wall to observe the activity. Her heart plunged.

Her one hope was to drag him out of there, telling him it was just a delivery and, surely, he would rather dance than watch anything so dull. But she had not taken more than a step before one of the strangers growled, "Who in hell is *that?*"

Kitty froze. Everyone in the barn stopped working to turn and stare at the interloper.

Johnny, finding himself suddenly the center of attention, straightened and casually inclined his head as though he'd just arrived at his club or somewhere equally innocuous.

"Good evening, gentlemen," he said amiably, strolling forward—*instead of backward and out the door,* Kitty thought furiously. "Forgive the intrusion, but what on earth are you doing?"

What on earth are you doing?

Loads were abandoned, directions changed. Everyone advanced toward Johnny, who seemed careless of the danger, although he moved no further inside.

"Whatever it is," Johnny observed when he received no answer, "I can't imagine Mr. Renwick would approve."

It gave them pause—because, in fact, Johnny was quite

right—but only for a moment.

"Get him," growled one of the smugglers, and as they swarmed toward him, Kitty, who had been creeping nearer, reached out to seize Johnny by the hand.

Before she could grab him, someone buffeted against her, shoving her out of the way to get at Johnny from behind. Only someone was before him. Recovering her balance, she saw a different brawny stranger lunge at Johnny, who took everyone by surprise by sidestepping his attacker and bringing him down with one swift kick behind the knees. Almost at the same time, his fist sent the next man flying into his fellows, and he spun just in time to block on his arm the massive blow coming from the man behind. He even managed to get in a punch of his own before his eyes suddenly found Kitty, who was staring at him, both frightened and astonished. Somehow, she had never imagined he could, or would, fight.

It was the tiniest instant of inattention on his part, and in truth, it could hardly have made any difference to the end result. He was seized by several men at once while the one facing him drew back his fists.

"No!" Kitty snapped, pushing past to stand with her hands on her hips, glaring at him, her back to Johnny. "What do you think you're doing, imbecile?"

The man blinked, scowled in bafflement, and looked wildly around him for support or at least explanation.

"Kitty?" came Dan's stunned voice. "What the devil are you doing here?"

Kitty swung around to face him, carefully avoiding Johnny's gaze although she knew he still struggled in the grip of several men.

"What am I doing here?" she raged. "What are *you* doing? While the Gardens are full of people? You must *all* be fools! Especially as you seem to be about to add assault—if not murder!—of guests to your idiocy."

"Don't be silly," Dan said uneasily. "We're not going to hurt him."

"You could have fooled me."

"Be reasonable, Kit. We can't let him go until they're clear away," Pete said reasonably, waving one hand to encompass the strangers, horses, and carts.

And then what? she wondered, feeling sick to her stomach. *You'll let him go to inform on you?* Neither Pete nor Dan were men of violence, but she could not say the same for the other ruffians. And her cousins might just be afraid enough of Uncle Bill to be persuaded to turn a blind eye.

Oh, God, how did I let him get into this…?

"In any case, you've no business here," Dan said severely. Since he had been brought up with her, he was always more likely to order her around like a brother. "You shouldn't even be out of the house."

"How could I help hearing this racket?" she retorted.

"Well, you're here now, so fetch some rope and tie him up while we get this done."

Are you insane? We can't go around tying up guests! Certainly not gentlemen guests… On the other hand, if she tied him up, it might stop the others from hurting him as a warning, or even killing him.

Without a word, she stalked to the shelf to find the various lengths of rope used for hauling and other purposes. By the time she marched back to the prisoner, who was watching her from heavy-lidded eyes without noticeable anger, he was being held at pistol point by only one stranger while everyone else, including Dan and Pete, finished unloading the carts.

The smuggler might give her the pistol if she asked. She could then tell Johnny to run. Only how long would it take one of the men to wrestle the weapon from her again? Of course, they should not be risking a firearms explosion with a ball in full swing, but then, they shouldn't be taking delivery of smuggled goods at such a time either.

"Put your hands behind your back," she told Johnny without

looking at him. She moved behind him, which was easier, except that he didn't do as he was told. She had a feeling he was smiling at the man with the pistol, who promptly cocked it.

"Watch what you're doing with that thing," Kitty snapped as she snatched one of Johnny's hands, and looped the rope around his wrist several times. She gathered the other and did the same, pulling the knot tight enough to be difficult but not cut into his wrists unless he strained.

Then she stood deliberately between Johnny and the pistol. "Sit down, if you please."

When he did not at once comply, she raised her eyes to his face, wondering desperately how to make him do it before the man behind her just shot him, or at least hit him with the pistol butt.

For some reason, in the midst of this disaster, it broke her heart that his once open, sunny gaze was now unreadable as it met hers. She opened her mouth to plead, but then, to her amazement, he lowered himself wordlessly to the straw-strewn floor, his back against the wall.

She knelt and bound his feet together without looking up.

By the time she had finished, the man with the pistol had vanished.

"*Et tu, Brute*," Johnny murmured.

"I haven't betrayed you yet," she muttered. "But don't tempt me. What the devil are you doing here?"

"I just followed my nose."

She met his gaze. "I don't mean the barn, although surely no one's stupid enough to have deliberately walked into this without a reason. I mean Maida Gardens."

She might have surprised him, for something glinted in his eyes, then changed into almost appreciative amusement. "There is more to you than mere beauty, is there not?"

"Oh, there's more to everyone," she said pointedly. "Why did you really come here, alone, poking around, asking about the Renwicks, following the carts? Truthfully."

His lips curved slightly. "Truthfully? I was thinking of investing in your uncle's hotel."

She closed her eyes. From the high point of the waltz and the kiss—*don't think about the kiss, don't dare!*—the evening was plunging ever deeper into disaster. Uncle Bill desperately needed further investment to build the rest of his hotel, and there was no way he would get it from this wealthy gentleman, not after he had stumbled onto a delivery of smuggled goods and was offered violence and imprisonment by the Renwicks and their associates. And if he told his friends…

"Another reason to shoot me," Johnny murmured, just as if he was following her train of thought.

"I'll shoot you later," she said, rising abruptly to her feet. "Don't make me gag you first."

One of the unloaded carts was pulling out of the barn. Kitty crossed behind it toward the shelves, and while money was changing from Dan's hands to the chief smuggler's, she picked up the sheathed knife used for cutting rope and hid it beneath her domino cloak.

"Pete, make sure they get off without trouble," Dan said as the strangers leapt onto the remaining two carts. "I'd better go and see all's well with Rob at the pavilion. You," he barked, spinning to point at Johnny. "Stay there. Watch him till I come back, Kitty."

Kitty nodded, and while she observed the carts leaving, followed by Pete and Dan, she walked slowly back toward Johnny, unsheathing the wicked-looking knife as soon as Dan was out of sight.

She turned her attention to Johnny, who sat very still, gazing steadily at the knife. Only when she knelt in front of him did he shift his eyes to her face. She sliced through the bonds at his ankles, then moved to do the same at his wrists, being careful not to cut his skin.

Then she rose and hurried to the back of the barn, unbolting the small, half-hidden door. She turned impatiently to find him on his feet but unmoving.

"Hurry up," she commanded. "They'll be back any moment. Jump the fence behind and follow the path."

He strode toward her, then, frowning. "You will be in trouble for this."

"Oh, we're all in trouble for this," she assured him. "Less if you can bring yourself to be silent, but you owe us nothing."

His frown deepened. He stood irresolutely, gazing down at her. "Come with me," he said abruptly.

She blinked, astonished and not a little shocked until she realized he really thought she would be in danger. She laughed. "That really is beyond flirting. Don't be silly. No one will hurt me. Go."

A smile flickered. Unexpectedly, he brushed his knuckles across her cheek and slipped out the door, which she bolted behind him. Then she sheathed the knife, put it back on the shelf, and walked out of the barn. She even closed the main doors before walking down the path back to the cottage.

CHAPTER THREE

John Winter, the fourth Duke of Dearham, strolled into his solicitor's office and smiled amiably at the clerk, who sprang to his feet.

"Good morning, Mr. Andrews. Is he in?"

"Yes, Your Grace. Allow me to just…" Andrews shot across the floor to the inner office, hoping for once to beat the duke, but His Grace, as usual, merely strolled past him.

"Morning, Dunne. Got a moment?"

Ludovic Dunne, who, these days, probably wouldn't have troubled to hide it if he were annoyed, smiled sardonically and rose, indicating the other chair. "Thank you, Andrews," he said resignedly, and the clerk effaced himself.

Johnny didn't shake hands since he had seen Dunne only yesterday. Instead, he lounged into the offered chair, laid his hat across the papers on the desk, and said, "I went to Maida last night."

Dunne's dark eyebrows, a distinctive contrast to his silvery fair hair, rose. "I told you she is never there in the evenings. Renwick takes too good care of her."

"She was there. She sneaks and mingles in disguise."

"So you met her? Did you tell her?"

"Lord, no." Johnny gazed thoughtfully at his gloves, then allowed himself a rueful smile. "She is rather delightful, but I have to say, I see no family resemblance. Which may be as well, for I'm not sure I care to deal with *her* family."

"Then you don't wish to pursue it?"

Johnny, who had no objections whatever to pursuing Kitty, murmured, "I didn't say that. Tell me more about Renwick."

"He's an old villain, though his income is largely legal these days. I still wouldn't play cards with him."

Johnny smiled involuntarily. "I wouldn't play cards with Kitty either. I once saw her plant an ace in a man's sleeve so fast I thought I'd imagined it."

"I thought you'd never met her."

"So did I until last night. I'd forgotten. Anyway, I have my doubts about the legality of Renwick's current business dealings. He was quite clearly receiving stolen or smuggled goods last night."

"So, whatever the truth of Kitty's birth, you wouldn't invest in his hotel?"

"Certainly not without letting you and your brother loose on his books."

Dunne sat back, watching him. "What have you really come to ask me?"

Johnny sat up. "Come to Maida with me this afternoon."

"Why?"

"I'd appreciate the introduction. Renwick will have no reason to trust me after last night."

Dunne sighed. "What happened?"

"I walked in on their delivery. Renwick wasn't there, but I suspect two of his sons were."

One of the things Johnny liked about the lawyer who had become his friend was that he rarely had to explain the obvious. Or even the slightly obfuscated.

"Then I should go, and you should stay well away until Renwick is made aware—"

"I can't," Johnny interrupted. He smiled apologetically. "I need to be sure the girl is well. She let me go."

"Ah." Dunne fixed him with his over-perceptive stare. "Renwick wouldn't hurt a hair on her head."

"Would his sons?" Johnny interrupted.

"I don't know the sons, but I can't imagine them putting themselves in the way of Renwick's wrath. Let me go and find out for you."

"No."

Dunne blinked.

Johnny stood up. "Come on. I'll treat you to lunch at my club first."

※

"AND YOU'VE NO idea who he is?" Vera said, sounding almost as intrigued as Kitty.

"I know he's a gentleman and a friend of the Earl of Wenning. Beyond that, no." Kitty had spent the morning with her friend, who lived with her parents in a rather pleasant set of rooms in Seven Dials. The area was poor and rough, but Vera's folks lived well and honestly, thanks to her father's building works. He had repaired this building outside and in, and since Kitty's childhood, had expanded his own dwelling into two other rooms. In fact, he part-owned the whole building now.

"Goodness," Vera said, gratifyingly impressed. "Don't you move in exalted circles these days!"

Kitty laughed. "Well, I get to glance into them every so often. Like when Lord Wenning lived in our barn, or the odd party of nobs deigns to visit the Gardens to see how the lower orders enjoy themselves."

"Is that why your Johnny was there?"

Kitty frowned. "He *said* he was there because he'd thought of investing in the new hotel."

"But you don't believe him?"

"Why would a man like that flirt with me to find out about

my uncle's business?"

"If he kissed you, he did rather more than flirt," Vera said flatly.

Kitty flushed. "So, I have even less reason to trust him."

"Maybe," Vera agreed. "Or maybe he just liked you, quite apart from his business interests."

Kitty regarded her friend, who was raven-haired, curvaceous, and rather spectacularly beautiful, with all the self-confident poise such looks could bring. "He could have any woman he wants. Why would he look at me?"

"He would look," Vera said, with the certainty of a friend. "But unless he's an idiot, he wouldn't touch Bill Renwick's niece. Of course, being a nob, he probably doesn't know much about Bill Renwick. Anyway, did Dan know you let him go?"

"The ropes were cut, so yes. He tried to tell me off until I demanded what he'd planned to do with his prisoner and if he imagined he could hide it from Uncle Bill along with the fact he'd received the smuggled goods too early in the evening. I also told him he was an idiot for attacking Johnny in the first place, and what he should have done was just say it was a late delivery and leave it at that. Now Johnny knows they were up to no good."

"Will he tell?"

"I'm sure Uncle Bill can talk himself out of any trouble."

"You don't sound very pleased about it," Vera remarked.

"Oh, I'm pleased about *that*."

"But you'd like to see this Johnny again. Gentlemen aren't for the likes of us, Kitty. Not unless you're prepared to do it all without the wedding ring, and there's no security in that. Besides, there's your uncle and your cousins."

"Vera!" Kitty protested. "I'm not planning on marriage or anything else! Unlike you."

Vera smiled, her eyes softening. "Was Luke at the building site when you left?"

"Yes. We waved to each other."

Kitty liked Luke. He was clever, amiable, and hard-working

and not remotely the sort of young man anyone expected Vera to set her heart on. For she was beautiful and charming enough to win anyone, including the wealthiest of established tradesmen, merchants, or bankers. Instead, she had fallen for the young architect who worked for her father and refused to be budged by her parents' disapproval of the match.

"What will you do if your parents keep refusing to let you marry Luke?" Kitty asked.

"Marry him anyway. I'm one and twenty. I don't need their permission."

"But you do need Luke's job," Kitty reminded her.

Vera smiled mischievously. "And Dad needs Luke. Luke's the one more likely to end that association when he's offered a better-paid position elsewhere. He'll come round, trust me. It's not even as if they don't like Luke. They just think I should marry someone richer."

"I would be surprised if Luke didn't *get* rich," Kitty mused.

"There, you do think beyond the moment," Vera said with a grin, just as the door to the parlor opened and her brother Toby came in with Kitty's cousin Rob.

"Ready to go, Kit?" Rob said. "I've got everything loaded, so we'd better not leave it for long."

"Stay if you like," Toby offered, his gaze too warm as it rested it on Kitty. "I'll drive you back out to Maida later."

"Thanks, Toby, but I have things to do," Kitty said hurriedly, for Toby's new attitude to her made her distinctly uncomfortable.

She jumped up, seizing her hat and cloak, hugged Vera, and ran after Rob, praying Toby wouldn't follow to hand her up to the cart. The last time he had done so, he'd contrived to brush against her and held her hand too long in his clammy fingers.

As it happened, both Vera and Toby came down to wave them off, but by then, Kitty had jumped up beside Rob, unaided, and there was nothing to do but call goodbye and wave.

It took the usual age to crawl through central London, even using back roads, but eventually, past Hyde Park, Rob relaxed enough to talk.

"You avoid Toby these days."

"He makes me uncomfortable," Kitty confessed.

"Because he admires you?"

"Because he seems to. He never says anything but—"

"Would you like him to?" Rob asked bluntly.

"No! Absolutely not. I'm avoiding him until he grows out of it."

Rob was silent a few moments. "You could do worse, Kitty. You're one and twenty, and Toby will inherit his dad's building works."

"I'm afraid it wouldn't matter if he inherited the crown," Kitty said frankly. "He and I would not suit."

"You could give him a chance."

She glanced at Rob. "Did he ask you to speak to me?"

"Yes," Rob admitted. "He's an old friend, Kit."

She thought about that. "I preferred him when we were children. Now he leers, and I'm not convinced he doesn't leer at every female under thirty."

"He's not considering marriage to the others."

"I doubt he's considering marriage to me either. He might be considering marriage to Bill Renwick's niece, but—"

"Dad's not so flush as all that. The Gardens cost an arm and a leg to maintain, and this hotel is not cheap to build, though it may make our fortune later."

Kitty considered. "I don't think it's just the money with Toby. I think he likes Uncle's...power. You don't *really* want me to marry him, do you?"

"No, you'd shab off to the city with him," Rob teased, "and work would double for Dan and me. Talking of Dan, what the devil was he about last night?"

Kitty groaned. "You don't want to know. Does Uncle?"

"I don't fancy Dan's chances of keeping it from him. Dan is an idiot. He just wanted the delivery done early so that he could take that new waitress home instead. I suppose I'll have to keep a closer eye on him," he added gloomily.

The idea didn't enter Rob's head any more than it entered Kitty's, just to dump the problem with Uncle Bill. They had always covered for each other without involving higher authorities. Although, as Rob pointed out, there was rarely any point, for Bill Renwick generally found out in any case.

So, she wasn't terribly surprised when, with the cart halted at the cottage back door, Uncle Bill wandered out to greet them. He was wearing his hat, so, clearly, he was headed for the Gardens, no doubt on his "rounds."

"Did you get everything?"

"We think so," Rob said laconically.

Uncle Bill nodded. "Good. Walk with me, Kitty."

Kitty, who'd just jumped down, exchanged rueful looks with Rob and trotted along beside her uncle.

"You were out of the house last night."

She sighed. Found out at last. "I was. Sorry."

"Why?"

"Honestly? I was bored and lonely, and I could hear the music. I wanted to dance."

Uncle Bill cast her a not unkind glance. "You don't get much fun here, do you? I keep you too close because I know how bad a place the world can be. And God knows we get all sorts here in the evenings. Hmm…how would it be if we got up a party with Vera and her mother, and you can actually go *safely* to one of the balls?"

Kitty realized her jaw was dropping and hastily closed her mouth and swallowed. "You'd let me do that?"

"If you're going to do it, I want it to be properly. Did you help Dan in that lunacy last night?"

"No, Uncle."

"I hope not," Uncle Bill growled, "because if I have the law crawling all over here again…"

Kitty stopped listening, for they were approaching the rose garden, where drinks and ices were served outside in the summer. For the chillier months, a small marquee was set up to provide shelter from wind and rain. Since it was a pleasant day, the sides of the marquee had been rolled up, giving Kitty an excellent view of a tall, broad, well-dressed back in a blue coat and a shock of thick, dark blond hair.

No. It can't be. Not twice in two days…

The fair man turned to his companion, and her heart lurched before seeming to stop altogether. It was Johnny, half-smiling as he listened to something said by the man sharing his table.

Kitty clutched her uncle's arm but tried desperately to keep her voice casual. "Uncle Bill, do you know who *that* man is?"

"Ludovic Blasted Dunne," her uncle said with a hint of bitterness. "If ever a man was put on this earth to cause bother…"

"Oh, I know *him*," Kitty interrupted, recognizing Johnny's companion. "But what of the man with him?"

Uncle Bill's eyes narrowed. He flung a suspicious glance at her. "Everyone knows who *he* is. That, my dear, is His Grace, the Duke of Dearham."

A duke? Oh, dear God…

"And you are to have *nothing* to do with him," Uncle Bill added sternly.

"Why not?" Kitty asked, intrigued in spite of herself.

"Because he's a damned rake," growled Uncle Bill.

As if she couldn't have worked that out for herself. He had told her as much last night, and flirting had seemed as natural to him as breathing.

"Anyway, I've said my piece," Uncle Bill added. "You'd better run along and sort out the provisions you and Rob brought from…"

Again, he broke off for both Mr. Dunne and Johnny—His Grace—rose to their feet, pushing back their chairs. Kitty, who should have fled on her uncle's instructions, found herself rooted to the spot by Johnny's enigmatic gaze. Why had she ever thought it open?"

Mr. Dunne ducked out of the pavilion, quickly closing the

space between them. He inclined his head. "Mr. Renwick. Miss Kitty."

"Mr. Dunne. What can I do for you? Kitty, run along now."

"If we might beg the favor of Miss Kitty's company, too? This concerns her."

Uncle Bill went very still. "Does it, by God?" he said with dangerous softness.

"Yes, but in no way that is an insult or a danger to her or to you," Mr. Dunne said evenly. "Please, hear us out."

For an instant, it hung in the balance, and then, for the first time ever, Uncle Bill placed her hand in the crook of his arm and walked with dignity into the pavilion, where the duke awaited.

He still stood by the table, which now boasted four chairs around it, and accorded them a small bow. Kitty bobbed a quick curtsey, forcing herself to meet his amiable gaze. She frowned deliberately and flicked her gaze toward Uncle Bill, hoping he would understand the need for silence.

His lips quirked, but beyond that, he gave no sign of compre-hending the gravity. Or perhaps he did. Was it not ominous he was with Ludovic Dunne, a lawyer?

"Your Grace," Mr. Dunne said, "allow me to present Miss Renwick and her uncle, Mr. Renwick, who, as you know, is the owner of Maida Gardens. And this is His Grace, the Duke of Dearham. Shall we sit?"

Under Uncle Bill's fierce stare, the duke held a chair for Kitty, just as if she were a great lady, and sat beside her. Uncle Bill sat on her other side and said, "It's getting to a busy time for us, gentlemen, so I must ask you to be brief."

One had to admire Uncle Bill. He seemed not remotely awed by the presence of such a high-ranking nobleman.

A pot of tea, three mugs of ale, and a bowl of flavored ices appeared on the table—brought, oddly enough, by Dan's waitress. When the ices were placed in front of her, she began to feel like a child being treated by the adults. Still, they were very good. She picked up her spoon.

Mr. Dunne said, "The matter is delicate. Several months ago, His Grace instructed me to find a lost member of his family, the child of a distant cousin who—er... fell on hard times but gave birth to a child before she died. It has not been an easy task, retracing the movements of this lady, let alone that of her child. I won't bore you with the details of my search, but eventually, I did find the last known address of the duke's cousin."

Kitty and her uncle looked at him expectantly. From the corner of her eye, the duke appeared to be looking at Kitty.

"A building," Mr. Dunne continued, "in Taverner Street, in Seven Dials."

Kitty paused, with her second spoonful of ice halfway to her mouth. "We have friends who live there."

"Yes, we do," Uncle Bill agreed. "But what of any of this is to do with us?"

"Miss Kitty is your niece, but not the child of your only sibling," Mr. Dunne said bluntly. "Or, at least, not that I can discover."

Uncle Bill took a draught of ale and sat back, his fingers curled casually around the handle. "I don't doubt your ability to nose out what's there. Truth is, she ain't my niece."

Kitty dropped her spoon. "I'm not?"

"No, I adopted you when your mother died. She lived in Taverner Street. She and Sal Harris were friends, lived across the landing from each other. Sal and Jimmie would have taken you in, but they already had two nippers, and Jimmie wasn't as flush then as he is now. Besides, I took a shine to you."

This took some getting used to. Kitty had assumed she was an illegitimate niece, or perhaps even Bill's own illegitimate daughter. Though Bill's wife, Aunty Mary, had always treated her as her own.

Instead, she wasn't related to any of them. It made her feel suddenly...adrift.

Bill's hand closed over hers on the table, squeezing almost fiercely. "Chosen family is best, and you've been more than any daughter to me. Rob and Dan ain't mine by birth either. They were Mary's sons, by her late husband, but they're mine in any way that matters, and so are you." He glared at Mr. Dunne. "Did you have to bring that up now before my girl?"

"Well, yes, we did," Mr. Dunne said apologetically.

"You're barking up the wrong tree, gentlemen. Kitty's mother weren't no duke's cousin, however distant."

"What was her name?" the duke asked, speaking for the first time since they had arrived.

Uncle Bill regarded him warily. "Maggie."

"My cousin's name," said His Grace, "was Margaret."

CHAPTER FOUR

JOHNNY HAD GONE along with Dunne's way of doing things because it made sense. It was important to see the reactions of Kitty or her family to this news, for, after all, playing a duke's cousin was a tempting prospect. But it hadn't entered his head, watching with secret, erotic pleasure as she enjoyed her ice cream, that Kitty would not know the story her uncle produced, that it would bring about that sudden, lost look of an abandoned child.

For the first time, he felt a complete scoundrel, as her uncle, not Johnny, comforted her with what was surely genuine anxiety.

"Margaret?" Renwick repeated with derision. "Maggie, Meg, Madge, and God knows how many other pet names. Got at least two of them working for me. Not exactly uncommon, is it?"

"That's true," Johnny agreed. "My own sister is called Margaret. Still, you must allow the coincidence to be great, to find a child of the right age, at the right address, with a mother called Margaret."

"Yes, well, much as I'd love to be on family terms with the likes of you, that Maggie weren't no lady. We're no gentlefolk neither, and no wish to be so."

Kitty was staring into her ice. Johnny poured a cup of tea, added a spoonful of honey, and pushed it toward her. She looked up at him blankly.

"You seem very certain, Mr. Renwick," Dunne observed.

"I am," Renwick stated.

Kitty blinked and picked up her tea. After sipping, she returned to the ice.

"If you don't believe me, go and talk to Jimmie and Sal. They'll tell you the same."

"What, that you never met Maggie?" Dunne said mildly. "That she died three months before you adopted Kitty?"

Renwick's hand slid away from Kitty's, and he rose to his feet. "A word, Mr. Dunne," he said pleasantly.

Dunne politely excused himself, and the two men walked out of the tent. Johnny dragged his gaze away from Kitty's lips savoring the ice, trying to look into her averted eyes.

"What about you, Miss Renwick?" he said. "Do you believe such a thing is possible?"

"That I'm your long-lost cousin?" she said derisively. "Of course not. I'm only surprised you'd pursue such a connection, rightly or wrongly. You can't *want* a cousin from the slums of Seven Dials or from Maida Gardens."

His lips quirked. "Why would you think that?"

He hadn't meant to flirt, but she seemed to take it that way. Her skin—soft, flawless skin, as he knew—flushed, and there was a faintly outraged expression in her beautiful blue eyes. He didn't blame her. This was not the time or the place.

"None of us can help where we're born, Kitty."

She lifted her chin. "All free and equal? What a very egalitarian sentiment for a duke."

"And what an educated vocabulary for a girl from Seven Dials. Or even Maida Gardens."

Her flush deepened. "I went to school. I can read."

She was full of surprises, this tempting creature who might or might not be distantly related to him. "What do you like to read?" he asked.

She blinked as though taken aback by the question. A tiny droplet of melted raspberry ice clung to the corner of her mouth.

"Whatever I can find."

He took his clean handkerchief from his pocket. "Novels? Books of travel? Philosophy? Science?"

"Not science, but—" She broke off, flinching back as he reached over to her mouth.

"But what?" he said, pretending to be unperturbed by her reaction. But he didn't like it, not when she had melted into his arms last night and kissed him so sweetly. Of course, that was before he had found her cousins with a crew of reprobate smugglers or thieves or whatever they were, and she had efficiently tied him up. Before he had told her she might be related to his noble family.

He paused for only an instant, then brushed the handkerchief across the corner of her mouth and sat back.

"A cousinly gesture," he assured her.

"I'm not your cousin."

"You might be. Would it be so very terrible? After all, the relationship is not close."

Kitty frowned at him. "Then why do you care? What do you want with her daughter, whoever she is?"

"It was a guilt inherited by my father from his father and kindly passed on me. I'm not a very responsible duke, but I thought this was one wrong I could manage to right."

"What wrong? If no one knew where to find her—"

"No one tried," Johnny said. "My grandfather forbade it, and everyone obeyed. Even though she had lived in his household for several years, as companion to his wife, the duchess."

A frown tugged at her brow, but Renwick and Dunne were returning, so he said, "We can at least be friends, can we not?"

She met his gaze. "We are not friends. Friends don't lie. You came to Maida last night to look me over."

"I came to meet you," he corrected.

"You pretended otherwise," she said starkly and stood up. Her curtsey was small and cold and, for some reason, cut him to pieces. "Good day, Your Grace."

Renwick nodded curtly and somewhat suspiciously and then walked away beside Kitty.

Johnny sighed and threw some coins on the table. "Shall we go?"

"By all means," Ludovic said. "Rebecca is coming up from the country and should be here by teatime."

"Give her my regards. I hope she feels free to invite me to dinner."

"Are you not bound soon for Dearham Abbey?"

"I will be, when I've seen Meg and Harry." He frowned as they walked down the main path toward the gate. "What did Renwick say to you?"

"He told me to stop upsetting his niece."

"Did you apologize?"

"Yes, though I upset him instead by reminding him—as he knew I would—that there was something of a riot in that particular building in Taverner Street around the time he adopted Kitty. And that a man vanished shortly after—Maggie's lover, if not Kitty's father."

"And you know this because...?"

"His friend Jimmie told Napper."

Johnny absorbed this. Only when they sat in his comfortable town carriage did he say abruptly, "She didn't know anything about that. The idea that she's related to me took her completely by surprise."

"Not sure it surprised Renwick, though," Dunne replied. "He knows more than he's saying."

"Then you still think it's possible?"

"Don't you?"

"The coincidences would seem too many," Johnny said slowly. "And she's been educated above her station. She even speaks better than her cousins."

"Meaning you could turn her into a lady if you wanted to?"

"If it was the right thing to do," Johnny said. He became gradually aware of Dunne's amused expression. "What?"

"Nothing. Just…for one tiny moment, you sounded almost *responsible*."

"Ha," said Johnny derisively. "Tell that to my mother."

"IS IT TRUE?" Kitty asked abruptly.

Uncle Bill, apparently forgetting about his "rounds," was walking beside her back toward the cottage. "It's true you're no blood relation, that I adopted you from Jimmie's neighbor in Seven Dials. But you're no more the duke's cousin than I am." He cast her a quick look. "Are you disappointed?"

She shook her head. "No, I'm just wondering how you can be so sure. They seemed to know an awful lot, and that Mr. Dunne—you've said yourself he's too damned smart."

"Watch your language, girl. There's no need to repeat my careless talk. Yes, Dunne is smart, and he's clearly done a lot of digging. He knows more than I thought anyone would find out. But the thing is, I know more."

She stared at the ground as she walked, then up at the clouds.

"You don't believe me?" Uncle Bill asked.

Again, she shook her head. "I believe you. Of course, I do. I'm just wondering why you never told me any of this before."

He sighed and put his arm around her in a quick, rough hug. "Because I didn't want to see that look on your face. A family's about more than blood. Doesn't matter to me whether you were born to my Mary, your Aunt Jane, or someone I never met. I'll tell you something else. You know how I felt for my Mary, but when I first married her, taking on Rob and Dan with her, it was to give you a mother who could bring you up better than I could. And now you're all my kids. Never forget that."

Kitty took his arm and gave it a squeeze. He was right, of course. Whoever had given birth to her made no difference to her life. *This* was her family, her home, and she would never want another. Certainly not some grand, draughty palace full of servants snootier than Aunt Jane with her "going-to-church" face, and great lords and ladies wearing a king's ransom on their backs and their noses held up in order to look down them at her. People who despised her or resented her.

Such a life held no warmth, no attraction. She was not sorry to be unrelated to the duke. Especially not, she told herself as his handsome face swam into her mind, when he had lied to her about his reasons for being at the masked ball. But...he had been sure enough to seek her out, not just at the ball, but this afternoon, with his very sharp solicitor in tow.

She could not help wondering if, on this particular occasion, Uncle Bill might be wrong. That he didn't *want* the duke to be right, in case it broke up his family. She didn't mind if that was true. It was the kind of lie she could live with.

⇥⟫⟫⟩⟨⟨⟨⇤

THE NEXT MORNING, as Kitty fed the hens, Vera appeared at the back garden gate.

"You ever thought about being a farmer's wife?" Vera teased.

Kitty laughed, tossed the rest of the feed in a heap, and went to meet her friend. "What are you doing here so early?"

"I came with Luke, and I'll go back with him, so rejoice. I can spend most of the day with you."

"Behold me speechless with pleasure. Not least because you were allowed to come with Luke. That is surely good progress."

"It would be if my parents knew," Vera said carelessly. "Don't lecture me. I left a message." She looked up the track toward the new building which was growing above the trees on the hill. "It's coming on, isn't it?"

"It is. Wouldn't it be good if it made Luke famous?"

"It would, providing he didn't forget me."

Vera's odd little vulnerabilities, rare but genuine, always took

Kitty by surprise. She nudged her friend over the fence. "Don't be silly. You're not exactly forgettable. Come and help me set up the garden for the lunchtime concert."

"Concert? Surely people won't sit still to listen in this cold!"

"It will be warmer by lunchtime," Kitty assured her as they walked. "Rain is more of a problem, but we have a little band-stand for the performers and a marquee for the audience. But most people wander about, stop to listen for five minutes, and then go off to watch the magician or the stilt-walkers."

"True. I think we should take Luke when he stops for mid-day."

"You can. Sadly, I have to work."

"He's a slave driver, your Uncle Bill."

"Hardly that!"

Vera sniffed to concede the point, though she immediately added, "You want to get your hooks into your masked gentleman and become a lady of leisure."

"Oh, Vera, you'll never guess who he is," Kitty said, suddenly overwhelmed once more.

Vera's eyes widened. "He's been back? For you? Goodness, who is he?"

"He's the Duke of Dearham, who apparently has a shocking reputation."

"But a delicious one," Vera interjected, clearly impressed. "Well, if he's coming here to meet you twice in two days—"

"He isn't," Kitty said flatly. "Or at least, not in the way you mean. He's got it into his head that I'm some sort of lost cousin."

Vera stopped and stared at her. "Stone the crows!"

"Oh, don't be too impressed. I'm not. But that's why he came. Both times."

A martial light flickered in Vera's gaze and vanished into a frown. "That doesn't make sense. What's he kissing you for if he thinks you're his long-lost cousin?"

"I'm not."

"No, but that's why he came in the first place. Only you

caught his attention and stole his heart, and he forgot himself."

Kitty couldn't help laughing, although a tiny pain had formed in her chest. "Don't be ridiculous. Wait until he meets *you*."

"Ah, but I'm spoken for."

"So is he, probably."

"No. The Society papers keep speculating on his prospective brides, especially since he inherited the dukedom, but he always avoids the marriage traps. Still sowing his wild oats, as they say, so you'd better be careful not to catch any."

"I have no idea what you're talking about," Kitty said with mock dignity.

Vera grinned. "That's my duchess."

VERA ENJOYED A very pleasant day with her friend and a special hour with her swain listening to very refined music and watching less refined jugglers and stilt-walkers before he went back to work. As a result, she was shining with happiness when Luke dropped her in Taverner Street with no more than a kiss to her hand.

She touched his hair, smiling tenderly. "Thank you for today, Luke."

"Thank me if your father doesn't forbid me the house and dismiss me for this day's work!"

She laughed and ran inside, where her mother stood with folded arms.

"Don't say a word," Vera commanded. "He was working most of the time, but I got to see him on the ride there and back and for an hour at midday. Even if you lock me in my room, it was worth it."

"Don't be dramatic, Vere," her mother said mildly.

"Besides," Vera said, dragging her mother upstairs, "I saw Kitty, too, and you'll never guess what's been happening with her!"

"She has a suitor?" her mother asked.

"Who has?" Toby demanded from the landing.

"Kitty, though not really. But this duke thinks she's related to him and has set the cat amongst the pigeons." For the sake of her brother's pride, she didn't add that Kitty rather liked the said duke.

Toby began to laugh derisively as he walked into their own rooms. "Bill Renwick related to a duke? Don't make me laugh."

"Not Bill," Vera informed him. "Just Kitty. She's not Bill's niece by blood. She's adopted. Did you know that, Ma?"

Her mother sighed. "Yes, I did know that." She shut the door firmly. "What duke?"

"Dearham."

Toby whistled. "Rich as Croesus, then."

"Yes, but Bill says it ain't true."

"It isn't," her mother said mildly. "Does Kitty want it to be true?"

"No. She's devoted to Bill and the boys." Though she clearly wished the duke liked her for herself rather than her possible blood line.

Toby threw himself down in the nearest chair, his eyes sparkling beneath his frown of concentration.

After one suspicious glance, Vera said to her mother. "Mr. Renwick suggested we go to one of the public balls in the Gardens. I think he realizes he can't keep Kitty cooped up forever and knows she'll be safe with all of us there."

"Who is all of us?" her mother demanded.

"Well, you and me and Da if he wants. And Toby, I suppose. And Luke."

Luke, of course, had not been mentioned, but Vera saw no point in missing the opportunity.

Toby, of course, had quite other opportunities in mind. "So, Kitty's *not* related to this duke?"

"Not according to her uncle," Vera said impatiently.

"But the duke still thinks she might be? Old Renwick's going soft if he can't see the fortune in that situation."

"What fortune?" Vera demanded.

"Dearham's. What's he looking for his relative for, if not to give her wads of money? Kitty could be a wealthy woman."

"Bill Renwick will see she is anyway," their mother intervened.

"Yes, but not by the Duke of Dearham's standards!"

"Well, since she isn't related to him," Vera pointed out, "it doesn't apply, does it?"

Toby grinned. "Yes, but the beauty is, she don't need to be related to him. He just needs to believe she is. And I'm sure, between us, we can come up with some kind of proof to keep his Nobleness satisfied."

Vera stared at him. "Toby, have you ever considered *working* for your living?"

Her brother flushed. "Don't nag at me, Vere. It's your friend I'm trying to help out. And Bill Renwick ain't so flush as everyone thinks. He was great at bringing in the readies when he was young, or so everyone tells me, and no one can deny he's got reach and influence in some very scary places. But he's sunk everything he owns in that money pit at Maida, and everyone knows if this new hotel of his doesn't save his bacon, he'll be quite rolled up. And then where will your Kitty be?"

"It's not as bad as that," her mother said uneasily. "Your da would know."

"It was Da who told me. Look, Kitty doesn't need to know. Neither does Mr. Renwick. We just need to find a way to get at this duke with proof, and then the money starts flowing to Kitty. And Mr. Renwick, and therefore Da and us. And Luke," he added to Vera as a masterstroke.

CHAPTER FIVE

"Dunne," Johnny greeted his visitor, who strolled into the breakfast parlor the following morning.

Dunne's eyebrows flew up. "Good God. I thought your man must be new that he sent me in here. What are you doing up at this ungodly hour? What of your thick head?"

"What of yours?" Johnny retorted. He waved one hand at the sideboard. "Help yourself. There's too much for me."

Dunne poured himself a cup of coffee and sat down beside him. "Busy day, Your Grace?"

"Early one. My sister Meg's had twins—again—and I was forced to entertain Harry to breakfast to hear all about them."

"They're in London?"

"Yes, with Harry's brother and sister-in-law. How is Rebecca?"

"Well, and invites you to dinner the day after tomorrow."

Johnny grinned. "How are the mighty fallen. You came at this hour to deliver a dinner invitation?"

"No, I came at this hour to tell you about a very odd encounter I've just had. When I went into the office first thing, some shifty fellow was all but threatening Andrews to let him see me. Turns out he only wanted me to give a message to you."

"About what?" Johnny asked, only half-amused. Most of his mind was still on his sister Meg and her twins, whom he hadn't yet seen, and the odd little tug of envy he had felt when Harry dazzled him with his pride and joy and relief at Meg's safe birthing.

"He says, if you want proof that Kitty Renwick is your cousin Margaret's daughter, you should go to the masked ball at Maida Gardens on Saturday."

Johnny blinked, dragging the remainder of his restless brain to Dunne's news. "What sort of proof?"

"He didn't say."

"Who was he? Or didn't he say?"

"Actually, he didn't. But Napper followed him to Seven Dials, where he lost him."

"He doesn't sound like a very reliable informant," Johnny observed.

"Didn't look like one either. My first thought was *flim-flam man*. Though an expensively dressed one, especially for Seven Dials. I don't advise you to go."

"No," Johnny said thoughtfully, "though I probably will. Trap or not."

Dunne sighed. "Very well, I'll come with you."

"No, stay home with your wife. She won't want to be at Maida in her condition. Though you could lend me Napper if he doesn't slope off back to Gorse before then."

"You certainly shouldn't go alone."

Johnny smiled. "I don't intend to. I shall get up a party of bored ladies and gentlemen and take my brother Peter for respectability."

"Is that the best gown you have?" Vera asked doubtfully on the evening of the masked ball. Leaving the others in the parlor, she had followed Kitty into her tiny bedchamber to help style her hair more elaborately.

Kitty looked down at the skirt of her deep autumn-red gown. Admittedly, it was not new. For nearly two years, it had been both her party dress and her Sunday best, and she rather liked both its simplicity and its soft, velvet feel.

"Don't you like it?" she asked, vaguely disappointed.

"Actually, I do, and the color suits your coloring beautifully. Apt for autumn, too. But it's not exactly a *ball* gown, is it?"

"I don't have such a thing, Vera," Kitty said dryly, eyeing her friend's delightful lace and embroidery confection with a sparkling gauze train. "There's never been any point. Besides, I'll have the domino over it."

"Let me see, what jewelry do you have?" Vera rummaged in the box and came up with the twisted gold-plated necklace Aunty Mary had given her for her seventeenth birthday. Tiny pearls were set in the apex of each twist, and there was a matching pearl comb for her hair, which Vera found unerringly. "I'd forgotten about these. They will be perfect."

Ten minutes later, Vera stood back, satisfied. She had rolled Kitty's hair up into a loose, high pile, held cleverly together with pins and the pearl comb. Only one skein of auburn locks fell artfully loose from her forehead to her right shoulder.

"Perfect," Vera proclaimed. "Mask and domino, and let's go!"

"At last," Rob grumbled as they emerged.

"Where's Dan?" Vera asked. "Is he not coming with us?"

"Dan's in the black books," Rob said cheerfully. "Punished by having to help Dad while Kitty and I go the ball. You'll probably see them both around the ballroom and the Gardens, though."

It seemed odd not to be sneaking out in the dark but to belong to a genuine party heading openly to the ball. She seemed to see everything differently, as if through the eyes of a visitor. She didn't even mind taking Toby's arm as her escort, Vera being firmly attached to Luke.

"You should wear your hair like that more often," Toby said warmly. "You look incredibly beautiful tonight."

"Thank you, But I couldn't work with hair falling over my

face!"

"You shouldn't be working at all," Toby said stoutly. "Lovely girl like you."

"We all do what's needed," she said vaguely, wondering what looks had to do with anything.

Uncle Bill, in his usual role of master of ceremonies, welcomed them into the pavilion and showed them to a table of honor with a view of the lantern-lit gardens from the window. He even supplied a bottle of champagne and a large jug of ale, and then, with a glance at Kitty that was part pride and part warning scowl, he walked away about his duties, for the orchestra had started up the first waltz, and the guests braving the Gardens began to spill inside to dance.

"Does he do this every night?" Toby asked, gazing after Uncle Bill as if awed.

"When there's a ball or other event, yes," Rob replied, pouring a small amount of champagne into each glass. "Unless he has other business, when I do it for him."

They all picked up their glasses and clinked, and Kitty had her first taste of champagne. It tasted better than it smelled, but it was odd and bubbly, and she wasn't sure she liked it until her second sip.

"Where's Dan, then? Serving the booze?" Toby asked with a hint of derision.

"If necessary," Rob said evenly. "Usually, he and I make sure there's no trouble, either in the grounds or the pavilion itself."

"And is there much of that?" Sal, Vera's mother, asked.

"No, but it happens," Rob admitted. "Don't leave things where they can be stolen. Also, it's polite to dance with whoever asks you, but you don't need to put up with…over-familiarity."

Vera laughed. "Don't you sound mealy-mouthed!"

"Will you dance, Vera?" Luke asked.

Vera smiled and stood, and they trooped off together.

"What does she see in that boy?" Sal wondered.

"I like Luke," Kitty said firmly.

"Oh, we all like him, Kitty," Sal assured her. "And trust him, too, for he's a clever lad, and Jimmie wouldn't be without him, now. But she could have anyone."

"Fenlow, the wine merchant, would have her in a trice," Toby said gloomily, "if she'd only look at him. And he's got a place the size of Apsley House. Luke's got two tiny rooms in Covent Garden. Come and dance with me, Kitty, cheer me up!"

It was inevitable that she would have to dance with Toby at some point in the evening, and it was hardly the first time. Family parties and Christmas parties were hardly the same as masked public balls, however. She had the feeling Rob's remark about over-familiarity had been aimed largely at Toby, and she was not looking forward to being mauled.

But Toby, it seemed, was happy to keep the line. He held her decorously and chatted amiably as they waltzed, and Kitty was happy enough to join in and laugh at his bad jokes. If he danced a shade awkwardly and missed the rhythm by a fraction all too often, well, she suspected Johnny had spoiled her for lesser men.

Johnny. The Duke of Dearham, God help her.

And then, as though she had conjured him from her mind, she saw him.

A tall, fair gentleman with a lady on his arm led a group of similarly dressed people toward a group of small tables. They were all masked and cloaked, but it was clear from the way they moved, all grace and languor and a subtle, superior amusement at their surroundings, that they were quality. Nobs, as Uncle Bill said.

Which didn't make the tall, fair gentleman Johnny. His Grace. She had only the tiniest glimpse beyond Toby's shoulder, and now she could only see his broad, cloaked back.

He could be any nob. And in any case, I'm not his cousin, and I don't even like him. He's underhand, dishonest. And I was an idiot to be taken in by well-practiced flattery. She would not think of the kiss, for that, she knew, was well-practiced, too.

She felt an odd pang of loss for the illusion she had harbored for more than a year, of the kind, open-hearted gentleman with the laughing eyes.

JOHNNY SAW HER from the table, almost as soon as he sat down with his brother and friends. Surprised, for he had the impression her visits to the masked balls were rare, he found himself unreasonably annoyed with her partner. This was a stocky, slightly overdressed fellow with extravagant taste in waistcoats. And jewels. Rings winked on his fingers, and his cravat sparkled.

But Johnny was not here for Kitty, not directly. Instead, he was here to meet the mysterious man who claimed to have proof Kitty was his cousin. How exactly he was supposed to recognize this man had not been revealed, though it really had to be someone close enough to the Renwicks to know anything about his quest. Johnny suspected one of her cousins, who perhaps looked on the situation less sentimentally than Bill Renwick.

While Johnny made sure his guests had wine and made amiable conversation, he kept a surreptitious eye on Kitty. Something told him she was not quite comfortable with her partner, although when the dance ended, she took his arm easily enough, and they walked without debate toward a table at the back. Another couple converged on this table, too, and they all sat down together. Three young fellows, Kitty, and another young woman, who were whispering together like old friends, and an older woman who raised a glass often to her lips but appeared to be a chaperone, at least nominally. Was this her family?

"What the devil are we doing here?" his brother Peter whispered in his ear. "It's downright vulgar."

"True. I'm seeing to your broader education."

Peter lowered his voice even further so that Lady Langtry next to him would not hear. "There must be better places to seduce your next mistress."

"Don't be presumptuous, Peter," Johnny murmured. "I brought her for you."

Peter blushed, which was one of his endearing traits, and glared disapprovingly at Johnny, which was not.

"Ask her," Johnny said provokingly, just loud enough for Lady Langtry to hear.

Inevitably, she turned to smile at them both. "Ask me what?"

"To dance," Peter said civilly, the flick of his eyes at Johnny promising retribution on a grand scale. "May I have the honor?"

When he had stood to wave them off, as it were, Johnny returned his attention to Kitty's table and noticed the man she had been dancing with was no longer there. He had no idea whether or not Kitty knew Johnny was present. But a moment later, while listening with half a smile to the banter of his friends, he noticed Kitty's erstwhile partner standing against a pillar not far from his table.

Interesting…

To test a theory, he excused himself to his friends and strolled over to Kitty's table.

She *had* known he was here, for there was no surprise in her eyes, only dread as she turned them up to his. That looked startled him, shamed him, though he had no immediate idea why. Unless it was that he cut up her peace with his presence, with his talk of her being one of his family.

Or perhaps because he had kissed her when her uncle had made sure she was more sheltered than his own sisters had been. That had not been well done of him perhaps, though it had felt quite delicious at the time, and she had melted most appealingly into his arms. He was too used to following his heart…or at least his bodily instincts.

Everyone at the table was gazing at him, agog. He bowed with faint amusement and met Kitty's suddenly determined gaze. Determined to refuse him or to speak to him?

He never found out, for a tap on his shoulder caused him to turn and face Kitty's erstwhile waltz partner.

"Your pardon, sir," the man said, dropping his gaze. "Might I crave the favor of a private word?" The submissive gaze shot up to see what impression he was making, and Johnny knew he had been right.

He bowed again to the table in general, noting Kitty's sudden frown, and turned to the young man.

"Would you mind walking?" the man asked. "Just to a more private spot."

Johnny swept his arm in front of him. "Lead on."

To his surprise, he was led right outside the pavilion, so he kept a wary out for likely confederates who might help rob him. But the man didn't lead him off the paths, merely to stand beneath a lantern to the right of the main door.

"Am I right to suspect I address His Grace, the Duke of Dearham?"

"My dear fellow, it's a masquerade," Johnny said amiably. "*You* can be His Grace if you like."

"I heard your friends address you," the man said. "And I saw the way Kitty looked at you."

"Am I to assume you have the advantage of me?" Johnny inquired.

"It was me you came to meet," came the blunt response. "I told your lawyer, if you want more proof Kitty's your relation, then I have it."

"You intrigue me," Johnny murmured, keeping his eyes on the man's face. "And you are?"

"My name's Harris. Toby Harris. I live in Taverner Street in Seven Dials. Next door to where Bill Renwick found Kitty." He delved in his pocket but radiated no hint of violence, so Johnny stood perfectly still until Harris brought out a gold locket on a chain, a dainty piece of female jewelry. On the front of it was a miniature portrait of a woman. "Perhaps you recognize this?"

Johnny gave it only a cursory glance. "I can't say I do."

"Maggie, Kitty's mother, gave it to my mother as a token of thanks because Ma looked after her when she was ill. Look."

Harris pressed a catch, and the locket opened to reveal a lock of fine, soft chestnut hair, almost the right shade to be Kitty's.

Harris closed the locket again and held it up toward Johnny, who suddenly frowned and took it from him, turning so that the lantern light fell on the young, beautiful face in the painting. It was, unmistakably Her Grace, Johnny's grandmother. He knew her at once because a larger version of the same portrait hung in the drawing room of Dearham Abbey.

Johnny's fingers curled around it. "May I borrow this? To examine it at my leisure. As soon as I have, I promise to return it to its rightful owner."

A twitch of Toby Harris's eye told him the young man did not like this idea, and Johnny watched the struggle wage across his face before he said, "Of course. We know where to find each other."

Johnny smiled faintly, inclined his head, and returned to the ballroom without another word.

CHAPTER SIX

"**I**S THAT *HIM*?" Vera whispered in Kitty's ear.

"Yes..." She gazed anxiously after the duke's retreating back until both he and Toby vanished from view. She knew a confused urge to follow them, as much to do with annoyance as protection, only why would she try to protect *him*?

"Now I understand," Vera murmured in awe. "He is...gorgeous."

"Yes, but what does Toby want with him? What is he up to?"

"Warning him off?" Luke suggested with a quick grin.

"Or standing up for Kitty's interests," Vera retorted.

"It's not his place to do either," Kitty said flatly. "Excuse me. I'm going to find out what they're up to."

"Here, where's Kitty going?" Sal's voice demanded behind her as she slipped around the edges of the dance floor. Rob and Vera's voices spoke soothingly back, and fortunately, no one followed.

Her uncle was in conversation with some people a few yards from the main entrance, so Kitty made a dash for the door, just as it opened, and she literally bumped into the Duke of Dearham coming back inside.

Before she could catch her breath, or her heart, his arm was around her, sweeping her onto the dance floor and into the waltz.

"It's polite to ask," she said coldly.

"And to accept. So, if you will forgive me my oversight, I shall forgive you yours."

Refusing to laugh, she scowled. "What do you want?"

"To dance with you again, of course. And to invite you to an assignation whenever you are tired of the dancing."

That took her breath away. "No," she managed.

"No, it's the wrong answer? Or no, you won't come?"

"Both!"

The beguiling, teasing twinkle faded from his eyes. "Very well, no joking. But I do need to speak to you without your family or mine hanging around."

She blinked, her eyes straying to the tableful of fashionable gentlefolk he had brought with him. "*That* is your family?"

"Well, the serious-looking fellow is my brother. The rest may be related somewhere. They often are."

Her quick glance gave her only a dazzling impression of elegance and beauty before the duke turned her, and she could no longer see them. She glanced up to speak seriously to him, but his gaze was as steady, his masked face so...not merely handsome but appealing, that the words fled. The mere pleasure of dancing with him had sneaked into her body at some point, smoothing away the awkwardness she should have felt. Why should it be so different dancing with him? Just because he danced better than Toby or anyone else who had held her like this.

"What about your friends?" he asked. "You have not slipped out in disguise tonight, have you?"

"No. My uncle gave permission to me and my cousin Rob. Partly, I suspect, to punish Dan for his idiocy the last time you were here. You didn't tell anyone about that, did you?"

"What makes you think so?"

"We've had no untoward visitors." She took a deep breath. "I should thank you."

"But it would choke you because of what you see as my dishonesty."

It wasn't a question, more of a wry statement, but she answered anyway, lifting her chin. "I am not so petty. I do thank you. What we did to you was unforgivable, and you have every right to bring the law down on us. We are all profoundly grateful that you did not, even if some of us don't quite know it."

For several moments, he actually seemed speechless. "That's a very handsome apology," he said at last, "especially considering you let me go. Did that cause you any trouble?"

"It earned me a mouthful from Dan until I pointed out his own utter stupidity and what my uncle would say if he knew the whole of it."

"Forgive my stupidity, but why didn't you simply say that at the time rather than tying me up?"

She dragged her gaze free and stared at the rather tasteful sapphire pin in his cravat. "Because the smugglers were there. If they didn't think we were taking care of the problem, they might have done so themselves."

"So, you waited until they were gone. You are quite alarmingly level-headed, aren't you?"

"I don't scream and faint when I encounter a problem, if that is what you mean." She raised her eyes to his once more. For once, though his eyes were warm and a little puzzled, he did not appear to be laughing. "I am not, after all, a *lady*."

Now the glimmer of a smile crept into his eyes. "Oh, nicely done, Miss Kitty. An insult and a denial at once, though I must introduce you to my sisters. But you do bring me back to the point. Walk with me? If I promise to be a gentleman."

"From what I have seen of gentlemen, that is no comfort. In fact, I shall need my cousin as—"

"My dear, you are relentless. Very well, I promise not to touch you, not to kiss you, or otherwise show you any sign of what *anyone* might construe as disrespect. Although, in my defense," he added as she flushed furiously, "I must tell you that I never kiss anyone I don't respect. Shall we?"

His arm dropped from her back, and he released her hand, offering her his arm instead. By giving her a choice, damn him, he took the wind out of her sails. And he had promised to be a gentleman. So why her heart pounded, she had no idea. For an instant, they stood thus, surrounded by dancers who didn't quite bump into them.

Then, almost impatiently, she seized his arm and strode through the waltzers. She had meant to tow him along, both venting her anger and proving her disregard for whatever danger he presented. But somehow, he walked by her side. The waltzers parted for them, as did the people milling between the dancefloor and the exit.

There was no sign of Uncle Bill or Dan. The staff she did see never looked at her. She suspected they would see only the duke in any case.

The cold air hit her, and she gulped it in with relief. Though what there was to relieve her in this situation remained a mystery. She was alone with a powerful nobleman, who had already taken advantage of her and who, for some reason, she didn't yet understand, wanted something she wasn't prepared to give.

And yet, walking beside him, among the other couples dallying beneath the trees, reality seemed to fade. As she held his arm and moved along the path leading beyond the pavilion toward the lily pond, he no longer seemed like a duke. He was the handsome young gentleman who had smiled at her more than a year ago and taken a heavy tray from her. He was the man who had danced with her earlier in the week, stolen kisses, and stood up to threatening smugglers, giving a pretty good account of himself, too.

He wasn't related to her, whatever he thought. But for the first time, it entered her head that she wouldn't mind. Why was that?

Unwilling to look further in that direction, she said abruptly, "What was it you wanted to discuss?"

This part of the gardens was quieter. No giggling came from the undergrowth, although it might just have been muffled by the gentle splashing of the waterfall.

"The man you danced with first," Johnny said unexpectedly. "Who is he?"

"Toby? An old family friend." She glanced at him, gathering her skirts to climb the steps to the pond. "What did he say to you?"

"I'll tell you in a moment. What's his name?"

"Toby Harris. He is my best friend's brother, the son of the builder, James Harris, who is one of my uncle's oldest friends. What did he want with you?" She sat on the first boulder, gazing up at him expectantly.

He took something from his pocket and sat next to her, almost touching. "Do you know what this is?"

A gold locket lay in his palm. In the dim light, it looked valuable, with the portrait of a lady painted on the front. "It looks like the kind of necklace Aunt Mary kept locks of our hair in. Does it open?"

He didn't look at it as he caused it to open. She knew he was watching her, though she didn't know why. Within was indeed a lock of dark hair. She closed the locket and bent over it, even taking hold of his wrist to bring the portrait closer to her.

"She's pretty. Is she a real person? Who is she?" She looked up and met his steady gaze. At some point, he'd removed his mask, and his lean, masculine beauty swiped at her breath.

"An ancestress of mine. My grandmother, in fact. Have you never seen this before?"

"No, but then—"

"Why would Harris have it?"

She blinked. "*Toby* had it? How on earth… He isn't a thief, I'm sure of it."

For some reason, she thought he relaxed, although he remained perfectly still. "He told me your mother gave it to his for her kindness in looking after Maggie."

A frown tugged at her brow. "That makes no sense."

"Unless Maggie was a Winter."

Her fingers curled in response, and she realized she was still grasping his wrist, which was strong and supple in her hold. She dropped it as though it burned her, muttering an apology, and tried to think.

"Why would Toby try to convince you I am this long-lost cousin of yours? Because I'm not, you know."

"Perhaps he's trying to do you a favor."

"How? It makes no difference to him whether or not…" She broke off as another unpleasant idea hit her. She dragged her gaze free of his, trying to think. "If I *was* your cousin," she said abruptly, "what would you do?"

He shrugged. "That would depend on what you wanted."

A home with his family, perhaps, or means to establish her independence… And Toby, both lazy and ambitious, kept trying to court her.

"You shouldn't believe anything Toby tells you," she said abruptly.

"He is a liar?"

She jumped to her feet too quickly, torn between truth and old friendships. Johnny stood up, too, steadying her with a hand on her waist.

"Toby plays his own games," she managed. "They aren't necessarily in your interest. Or mine. I have to go."

"Stop," he said mildly. Both hands were on her waist now, but lightly, unthreatening, although somehow, they seemed to burn through the fabric of her gown. "You'll fall down the steps. I didn't mean to agitate you."

"But you meant to find out if I was part of Toby's scheme, whatever it might be?"

"Yes, though it made no sense to me."

She became aware of a growing pain in her mind. She rubbed half-heartedly at her forehead, then, understanding, dropped her hand with a sad little laugh. "Do you know what's really funny? What I first liked about you was your openness."

He blinked. "We were both masked."

"Not then," she said impatiently. "Before."

A smile tugged at his lips. "Really? You remember me from Wenning's bizarre revenge party?"

"I have a good memory for faces," she said with dignity. "Let me go. I won't fall down the steps I've been running and jumping on since I was ten years old."

At once, his hands fell away, although he walked in front of her to help her down, still treating her as a lady, which for some reason annoyed her even more.

"I suppose you were always this...convoluted," she said shrewishly. "I was just too foolish to see it."

His lips quirked. "Thank you for looking. I like to think I am open with friends. But one cannot grow up as heir to a dukedom without a hint of cynicism."

For the first time, she considered that—the toadying and the flim-flam and the concentration on his rank rather than his person. Something pulled at her that she couldn't quite grasp.

"Even you," he said softly, "cannot be kind and sunny all the time."

She swallowed, secretly loving his strong grip on her fingers, and wished she didn't. "Most of the time," she managed and looked up to meet his gaze. "I am lucky in my life."

An arrested look entered his eyes before his eyelids drooped like hoods. And she recognized at last what had been pulling at her.

His loneliness.

And in some almost hidden part of her, her own.

JOHNNY FELT AS if someone had hit him with a sledgehammer.

Stupidly, not once in his pursuit of righting the wrong done to his kinswoman, had it entered his head that her daughter would not want to be reclaimed by the Winters. That her life now was actually preferable to the one he was offering her. Of course, if she had chosen to mix with the Winter family, she would have found things new and unfamiliar, difficult at first, in terms of manners and surroundings. But he had never doubted Kitty's ability to adjust. Or that anyone would want to.

That he was, in fact, upsetting her contentment, *annoying* a life much more pleasant than his own, in terms of everything but money, was something even an imbecile should have seen. But he, God help him, was blinded by her, by whatever feelings it was she churned up in him. Protectiveness and attraction, definitely, but beyond that, something else that was quite unfamiliar.

"I'm sorry," he said abruptly as they walked in silence toward the pavilion once more. "Please believe I meant it for the best."

She cast him a quick glance, but he was putting his mask back on—without her help—and he could not bear to see her expression. Instead, re-masked, he drew her hand jauntily back through his arm to enter the pavilion and parted from her the only way he knew how.

He bowed and lifted her hands to his lips, one after the other, and left her with his most dashing smile. He never once glanced back as he strolled back to his table and sat beside his brother. Most of his party seemed to be dancing.

"Who is the girl?" Peter asked him disapprovingly. "Your latest conquest?"

"No, just a girl. What of your own?"

Peter scowled. "If you mean Lady Langtry, I am not in the market for a mistress, and I refuse to commit adultery. Besides, I would never touch your cast-offs."

Johnny buffeted him on the shoulder. "You are a miserable old grump, Peter. I may have once considered pursuing her ladyship—you can't deny she's beautiful and charming—but she was always more taken with you." He smiled into his brother's disbelieving eyes. "And you should be aware, she is a widow, not a wife."

CHAPTER SEVEN

THE DISTANCE THE duke achieved while still flirting with his smile and his hand-kisses chilled Kitty to the bone.

Thinking about it as she flopped back down beside Vera, and as she danced with Luke, and with a stranger from the next table, and with Toby again, she realized something she had said had changed his mind. Either he no longer believed she could be the cousin he sought, or he had decided he did not want her to be.

Which should have felt like a relief, not a rejection. No friendship was possible between Bill Renwick's niece and the Duke of Dearham. And nothing warmer was acceptable to her, so it was as well as he had decided to abandon her.

So why did she watch him dancing with those beautiful women of his own party and once with a dashing lady in yellow? Why did her heart cringe and her stomach tighten with something alarmingly like jealousy?

Because she had once been dazzled by a romantic illusion. And although that illusion had never had anything to do with reality, she was foolishly reluctant to let it go.

One thing she could do, though, and she did as she walked beside Toby back to the cottage after the last dance of the evening. She took his arm to hold him back a little from the others.

"Wait a moment. I want to talk to you in private."

He smiled at that and covered her hand with his. "I wondered how long it would take you," he said smugly.

"Oh, you aren't going to enjoy it," she said grimly. "What do you mean by interfering in my business with the Duke of Dearham?"

"Just doing you a favor, sweetheart."

"Don't call me that. You mean, you hoped to extort money from him by pretending I am his wretched cousin."

"Money for you," Toby corrected. "You can thank me later."

"Money for me because you think I'll marry you? I won't, Toby. I don't know where you got that locket, but—"

"From Ma, of course."

She cast him a disbelieving glance. "I'm not so gullible, To-by."

"Ask her," he insisted.

"I will, but it makes no difference. I won't beg via you or anyone else. And whoever I am, I am not related to the Dukes of Dearham!"

"Keep telling yourself that, love," Toby said with maddening condescension. "You may not want the life of a nob—after all, it would take you away from me. But we can have the best of both worlds."

"Toby, you get neither me nor the duke's money. Good night." She tugged her hand free of him and marched ahead to join Sal.

For the first time ever, Kitty was ambivalent about Vera staying overnight at the cottage. Probably because, for the first time ever, she didn't know, apart from annoyance with Toby, exactly what she felt. But sharing a room and a bed with her friend, there was really no way of avoiding late-night confidences.

"I like him," Vera said dreamily. "Your duke. So handsome and tall, and those smiling eyes of his must just drop women in his lap."

Kitty really didn't want to hear this.

"Will you still talk to us in the lower orders once you're a duchess?"

"Duchess?" Kitty repeated, startled. "Don't be so ridiculous! I'm not even his distant cousin, though Toby seems to be trying to persuade him I am. I don't want to be his family, Vera. I want to be left alone as I am."

In the dark, she couldn't see Vera's eyes, but she could imagine them, penetrating and shrewd. "And marry Toby?"

"No. Toby and I would not suit."

"I told him that."

"So did I," Kitty admitted. "But I'm not sure he believes me."

"He never used to be so full of himself," Vera said sadly. "I think a little success with certain females has convinced him he's irresistible." She giggled suddenly at the idea of her brother's irresistibility, and Kitty couldn't help joining in.

After a few moments, Kitty said sleepily, "Feeling as you do about Luke, do you ever look at other men?"

"I look," Vera admitted. "But I don't ever want them. I only want Luke, and I always will."

It was a warm sentiment to fall asleep with. But as Kitty closed her eyes, it wasn't Luke and Vera she saw, but the duke's distant smile as he bade her farewell.

IN THE MORNING, Vera's dad appeared to inspect the work on the hotel and to bring a couple of burly new workers to speed things up. Like several others, Mr. Harris said, they would sleep rough in the part of the building already roofed to make sure there was always an early start. While Luke put them to work, Mr. Harris and Uncle Bill sat in the corner of the kitchen discussing business. Rob and Dan went off on their duties about the Gardens, and Vera accompanied Kitty on hers. Toby sat in the parlor with a newspaper on his knee, watching them leave.

"What does he do?" Kitty asked Vera.

"Wanders about with my father sometimes, apparently learning the business," Vera said wryly. "But between you and me, he's never done a hand's turn in his life either in the house or the office or on a building site. But then, neither have I. Not like you."

"You help in the house, though. So when you marry Luke, you'll make a fine home."

"I think Toby imagines he'll have a wife and servants, and probably Luke to run his business when Dad steps back. Not sure Luke will like to answer to Toby, though."

"Is there nothing Toby wants to do?" Kitty asked.

Vera shrugged. "He did say something once about working for your uncle, but Dad scoffed at him."

"Why would he want to work here?" Kitty asked. "He's never shown any interest in the place."

"Not sure it's the place so much as your uncle," Vera said. "Toby admires him, thinks everyone looks up to him. And by everyone, I mean the people your uncle doesn't let you meet."

JOHNNY SURPRISED HIS sister and brother-in-law, and the whole Staunton family, by joining them for breakfast, a chaotic affair since both Lord Staunton's children and Meg's older twins were with the adults. It reminded Johnny a little of long summers spent in the country when he and his siblings had been inseparable from Staunton and his. Of course, Johnny had not been the duke, then, and Robert had not been Lord Staunton. And now their children seemed to be forming the same kind of bonds.

After the well-ordered quiet of Dearham House, he rather liked the noise and carnage of breakfast with the Stauntons. He even helped the children create more.

"How are my new nieces?" he asked Harry at last. "Are they and Meg visitable?"

"Of course," Harry said at once. "Meg will be glad to see you. She comes down for meals occasionally, but the little devils are quite demanding."

In fact, Meg was discovered in a bright new dressing gown, laying the tiny bundles of difficulty in their cot. She looked tired but happy and smiled as she beckoned Johnny over to see her new babies. He duly admired them. Although there was little to distinguish them from others of the same age, the perfection of their tiny features always took him by surprise.

"You look well, Meggie," he told his sister when they had crept into her sitting room.

"I am. Harry and I are going for a walk this afternoon with the boys and then tomorrow with the babies. And then it's our reunion at the Hallands'."

"Are you feeling up to all this?"

"She planned it," Harry said wryly. "But don't worry. I won't let her overdo it."

"You always were the only one she listened to." Johnny stuck his hand in his pocket and brought out the locket Harris had shown him last night. "Have you ever seen this before, Meg?"

Meg took it and turned it in her fingers peering at the painting. "Oh, it's Grandmama when she was young before she became the duchess."

"I thought so, too."

She glanced at him quizzically. "You're not sure? It looks like a miniature of the portrait in the drawing room at Dearham Abbey. Where did you find it?"

"A complete stranger showed it to me. Do you suppose Grandmama gave it to Cousin Margaret as a keepsake?"

Meg frowned. "I've a feeling we were never to mention Cousin Margaret, though I can't remember why. I certainly don't remember her. Why?"

Johnny shrugged. "I've had someone looking for her daughter," he said vaguely. "No matter. So, tell me about your new posting, Harry?"

After an hour with Meg and Harry, he took himself off to the jeweler who had enjoyed Winter patronage since time immemorial, and in the privacy of the back room, showed him the locket, too.

"It's not my work or my father's," the jeweler said at once. "Although I can point you to one or two likely candidates."

"I don't think that will be necessary. I was hoping you could simply tell me the age of the piece. Is it new?"

"Not especially, no." The jeweler peered at it through his glass. "I would say it's fifty or sixty years old. Which fits with the lady's costume."

Johnny nodded and stood up. "Thank you. That's what I thought."

His next visit was to the city, where he found Ludovic Dunne about to leave his office, although he returned to the inner office as soon as he saw Johnny.

"You have news?" Dunne asked.

Johnny produced the locket and set it on the table in front of Dunne. "I'd like you to send someone to the house in Taverner Street to return this."

Dunne's eyebrows rose. "It came from there?"

"At some point. I think it was Margaret's. She was my grandmother's companion for a few years, and this does appear to my grandmother. Apparently, the dying Maggie gave it to Sal Harris."

"Then Kitty Renwick is Margaret's daughter?"

"Possibly. Someone is certainly anxious for me to believe so, although there's an air of the flim-flam about him. Kitty herself knows nothing about this and has no interest in being adopted as a Winter. So I think we just have to leave it. Some wrongs cannot be righted without making the wrong worse."

FOR KITTY, THE chill of autumn seemed to seep into her bones. It was the start of the Gardens' quiet season, so there were fewer events and entertainments to keep her busy. They had a real masquerade ball for the children at Hallowe'en, with all the guests dressing up, and one with fireworks to celebrate Guy Fawkes Night. And in the daytime, people brought their children to walk and play, but it was often too wet or cold to linger.

If Kitty had hoped to see the duke's tall figure wander through the Gardens to speak to her, she was disappointed. She could not help feeling hurt that he had abandoned her, although it was what she had told him to do. And she went over and over their final conversation, wondering what she had said to make him decide so suddenly to walk away.

She suspected it was something to do with the locket. He probably thought she and Toby between them were somehow trying to push him into the belief that Kitty was his cousin. Though where Toby had got the wretched locket was anyone's guess.

By the night of the firework ball, Kitty had convinced herself that he would make an appearance then. She refused to go looking, either in the pavilion or by the lily pond. But she did stand by the garden gate to watch the fireworks for quite a long time before they began and for quite a long time afterward.

Uncle Bill put on a good show, lighting up the sky with beautiful colors and patterns. She could hear the frequent "Ooh!" of the watchers, even through the hissing and banging. And it was well attended. Even the builders who lived on the hotel site had been there, according to Rob, as he passed through for a sustaining bite to eat. And, certainly, Kitty saw movement up there until late. She doubted there would be an early start the next morning.

But, shivering in the cold as it began to permeate her bones, she acknowledged that the duke would not be coming. She turned back inside, hung up her cloak, and huddled before the parlor fire. In her heart, she recognized a lost chance, though the chance of what was a question she couldn't answer. It hardly mattered if she was never to see him again.

And then she heard the creak of the gate, quick, quiet foot-falls, and in spite of herself, she jumped to her feet. But she heard no knock on the door over the drumming of her heart. Though…was that the gate clicking shut?

Oh, no, have I lost him again?

The thought may have been idiocy, but it got her to the front door in an instant, letting chill air into the cottage. But no one stood on the doorway or the path, and there was no movement beyond the gate.

Slowly, she shut the door again, trying not to care. Something rustled beneath her feet, and she bent and picked a piece of folded paper off the floor. Her fingers flew to the base of her throat, for by the light of the lamp, she saw it was addressed in a bold hand to *Miss Kitty*.

She made her way back to the parlor where there was more light and sank on her knees before the fire.

Hotel, 3am. Dearham.

She stared at the few terse words, so un-Johnny-like. Disappointment warred with fresh curiosity. Why did he want her to meet him at the hotel? The structure was little more than half-built, although there was some shelter. Perhaps that was the reason.

And why three am? The Gardens were usually locked by one of the clock on a ball night, and her family in bed before two. A warning bell rang, a feeling that this was not right, not in character for him or for herself.

And yet she knew she would go.

When Uncle Bill and the boys were safely in bed, and the house was dark and silent, she crept down from her attic bedroom, already cloaked and booted. She eased back the bolts on the door, picked up the lantern, and crept outside, closing the door softly behind her. She had only starlight to guide her along the familiar path because she couldn't risk lighting the lantern until she was distant enough from the cottage.

The track up to the building site had grown unfamiliar with the changes wrought by various carts and builders' boots, and she rarely walked in this direction except, occasionally, to speak to Luke. She found herself glad it was not Hallowe'en, when spirits and all manner of wicked, unearthly things were apparently free to roam the earth. Not that Kitty believed such nonsense, but even once she had lit the lantern, she found herself curiously unnerved.

The building site was large, the building already showing signs of its fine façade. It was going to be four floors high in the center, a small, two-story wing on either side. The side wings were already roofed. In the nearest of those, slept the builders who did not go home at night. All was quiet and dark there, so Kitty hurried past, as quietly as she could, searching for another light or any sign of the duke's presence.

With half her mind constantly speculating on the reason for this meeting, she felt more relief than unease when a light glimmered at the far end of the building. She strode toward it, paying less attention to silence now.

The light shone through the open door at the end of the building. As she drew even with it, she glimpsed a distortedly large figure behind it. Then it moved inside, and she followed impatiently.

The thought came to her that she had never known the duke so ill-mannered.

"What *is* this about?" she demanded sharply, trying to shade her eyes as the light blinded her. Oddly, a stale odor of onion, beer, and tobacco assailed her. And then something large swept viciously toward her, and the face behind it was that of a complete, brutal stranger. "Johnny!" she got out in panic and something horribly like disappointment, just as the object struck her with agonizing force, knocking her to the ground.

The world went black.

CHAPTER EIGHT

T HE PAIN IN her head was blinding. She could not breathe and didn't really want to, for her nose and throat felt so hot and dry that every attempted inhalation was agony. She felt as if she could not see, and yet the bare room was lit by an otherworldly glow. And a vile stench of burning.

Oh, dear God, I'm in the hotel, and the building is on fire! She leapt up and almost lost consciousness again as the pain battered at her. Disoriented and dizzy, she stumbled through burning, choking smoke toward what had to be the front door she had entered by. The handle seared her fingers, causing her to cry out. Using her cloak as feeble protection, she tugged uselessly. The door was locked, and there was no key on the inside. Whoever had hit her and locked her in here to burn.

Fire crackled, the heat and smoke were unbearable, but beyond the door, she could hear the clank of buckets, the yell of voices, warning as things fell from the burning building. Something fell from above, hot and heavy on her shoulder, knocking her down again. She barely noticed as the wood burned at her feet. She kicked it away, then threw herself bodily at the door, yelling as loudly as her poor, damaged throat would let her.

Pain no longer meant anything, only survival, and she would not give up.

And then, when the shouting and the ringing in her ears were one, the door suddenly seemed to push back at her. She was lifted in strong arms—either to safety or to God, she could no longer tell which. And the world receded once more.

LUDOVIC DUNNE WAS enjoying breakfast with his wife, Rebecca, and small stepson, Tom, when Dawson the butler entered to inform him with an air of disapproval that a person requested to be seen. Dawson delivered the card on the usual silver tray, and Ludovic, not best pleased to be disturbed during private time with his family, scowled at the inscription.

William Renwick, Esq.
Proprietor, Maida Pleasure Gardens

"Shall I have the person removed, sir?" Dawson asked hopefully.

"No," Ludovic said, rising reluctantly to his feet. "I'd better see him. Sorry, Rebecca," he added to his wife, who merely smiled and saluted him with her coffee cup.

"Come home early instead," she suggested.

"What an excellent idea," he agreed with a grin of promise.

He ruffled Tom's hair and strode off to the reception room. Many things about this visit disturbed him, mainly the fact that Renwick would seek him out deliberately and that he would do so at his home, which Renwick should know nothing about.

Renwick stood by the window, facing him.

"Two things," he said without greeting. He held out a scrap of paper. "I want to know who he really is and where he is. Secondly, I want your company in order to get into your tame duke's house."

Ludovic took the scrap of paper and glanced at it. The name meant nothing. "Three things," he said evenly. "First, good morning. Second, what is this man to you? Thirdly, if you refer to

His Grace of Dearham, he is neither mine nor particularly tame that I have discovered."

"I don't have time for any damned nonsense," Renwick snapped, pacing across the room and back like a caged beast. He flung out his arm, pointing at the scrap of paper. "That man set fire to my hotel last night, almost killing my niece, and I want him found."

"I'm not surprised. How is Miss Kitty?"

"Alive, but only just. Will you help me?"

In all the years Ludovic had known him, Bill Renwick had never asked him for anything, let alone for help. "Of course," he replied, glancing once at the unknown name. "How do you know it was this man?"

"He was a new worker. Jimmie Harris brought him and another up to start, two or three weeks ago. They lived on the site. Last night, the building was set on fire, with my niece attacked and locked inside. Everyone's accounted for but one of those new men, Albert Franks, *him*. He's not at the site, and he's not at the address he gave Jimmie when he took him on. In fact, the landlady knows nothing about him. Apparently, I don't have time to look, Mr. Dunne. I have to keep my family safe."

"Of course," Ludovic said.

"It weren't an accident, not with her locked in there."

"What was she doing there in the first place?"

"She says she had a note from Dearham to meet him there."

"No," Ludovic said with certainty. "He wouldn't—"

"It wasn't him who hit her," Renwick interrupted. "But I need to speak to him all the same."

"Yes, I think we both do," Ludovic said grimly.

Ten minutes later, they were shown upstairs to the private sitting room Ludovic had been in before. The duke, coatless and yawning, his hair uncombed, wandered in from the dressing room door.

"Good morning, gentlemen," he said, waving one careless hand by way of invitation to sit while he threw himself onto the window seat and rubbed at what was, presumably, his sore head. "What can I do for you."

"Did you make an assignation with my niece in the small hours of this morning?" Renwick demanded before Ludovic could say a word.

Dearham blinked. "My dear sir, by three o'clock this morning, I was no use to any lady. Or even my valet, who gave up on me."

Ludovic had the impression the duke's mouth was moving without permission while he forced his brain to work, for without even drawing breath, he demanded. "Has someone taken advantage of Miss Kitty's good nature?"

"Someone enticed her up to the construction site, attacked her, and set fire to the building."

The duke's face whitened. "Is she—"

"Alive," Ludovic assured him while Renwick merely stared. "She was rescued just in time."

"Thank God." The duke stood up as if to do something urgent and sat back down again, gazing at Renwick with odd helplessness. "What can I do?"

"That depends," Renwick said harshly, "on whether or not you sent your bullies to work for me and destroy me. I'm not blind to the way you looked at Kitty. Nor the way she looked at you. And I know she sent you away. But I swear to God, if this is your idea of revenge for—"

"Revenge?" Dearham interrupted, startled. "For what? Dear God, man, I have nothing to reproach her with, and if I had—"

Renwick slammed his fist into the back of the chair he stood behind and cursed fluently. His glare shifted to Ludovic. "I can't bloody tell with you nobs! Is he lying to my face?"

"No," Ludovic said mildly. "Sending bullies to burn alive a girl who had refused his advances is really not his style. In fact, I'm not sure any advances were made *or* refused. It makes no difference to the current problem."

Dearham grasped his knee with fingers that were not quite

steady. "You had better tell me."

Ludovic explained succinctly what Renwick had told him, while Renwick gazed at his clenched hands, and Dearham watched Renwick.

"I've asked Mr. Dunne to find this man," Renwick muttered. "While I look to the safety of my family and my interests."

"You think they're still in danger?" Dearham asked.

Renwick nodded once. "I'm afraid of it."

"Then hadn't you better tell Dunne everything?" Dearham suggested.

Renwick scowled impatiently. "I just bloody did!"

"No, I think you have your suspicions."

"What makes you say that?" Dunne asked with interest.

"I think he's too used to keeping things to himself, even when it doesn't matter, or it's against his interests. I thought he knew more about Kitty's origins than he let on at our discussions. And he has that same look about him now."

"Cursed nobs," Renwick said bitterly. "You think everything's your business because you say it is. It ain't!"

"No, but if you want to get at the root of the problem, get Kitty's attacker before the law, and keep your family safe, hadn't you better give him *everything* he needs?"

Surprised by Dearham's insight, Ludovic glanced from him to Renwick, whose fists tightened and then relaxed. At last, the man sat and rubbed his knuckles across his forehead.

"It's the connection that bothers me," he admitted at last. "Burning my hotel to get at me is one thing. Deliberately involving Kitty is another. There's no denying she's special to me, and I've never hidden it. I haven't always been the most law-abiding man, but I try to be, for her and the boys, and these days, I don't know anyone mean enough to be revenged on me through her."

"Except?" Dearham prompted gently.

Renwick stared at his spread hands. "Alf Smith." He raised his eyes to Dearham's. "He lived in Taverner Street, eighteen years ago. I went there because he'd stolen from me. I went and took back my stuff, gave him a thrashing…and took Kitty from him. She was filthy, bruised, and neglected. I don't think she was his, but he lived with her and her mother for a bit. He knocked both of them around—a sick woman and a *baby!*" Renwick glared, then coughed. "I took the girl before he killed her. Best thing I ever did. For her and for me."

"And you think this Alf Smith is now Albert Franks?" Ludovic said steadily.

Renwick shrugged. "He could be. His name was Alfred Francis Smith, so there's some similarities. Maybe I'm being fanciful, for I certainly didn't recognize him when Jimmie brought him to Maida. But I barely looked. His laborers are his business and young Luke's. None of them ever misbehaved. But it *could* be him. And the fact that he enticed Kitty there *bothers* me."

"Oh, I think that bothers us all," Dearham said with rare savagery. He stood up, dragging his hand through his rumpled hair. "And you're worried he might still come after Kitty. To hurt you."

"And her. He was sick enough to beat a tiny child. God knows how his mind works. If I'm honest, I fear for my boys, too, but Kitty's our shared past, and the boys can take care of themselves pretty well. She can't."

Dearham drew a deep breath. "She can come here, with me. Don't glare at me, Renwick. I'm not offering to seduce her. My sister is in London, with her husband's family. I'll ask her to remove here. She'll like the company and some help with the babies, too."

"Are you offering her a job or making her your family?" Renwick snarled.

"Is she my family?" Dearham asked steadily.

Renwick sighed and sat back. "Truth? I don't know. What I do know is, she's mine to care for, and last night I did not do well enough."

"You rescued her in time," Dunne pointed out. "I don't think any parent in the world would have foreseen that kind of danger."

Renwick swallowed. "She'd be safe with you? Guarded by your army of servants? They won't look down their superior noses at her while someone harms her?"

"They'll do as they're bidden, whoever she is," Dearham said flatly. "And why would anyone look for her here?"

"Because they already know of a connection between you and her," Dunne reminded him. "They used your name to entice her to the hotel. On the other hand, you can easily keep strangers off the premises. Mr. Renwick can't, not if he wants to keep running his business."

Renwick scowled. "She can stay here until we have Franks. Or whoever committed the crime." A brief smile lightened Renwick's anxious face. "If she'll agree."

"Is she well enough to be removed here?"

"I don't know," Renwick replied miserably. "Not today, I don't think."

"May I see her?" Dearham asked.

KITTY'S EMOTIONS WERE all over the place. From sheer gratitude for the life she had almost lost, to anger at her own stupidity in going to the building site at night, to wonder at the obvious love and care of her family and friends.

Uncle Bill had carried her home while the rest of the fire was put out. The shepherd's wife, who was their nearest neighbor, had rushed over to help bathe her and anoint her burns and assist her into a clean bed where, despite her pain and the discomfort of her throat and chest, she had slept. But they had not left her alone. Rob and Dan and Uncle Bill had taken turns to sit with her, their faces so anxious that in her odd moments of wakefulness, she tried to tell them she was fine. Dan wiped his eyes.

By the time the doctor arrived, Sal and Vera were there, too. They had driven out from London with Mr. Harris as soon as Uncle Bill's messenger reached them. The doctor examined her burns and peered into her throat, and pronounced kindly that she would live.

"Rest in bed for a few days while your throat and lungs heal. The dressings on your hands and shoulder should be changed frequently. I'll call back in a few days to see how you do, but I'm sure you will be fine."

"Thank God for that," Vera said as her mother showed him out. "My God, Kit, you gave us such a fright."

"I was a bit frightened myself," Kitty admitted in her new, hoarse voice. Vera passed her a cup of water. "Where is Uncle Bill?"

"He went to London to see about finding that missing laborer. They think he started the fire."

Kitty nodded. She already knew that. Though her mind still whispered, *Why would he do that? And how did he know about the duke?*

"How bad is the hotel?" she asked.

Vera shrugged. "I don't know. I haven't been up there. Dad's gone to look at the damage with Luke, see what's best to be done. Tell you what, though, I wouldn't like to be in that arsonist's shoes when Uncle Bill gets hold of him. And the boys. I've never seen them so riled up, even Rob, who's *always* so calm." Her voice broke. "I'd hug you, Kitty Renwick, if I wasn't so scared of hurting you more. But I'll settle for having a go at that—"

"Don't go upsetting Kitty with your own anger," Sal said, coming back into the room. "Why don't you go and make a nice milky custard for Kitty?"

"One of the serving girls from the Gardens is already in the kitchen," Vera said, going to the door with a quick smile at Kitty. "But I do make a wonderful custard."

"I brought her up to be modest," Sal said humorously. She

chatted for a little, making Kitty smile, although waves of weakness seemed ready to hit her and make her cry for no reason.

Distracting herself, Kitty remembered that this was the first time she had been alone with Sal since she had found out about the locket.

"Mrs. Harris," she asked with difficulty, "did my mother really give you that locket Toby showed the duke?"

A flurry of confusion crossed Sal's face as though she had forgotten all about it. Or perhaps Toby hadn't got it from her at all. If so, she covered for him. "Yes, she did. Night before she died. She were a sweet girl and kind." She smiled. "Like you."

Which made Kitty want to cry again. Instead, she obediently ate Vera's milky egg custard, which was indeed very smooth and soothing on her tortured throat. And then, she lay down and fell asleep once more.

When she woke, the guard had changed, and Rob was in the room, gazing out of the window.

"How's the hotel?" she croaked.

"Bit of a mess at the wing where the fire started. Jimmie says it will set us back a week or so, but it hasn't completely destroyed the construction." He came toward her, shrugging. "Could have done without the added expense, to be honest, but at least we still have you. How do you feel?"

"Better. Is Uncle Bill back?"

"Just now."

"Tell him I'm sorry," she whispered, and her voice broke.

Rob sank onto the bed beside her, grasping her good shoulder. "Kitty," he said helplessly. "It's not your fault. None of this is your fault."

He passed her a cup of water, and that helped steady her as she heard footsteps on the stairs. Her bedchamber door opened, and Uncle Bill walked in, his anxious gaze locked on her face. Behind him, filling the little room, came the Duke of Dearham.

CHAPTER NINE

"What's *he* doing here?" Rob demanded.

"He's come to help," Uncle Bill said shortly. "He'd no more to do with this than you or me. Go and help your brother in the Gardens. Kitty's got enough guards for now."

Rob hesitated, then left the room, leaving Kitty grasping the bedclothes with her bandaged hands and staring wildly from the duke to Uncle Bill.

"Do you mind if I stay?" the duke asked. At least she could read no pity in his eyes. "Just for a few minutes?"

She shook her head. Although she had been so unforgivably stupid, she couldn't bear him to leave just yet. He'd come all this way to see her, and it made her want to cry. Again.

The duke glanced at Uncle Bill, who stared back, then growled, "Five minutes, and I'll be right outside."

Panic surged and ebbed as the door closed behind her uncle, and the duke came closer and eased himself down on the bed. He looked so large and elegant and out of place. And yet, for some reason, there was no one she would rather be there. Even though she was in her night rail, puffy on one shoulder with the bandage, her hair pushed askew by the dressing on her head, and her hands bound.

He had kept the pity from his face and voice when he first came in, but his expression now had no name. "Oh, my poor

Kitty," he whispered.

She gasped, hard, in a last attempt to stop it, but the tears came anyway. She jerked her head to one side to hide, but his arms came around her, and, somehow, she found herself cradled against his chest. How did he know that was exactly what she needed when she hadn't known herself? His strong arms were gentle, but he held her in a definite hug and let her cry.

It was only for a few moments. As her heaving sobs stilled, he rested his cheek against her hair, avoiding the dressing on her head. "I've never come across a woman who weeps silently."

"Most women do," she croaked. "Except for effect."

"So young and so cynical," he murmured, and this time it was a sob of laughter that escaped her.

"They're afraid to touch me in case I break," she confided. "I'm sorry. I keep wanting to cry. It's not the pain, it's not even the fire, just…that someone chose *me*, deliberately hurt *me*. No one…"

Softly, he stroked her hair. "I know. But you don't believe I did this, do you?"

She shook her head, forcing herself to sit back on the pillow. "I was stupid. The note was signed Dearham, but it didn't *sound* like you. I should have known you would never try to make an assignation with me in the middle of the night, in that place…" She had wanted to believe, that was the trouble. But she couldn't tell him that.

"May I see the note?"

She made a movement to rise, and his hand on her good shoulder pressed her back. "Tell me where."

"In the first drawer of the chest. There's a little box."

It seemed even odder to watch him opening the drawer, rummaging among her things, and emerging with the box, his brows raised. She nodded, and he opened it to reveal her paltry treasure—Aunty Mary's locket, a ring from childhood, and the necklace she had worn to the masked ball. And the note that had taken her out last night.

He sat down again and looked at the note, frowning. "If I ever command you so rudely, you may hit me. I expect that's what you went there to do."

"I expect it is."

He dropped the note on her lap, then took a card and a pencil from his pocket. On the back of his card, he scrawled *Dearham*. And showed it to her.

She swallowed. "I know. I know it was not from you. And I can't help thinking that if I hadn't been so stupid, the fire would never have happened."

"I suspect the grudge was never against you but against your uncle."

She met his gaze. "I was used to hurt him?"

The duke nodded, and she felt herself wobble again.

"I have an idea," he said, "that...well, that might kill two birds with one stone. If you come and stay in London with my sister and me, you will be safe while Dunne and your uncle find the person responsible. And you will also get to know my family, which is almost certainly yours."

Her jaw dropped. And then she smiled with genuine amusement. "Don't be silly. I can't live in a duke's palace."

"It's not a palace, just a fairly spacious townhouse. My sister is fun and kind. She is one of twins and has two sets of twins of her own. The second set are only weeks old, so she would value your companionship. Her husband is a soldier and will be there, too, at least for the next week or so before he takes up his new post. You'll like him, as well. We are old friends. When we were children, his family and ours spent a lot of time together, and we got into a lot of mischief. The next generation bids fair to outdo us."

"Oh, you are kind and trying to make me comfortable, but it would not work. I could be your sister's nursery maid, only not like this." She held up her bandaged hands.

"No," the duke said. Not fiercely or even sharply. On the contrary, his voice was quiet, and yet...implacable. "I have servants. You are my cousin."

"If I am, I'm a very distant one, and not in any way that matters."

"It matters," the duke said. "You matter."

"I matter to my family," she retorted, waving her bandaged hand to encompass the cottage. "*They* are my family."

To her surprise, the duke nodded. "Yes, they are and always will be. But now you also have us."

"Your Grace's world and ours do not mix," she said dryly.

"They do here at the Gardens," he pointed out. "Why not elsewhere?" He held her gaze. "Kitty, I would like to give you time to think about this, to come to us when you are comfortable with the idea. But circumstances have pushed us all to some…urgency. Your uncle fears for your safety here. His enemies have already got to you once."

"Through you," she pointed out, flicking her fingers over the note in her lap. "They know already of some connection between you and me."

"Which is a matter for further investigation," he said pleasantly, although with a hint of grimness in his fine eyes. "For the moment, I am in a position to have a large number of loyal servants who can protect you constantly, whether you are outdoors or in. No one will get to you who should not. On the other hand, the Gardens are open to the public, which means all sorts of people are around all the time. To run the Gardens, your uncle and your brothers are constantly out and about where you are not. They cannot protect you as they would wish."

There was truth in that, but still… "I don't *want* to be protected!"

He smiled. "Yes, you do. It's *having* to be protected that grates on you. And on me. But we have to work with the hand we have now until we can change it."

"But we are agreed the fire was to hurt Uncle Bill," she protested, frowning with fresh fear. "Who will protect him?"

"Your uncle assures me he has ways to protect himself. Now

that war has been declared, I don't fancy the chances of his enemies."

She stared at him. "And you don't mind that? That we live on the edges of the law? That my uncle made his first fortune, probably, on the wrong side of it? Probably with *violence?*"

The duke's smile was crooked. "My dear girl, most of the aristocracy is descended from robber barons of one kind or another. I am not so hypocritical as to condemn someone's family for doing what my own did a few years previously."

As she frowned over that, he added, "Whatever he was in his past, I believe your uncle is a good man. And the transformation, if there was one, is due to you and your cousins."

"He cheats at cards," she said desperately.

"So does my Great—Aunt Augusta. In fact, I'd like to see you sharp her."

In spite of everything, laughter caught in her throat and started a painful coughing fit that brought Uncle Bill back into the room. By then, the duke was holding the water to her lips and helping her drink, but over the cup, her gaze met her uncle's, and she saw that he had made up his mind.

"Even your lowliest servants will be too superior for me," she said desperately. "I will shrivel and fade to nothing amongst your aristocratic family,"

"Nonsense." The duke smiled, snatching her breath all over again. "Whenever I have seen you among the aristocracy, you shine."

And that deprived her of words long enough for him to stand and bow with no trace of irony and walk out of the room.

"YOU WANT *WHAT?*" Meg asked, staring at Johnny across the drawing room table.

"I want you and Harry and your tribe to remove round to

Grosvenor Square in order to chaperone a young lady I believe to be Cousin Margaret's daughter."

"I thought that's what you said," Meg said weakly. "Couldn't she just go to Mama at Dearham Abbey?"

"Perhaps for Christmas. I don't think she's ready yet for Mama."

Meg had never been slow. "Why, who is she?"

"She's the adopted niece of one William Renwick, who owns Maida Pleasure Gardens."

Meg caught her dropping jaw and swallowed. "Oh, dear."

"She needs to be able to hold her own at least among the family. Learn to be a lady."

"Johnny, I can't teach her to be a lady," Meg scoffed. "I spent most of my life being told off for hoydenish behavior."

"Which is why you will be so good for Kitty. She is spirited and kind and likes to laugh. And she is better educated than many debutantes it has been my misfortune to stand up with. But you will see for yourself. She is coming to Dearham House tomorrow."

"Tomorrow!"

"She has been the victim of an accident and has been injured. She may also still be in danger, so I will be instructing the household and Harry accordingly."

"You're very high-handed all of a sudden. Harry won't just jump to your bidding, you know."

"Of course I know," Johnny said cheerfully. "Which is why I rely on you, sweetest sister, to persuade him."

Meg uttered a word that was not remotely sweet or even ladylike and left the drawing room to see to her babies.

BY THE FOLLOWING morning, Kitty felt much less shaky. Her headache had faded to manageable proportions, and the burns on her hands and shoulder had settled into mere aches. With Vera's help, she went downstairs and had breakfast in the kitchen—scrambled eggs this time—and was touched when her uncle and cousins joined her, looking ridiculously pleased with her progress.

After breakfast, the boys filled the bathtub and departed, leaving Vera to help her bathe and wash her hair. After which, wrapped in the biggest towel, she went back upstairs to dry. Vera brushed out her hair, carefully avoiding her head wound and her burned shoulder, re-dressed her injuries, and helped her into the autumn-red dress.

"You would be better at this than I," Kitty muttered.

"No, I wouldn't. For a start, I'd say *better than me*, not I. You're the one who listened at school."

"They never taught us to speak like ladies, though, did they? How to eat like a lady, how to curtsey like one, how to make conversation like the nobs."

Vera nudged her. "You're half a nob already. You can pass everything you learn on to me, so I'll be a credit to Luke when he's building palaces for the prince."

"I won't fit in. His sister will hate me for the imposter I am."

"The duke don't think you're an imposter. Chin up, Kitty, it only needs to be for a little while, and then you can come home if it's awful. Or even if it isn't. Come on, I can hear a carriage at the back gate."

Since it was a Sunday, the Gardens were closed, but the duke had arrived in a massive traveling coach with no crest on the sides. He sprang out without help and let down the steps himself before strolling forward to meet her entire family gathered before the back gate.

"I will look after her to the best of my ability," he promised Uncle Bill. "And keep you informed."

Uncle Bill nodded curtly and offered his hand, which the duke shook cordially. "I'll see Miss Harris is taken home, too." He touched his hat to the others and offered his arm to Kitty. She took it rather blindly but found Rob waiting to hand her into the carriage.

With a gasp, she hugged him, then Dan and Uncle Bill, and let Rob help her inside. Vera followed, twitching at silken cushions to ensure Kitty's comfort. Finally, the duke followed, filling the space, and then the horses started off, and Kitty stared blindly back at her waving family.

"Give over, Kit, you're not going to another country," Vera scolded. "You're no further from them than you've been from me since you moved out to Maida."

"I know," Kitty said, trying to smile. "I just feel this is all happening to someone else. That when I leave, I'll never get myself back again."

She was grateful that the duke did not appear to see the need to make conversation with her. He and Vera had the odd humorous exchange while she watched out the window in silence until they reached Hyde Park and the huge, fashionable houses nearby. She had never been in this part of the city before, and it left her speechless and even more intimidated.

The carriage drove into a large, gracious square and pulled up in front of an impressive front gate. Liveried footmen ran down the front steps.

"Oh my," Vera mumbled, and Kitty giggled. "Off you go, Highness." Vera grinned and winked. "You know where I am."

"Stay in the carriage," the duke said to Vera. "It will take you home."

"Don't be daft," Vera said as one footman opened the door and another let down the carriage steps. "Rig like this'd be in bits in no time round Seven Dials. It can drop me at a hackney stand if you insist."

"I do," the duke said, casually depositing some coins in her hand before he got out with perfect grace and waited to hand Kitty down.

Kitty drew in her breath, twitched her eyebrows in her friend's direction, and laid her hand in the duke's.

CHAPTER TEN

S HE WALKED UP the steps on his arm and inside a wide entrance hallway. She tried not to gawp as the duke gave his hat to a bowing, very superior servant, and then turned to her.

"Collins will take your bonnet and cloak," he said. "Let me help you."

Her hands lifted of their own volition to perform the tasks herself, but her bandaged fingers were clumsy, and she let them fall again. His were deft, untying her bonnet ribbons and the frogs of her cloak, a curiously intimate service that made her flush all over. And yet she felt bare and exposed as he unwrapped her and handed her outer garments to the butler.

She tried a smile at the servant, who surprised her by smiling back.

Thus encouraged, she took the duke's proffered arm again to climb the elegant staircase. "Is Lady Meg in the drawing room?" he asked the retreating butler over his shoulder.

"I believe so, Your Grace."

Kitty did not look forward to meeting his sister. Lady Meg would be justly suspicious of her so-called relationship to the family and probably of her intentions toward the duke. She would be everything Kitty was not and never would be, and the woman had no reason whatsoever to be more than coldly civil to her in front of His Grace. She would be appalled by Kitty's appearance, speech…

"Meg doesn't bite, you know," the duke said mildly. "Though she is curious by nature."

And then they were walking through open double doors into a magnificent drawing room that was bigger than the whole cottage at Maida Gardens. A polished parquet floor with two fine, matching carpets, elegant cabinets, and tables scattered throughout, with beautiful porcelain and silver ornaments. Tasteful silk wall coverings. Two crystal chandeliers hanging from the ceiling that must have contained enough candles to light up the whole Gardens on a winter night.

And in the midst of this splendor stood a cradle. An expensively dressed lady paced beside it, the baby in her arms making small, annoyed noises that weren't quite crying while it wriggled and threw its arms around.

The lady paused in her perambulations and glanced toward them, a frown of worry tugging at her brow.

"Meg?" the duke said, as though calling her to attention. "Allow me to present Miss Kitty Renwick, Cousin Margaret's daughter."

"Possibly," Kitty muttered.

"Kitty," the duke continued as though he hadn't heard, "my sister, Lady Henry de Vere. Though we all call her Meg."

Lady Henry de Vere came toward her. "Of course, how do you do, Miss Renwick?" she said hurriedly, holding out one hand while she grasped the tiny, wriggling baby in the other. "Do you know anything about babies?"

"Only that I was one."

Meg gave a snort of laughter. "Trust me, it doesn't help. Nor does the fact that she is my fourth child and yet does not behave like any who have come before. Her sister lies peacefully asleep, while she won't settle at all. Perhaps she wants Harry."

"Where is Harry?" the duke inquired.

"Horseguards or somewhere. He shouldn't be long. Would you mind, Miss Renwick?"

As her ladyship held the child out, it was instinct to take her, holding her upright against her good shoulder.

"Oh, your poor hands," her ladyship exclaimed. "Johnny told me you'd been in an accident but...if it hurts, give her back to me."

"She weighs nothing," Kitty said in amazement, walking with the tiny creature to the window, where she turned her back to let the baby see out.

"She's stopped wriggling," Meg noted in triumph. "Do you know, I think she was bored?"

"I'm sure you were exactly the same," the duke said wryly.

"Then I need to speak to Mama, don't I?" she retorted. "She's usually happy to deliver advice. Ring for tea, Johnny, I'm parched. And with any luck, Rosie will fall asleep, and we can put her in the cradle beside her sister."

"Or you could give them both to the nursery maid," the duke said wryly, walking over to pull a silken cord.

"I could," Lady Henry agreed with the ghost of a smile. "But where's the fun in that? Sit down, Miss Renwick, if it's more comfortable."

"Would you mind calling me Kitty?" she blurted, emboldened by the small aristocrat on her shoulder. "No one calls me Miss Renwick."

"In fact, no one should while you're here," the duke said. "We shall call you Cousin Kitty, and you'll be Miss Kitty to the servants. But you will need a surname for introductions."

Kitty frowned. "Introductions to whom?"

"Anyone who calls on us. Fortunately, there shouldn't be many, for there's little fashionable company in London at this time of year." He glanced at his suddenly curious sister. "We think Kitty's...accident was part of an attack on her uncle. So she needs another name if we are to hide her."

"Then something like Smith is too obvious," Lady Meg declared, "How about Rennie? It's enough like Renwick to be familiar for Kitty but a completely different name in its own right.

Cousin, is that child asleep?"

"I think so. She's quite slumped."

Lady Meg detached little Rosie and laid her in the cradle beside her identical sister. Tea was brought in by two footmen, accompanied by a splendid array of cakes and scones and tiny sandwiches. Kitty's stomach rumbled. She wondered if her throat was up to real food. If her manners were up to eating it in this company.

She accepted a cup of tea from her ladyship with a murmur of thanks, though her bandaged fingers made it awkward to lift the cup.

"Just use both hands," the duke said. "There's no one here but family."

Lady Meg glanced at Kitty at the last word, and Kitty hastily hefted the cup to her lips.

During tea, the duke and his sister exchanged mostly chatter about family and friends, which they explained to Kitty as they went. She felt both impatient and ashamed of the silly charade, though the others seemed quite happy with it.

Seemed.

After tea, her ladyship took Kitty up to her bedchamber—another big, gracious room, with a huge bed and two bedside tables, a dressing table with a looking glass, a desk, a massive wardrobe, and another looking glass taller than she was. Her small carpetbag had been set on a chair by the dressing table.

"You didn't bring much," Lady Meg said.

"I don't have much," Kitty replied lightly.

"We should go shopping. What a pity Martha isn't here. She's much better at clothes than I am."

"Lady Martha is your twin sister," Kitty recalled.

"She is." Lady Meg sank against the foot of the bed and regarded her. "Are you really Margaret's daughter?"

Kitty met her gaze. "My mother was called Maggie. I've no idea if she was your Margaret or not. She died when I was a baby, and Uncle Bill took me in. His Grace thinks I'm his cousin. But it seems unlikely to me."

"I can't help wondering what he means by you," Meg said abruptly. "You're not his usual type at all, and in any case, he would never bring that kind of woman here to me. Are you just his latest cause?"

"Does he have causes?"

Meg's smile was cynical. "Pursuit of pleasure, as a rule, dragging scandal in his wake."

Kitty dropped her gaze to the bag.

"You don't like that idea," Meg observed. "Which is interesting."

"Why?"

"Most women are either intimidated or attracted by his rakish reputation," Meg said frankly. "You don't appear to be either."

She lifted her chin. "I'm not." His reputation was not the man. "What other causes does he have?"

"Oh, various charities among the poor. And injustice among his friends."

Kitty frowned. "I suppose I must be an injustice, then, although I am hardly a friend."

"You appear, my dear, to be family."

"Maybe," Kitty said restlessly. "But frankly, I don't see how you can introduce me as such to your friends."

Meg shrugged, her gaze appraising. "Oh, I don't know. A few rough edges to your accent, perhaps, but you speak well, and your basic manners are sound. But, forgive me, you seem less than wholehearted about the enterprise."

"I don't like being a fraud."

Meg searched her face. "Johnny doesn't think you are one. Neither does Ludovic Dunne, whose opinion one should never disregard because it is based solely on evidence."

"But it doesn't matter whether I'm actually your family by blood or not," Kitty blurted. "In any way that matters, I'm Bill Renwick's niece, who waits at Maida Garden tables and plays card tricks on Uncle Bill's friends."

"Is that all you *want* to be?" Meg asked. "Is it…enough?"

Kitty stared at her. "I don't know. I'm not even sure what you mean."

Meg moved restlessly from the bed to the window seat. "We are all born into a family or a circumstance that comes with certain…expectations. For example, I was born the daughter of a wealthy, powerful duke, and my one purpose was to marry well in order to bring my family even more wealth and power. But I wanted more. I wanted fun and adventure. I wanted to see the whole world and write books. I was such a trial to my family that they sent me to be a lady-in-waiting to the Princess of Wales, who was always talking of going abroad."

"Did you go with her?"

"Lord, no, she took others instead, but that's a different story. The point is, I did not *settle*."

"But you are married now," Kitty pointed out.

"For love," Meg said. "Which changes everything. I saw Europe with Harry instead, and we live our own lives. Johnny expects nothing of me, except that I be happy."

"Is he happy?" Kitty asked curiously.

"Good question," Meg said, her eyes suddenly shrewd. "And not one people normally ask about my amiable rake of a brother. Of course, there were expectations on him, too. He was brought up to succeed our father as duke, but *he* wanted more. He wanted fun and adventure, too. But my father died too soon, and suddenly Johnny was the duke. He does his duty, but I think he still wants more."

"In what way?"

"Ah." Meg's smile was fleeting. "Well, that is something you will have to ask him. And yourself. Would you have been happy spending the rest of your life at Maida Gardens? Does the life of a poor relation to the Duke of Dearham appeal to you any more than it did to your mother?"

"I'm only here until my uncle has dealt with his enemy," Kitty said stiffly.

"Of course you are," Meg said soothingly. She stood up. "I'll leave you to get comfortable. If you need anything, ring the bell beside the bed, and a maid will come. She'll help you change for dinner, too."

"Ch-change for dinner?" Kitty stammered. "But I have nothing more suitable than *this*." She spread her bandaged hands over her skirts.

"It's very pretty," Meg said kindly. "And will do for this evening. After all, there will only be the four of us. I'll talk to Johnny."

When she had flitted off, no doubt back to her babies or to her other children, probably corralled in a nursery, Kitty unpacked her meager bag, hanging her second-best dress in the wardrobe, and placing her spare shifts and night rail on the shelves. She put her hairbrush and comb on the dressing table, together with her pin box, and shoved her sewing kit in one of the drawers. Her spare bandages and salve for her burns, she put in one of the bedside cabinets, and then hung her old dressing gown over the bedpost.

After a moment, she took off her boots, slipped her feet into old slippers, and shoved the boots at the bottom of the wardrobe.

Then she sat down on the bed and wondered what she was supposed to do until dinner. And whether or not she would be able to eat it.

⇶⇷

HAVING EXPLORED THE house except the bedchambers, which seemed all to be on the same floor, and nodded amiably to the often surprised but well-mannered servants she encountered, Kitty returned to her own room.

Although she did not ring, a maid appeared to see if she needed anything.

"Oh, no. Thank you," Kitty managed.

"I can help with your hair, if you like," the maid offered.

"Is it a mess?" Kitty asked anxiously.

The maid grinned, making her appear younger than she had first appeared. "It's coming loose, Miss, but we'll fix that in no time."

Obligingly, Kitty sat before the dressing table mirror, and the made unpinned, brushed, and re-pinned her hair into a rather flattering style that Vera would probably have approved.

"Thank you," Kitty said, impressed.

"You're welcome, Miss. Just ring if you need anything."

The problem, Kitty realized only when the girl had gone, was that there was nothing to do in her room. Kitty was not used to being idle, and in her precious time alone, she would read whatever books she found in the cottage.

One of the rooms she had discovered today was a library so impressive she had crept out again. But surely the duke would not mind her using it? Accordingly, she left her bedchamber and ran down to the floor below, making her way past the drawing room, formal dining room, and around the corner to the library.

She opened the door and went in to discover it already occupied by the duke and a handsome young army officer in uniform. They sat in comfortable armchairs close to the fire, each with an elegant glass containing an amber liquid she guessed was brandy. They appeared to be in comfortable yet intense discussion, so Kitty backed hastily out again.

Unfortunately, the duke glanced up and saw her, and rose to his feet. "Kitty. Come in and meet Harry."

"Oh, I won't disturb you."

"Exactly. We were talking about you, so it's only fair. Harry, in case you hadn't guessed, this is my cousin, Miss Kitty Renwick, henceforth known as Miss Rennie. Kitty, my old friend and brother-in-law, Colonel Lord Henry de Vere."

The colonel, who had risen to his feet also, bowed and smiled disarmingly. "Call me Harry. Everyone else does."

Kitty bobbed a curtsey and looked a little wildly to the duke for help.

"A glass of sherry, perhaps?" he offered, already walking to the decanter, while Lord Harry set a chair for her between them.

"So, you are the young lady of miracles who soothed my daughter's fidgets?" Lord Harry said.

"Beginner's luck," Kitty said, taking the glass from Harry with some difficulty. "I know nothing about babies."

"Neither do we," Harry said. "Because as soon as you think you know something, the next one proves you wrong. For instance…"

He launched into a baby tale that made her laugh, especially when it led him and the duke into bantering reminiscences that were mostly insults. Once, she glanced, smiling from Harry to the duke, and found him watching her, a faint, warm curve to his lips.

Perhaps fortunately, Meg appeared at that point, looking beautiful but flustered in a fresh evening gown of pale lavender.

"Oh, there you are, Kitty. I thought you'd run away," Meg exclaimed. "And you've met Harry. Your hair is pretty like that." She sank down in Harry's proffered chair while her husband leaned casually on the arm, and the duke gave her a glass of sherry, too.

Bizarrely, the company began to feel comfortable, almost normal. As though she weren't really sitting in a ducal mansion, drinking His Grace's sherry, in the company of the duke himself, his sister, and her husband, who happened to be a marquess's son and a colonel of cavalry.

Before she could be overwhelmed again, the butler announced dinner, and Meg led them into the formal dining room where, thank God, the places had all been set at one end of the massive table.

The duke held her chair, and she sat, gazing at the daunting array of cutlery and glasses before her.

"You may serve the soup, Collins," the duke instructed. "We'll ring when we're ready."

A footman ladled soup into each fine, porcelain bowl, then replaced the lid on the tureen, bowed, and departed, two other footmen and Collins the butler following in his wake.

"I expect you're not used to so many courses," the duke said bluntly. "But it's not as impossible as it looks. As a rule, you simply begin with the cutlery on the outside and work inward with each course." He picked up his spoon.

Kitty lifted hers, trying to hold it as he did, although it was difficult with the bandages. "How many courses do you eat? I don't know why you're not all as fat as whales."

Meg laughed. "The courses are not large, and it's considered polite for some reason, for ladies only to eat tiny amounts of each. But you're entirely right, it's silly and wasteful, especially when the streets are full of the poor and hungry."

"My sister has Jacobin tendencies," the duke said.

Kitty's eyes widened. "Truly?"

"Yes. I'd cut off dukes' heads in a trice," Meg retorted, smiling sweetly at her brother. "For one thing, they seem incapable of thought. For example, you have brought Kitty here as our cousin, with one morning dress. Have I your permission to take her to the dressmaker's tomorrow?"

"Of course."

"No," Kitty said in alarm, and they all looked at her. She swallowed. "No, thank you."

The duke laid down his fork. "Really? You're the first female I've met to turn down new gowns."

"You just know the wrong kind of females," Meg told him before turning to Kitty. "The thing is, you would be doing us a favor if you accepted. It does the Winter honor no good to have a relation with only one gown. And if we're to carry this off, you really have to dress accordingly."

"I've never had to," Kitty said stiffly. "But my uncle will buy anything I ask him for."

Meg glanced at her brother. "Well, perhaps Johnny can arrange that with him. Meanwhile, you and I will go and choose a few new gowns. For every day, we can alter some of mine."

THE NEXT FEW days passed in a whirl of activity that left Kitty little time to brood or miss her family at Maida. Lady Meg, the children's nurse, and the duke's housekeeper conferred daily over the dressing of Kitty's injuries and debated treatments while agreeing they were healing well. Even the wound in her head was less tender, and she rarely had headaches from it. She was introduced to Meg and Harry's twin boys, who were three years old and full of energy, mischief, and good nature. Kitty played with them, accompanied them to the park with their parents—and two sturdy footmen—and gradually began to let down her guard around them.

She also seemed to spend an inordinate time at the dressmaker's and soon found herself the proud owner of two morning gowns of finest muslin, with warm, matching pelisses, two silk evening gowns fit for a princess, and a fur-lined cloak. She also had a smart new hat with dashing feathers, new undergarments, and a pair of evening slippers. And the finest ballgown she had ever seen, even though she still could not imagine herself attending anything grander than a public ball at Maida.

As if that wasn't enough, the household conspired to alter several of Meg's gowns to fit Kitty.

"But I will never need all these clothes," she protested.

"You might. Among other things, we thought we might go to the theatre," Meg said casually.

"The theatre?" Kitty repeated, instantly distracted. "My uncle took us once. It was wonderful. Like being in someone else's life."

"Is that what you wanted?" Meg asked evenly.

Kitty shook her head. "Not really. It was just…interesting. *Exciting*. To see, rather than just imagine, other people's stories, whether now or hundreds of years in the past."

Meg regarded her with a rather strange expression, from which Kitty could make out mainly curiosity and a hint of affection. "Do you know, you are really not what I expected? I'm not even sure you *like* Johnny."

"Of course I like Johnny," Kitty blurted, her entire body flushing with embarrassment. "That is, His Grace. When do you think we'll go to the theatre?"

Meg's gaze had grown speculative, and Kitty was terrified she would pry further, but in the end, she allowed the change of subject, and Kitty breathed again.

For she already knew in her heart that the strangely magical nature of the last week was due to Johnny's presence—amiable, bantering, and somehow larger than life. More than that, the warmth she occasionally glimpsed in his eyes thrilled her. She liked his teasing, his sense of fun, and her occasional glimpses of the much more thoughtful man beneath. That breathless sense of intimacy that had seized her when he had first smiled at her more than a year ago seemed now to be with her all the time, intense and wonderful and terrifying. But she absorbed that, too, as part of the whole bewildering change in her life, without pausing to think of the dangers.

Until the night she met him on the staircase.

CHAPTER ELEVEN

PERHAPS IT HAD even begun during the evening in the drawing room, when Meg and the duke had entertained them with a comic duet on the pianoforte.

"Do you play?" Harry asked Kitty, smiling at her delight.

She shook her head. "No, I've never needed to learn. We have musicians at the Gardens."

"It's considered a necessary ladylike accomplishment," Meg said, wrinkling her nose as she stood up from the piano. "Though since most ladies never play again after their wedding, I've never understood why it's meant to attract a husband."

"You and Martha were pretty good," the duke recalled, wandering over with the decanter to refill Harry's glass.

"We never took it seriously," Meg recalled. "I think it should be for amusement."

Kitty, suddenly restless because she thought the duke might sit beside her on the sofa, and she wanted it too much, stood up and wandered away to the pianoforte. She sat and touched a few notes, with the two undamaged fingers of her mostly unbandaged right hand, enjoying the sound, even though it was no tune.

With the background of the chatter behind her, she tried out notes with one hand and even found the first line of a song she had heard in the Gardens. Pleased with herself, she tried it again. And then the duke sat down beside her and played the same notes at the same time but further down the keyboard, filling out the sound.

Kitty smiled without looking at him, and they played again, and this time he embellished between each note, and she laughed. Enjoying herself now, she played again, and he joined in with increasingly elaborate accompaniment.

She only stopped when she realized she could no longer hear Meg's or Harry's voices. She knew suddenly they had stopped talking to watch her and the duke, and the physical awareness that had been with her since he had sat down beside her suddenly soared.

Dear God, she could feel the warmth of his thigh through the thin layers of Meg's altered gown. His arm touched her shoulder. His long, elegant fingers remained poised on the keys, his face turned toward hers. She risked a fleeting glance up at him, and all the breath seemed to leave her body. He held her stricken gaze, his own intent and glinting with warm wickedness and fun. God help her, he was beautiful, and she had no idea what to do about it.

In panic, she stood up, and so did he, which somehow brought them even closer and yet not close enough.

What is happening to me? What is the matter with me?

Nothing, you imbecile, came her brain's tart answer. *It happened long ago when he smiled at you and took the tray you were carrying to his crowded table.*

Oh, no, I can't fall in love with him. I can't.

Too late…

Somehow, she was smiling and taking his teasingly offered arm, but she made sure not to sit beside him while she let the talk of the others flow over her, and she refuted her own foolish allegations.

He was an attractive man. Everyone said so. And she was not used to meeting attractive men, certainly not to being thrown into such intimacy with them. It wasn't surprising her body stirred in close proximity to his, but that was something she could and would control.

By willpower, she focused on the conversation and forced herself to join in. And then, it really was easy because he didn't really look at her again, except to say a casual good night when she went up to bed.

She walked up with Meg, who was going to visit the babies and look in on her boys. They parted amiably, and Kitty was glad of the initially irksome new routine with Jilly, the maid, who unpinned and undressed her, brushed out her hair, and braided it loosely for the night.

"Just leave the lamp," she said as Jilly began blowing out candles. "I think I'll read a while." She would have to distract herself from all these feelings which threatened just below the surface of her deliberate calm.

Jilly bade her a cheerful goodnight and departed for her own bed while Kitty picked up the novel she had been reading and read the final few pages with satisfaction.

Except, of course, that it meant she had nothing more to read. She sighed, turned down the lamp, and nestled down into the covers. She tossed and turned for ten minutes before she sat up and re-lit the bedside candle.

The house was quiet. She was sure she had heard the duke's and Lord Harry's voices earlier, their parting footsteps as they retired. Restlessly, she got up and felt for her robe at the foot of the bed. Donning it for warmth rather than decency, for she didn't expect to meet anyone, she seized the candle and set off to the library to swap her finished novel for something else. Anything else.

She was used to this house always being lit when she moved around it, so it felt strange in the dark, negotiating the turns and the stairs and the passage to the library. Only when she reached the door did she realize she might find him there. She listened intently and, hearing nothing, went in.

The place was in darkness. Hastily, she lit a branch of candles from her own, giving her enough light to return the novel where she had found it, and snatch up a book of travels in the east. For good measure, she added another novel she found lying on the table, written by *A Lady*.

Thus supplied, she blew out the library candles and retreated with her own. As before, she focused the candle and her attention on her feet to make sure she found the curves in the staircase. The last thing she wanted was to stumble, make a racket that wakened everyone or even set fire to the carpet.

So it was that she saw the bare, male feet an instant before she collided with their owner. The candlelight swirled crazily as she leapt back against the wall. Strong hands seized her by the arms, causing the books to slither free and drop to the floor. The scream surging up her throat died in a gasp as the flickering flame played over her the familiar features of the Duke of Dearham.

For an instant, she went limp against the wall from sheer relief. But he followed, a frown of concern pulling down his handsome brow. That was when she realized what was different about him.

It wasn't just his feet that were bare. He wore no coat or cravat or even buttons to his shirt sleeves which flapped about his elbows. As the candle dipped, she could make out the muscles and veins of his forearms. And when she raised it again, she became fascinated by the golden column of his throat and his strong, prominent collar bone.

Her heart was still thudding, but no longer with fear of an attacker looming out of the darkness. Instead, every sense, every nerve and hair on her skin was aware. Like at the pianoforte, only more so, because his hands were on her arms, his hips touching hers, and her whole body seemed to melt.

With conscious bravery, she raised her eyes over his sculpted, parted lips, to his lean, strong cheekbones and up to his tousled hair. How could he be so rumpled and yet so…?

Beautiful, she thought in wonder as she finally met his deep, unblinking eyes.

They were intent on her face, the lids heavy like hoods. His gaze fell from hers to her lips, and the butterflies in her stomach plunged and rioted.

This is desire. Lust. Need...

His gaze dropped further, over her throat, where a pulse beat madly, and downward over her robe. God knew what he saw, for her robe was agape, and she could barely breathe, but his eyes had clouded as they once more found hers. Tiny glints of amber gleamed there, like flames, perhaps reflecting the candle or her own desperate heat.

He released one of her arms and stepped even closer, resting his hand on the wall just to the left of her head, forcing her to hold the candle out to the right. His other hand slid up her arm, over her shoulder to her neck, and she had to smother a gasp at his touch on her skin. His fingers moved to her nape, and fresh fire sparked through her veins, for the caress was exquisite. His head bent, and he paused with his lips so close to hers she could taste his breath—coffee, a hint of brandy, *him...*

I want...

Oh God, had she said that aloud? A smile touched his lips just before they covered hers and sealed.

This was different from the kiss at Maida. This was suffused from the beginning with utter sensuality, as though he recognized and fed her wild, unfamiliar lust. His tongue caressed her lips, her teeth, until she found it with her own. The length of his body from thigh to chest pushed her into the wall, which was as well, for her knees threatened to give, and without the wonderful pressure, she might well have fallen. As it was, she gloried in his hard strength, in particular the rigid column pressing into her abdomen. If she hadn't been so giddy with delight and need, she might have been shocked. As it was, she accepted every delicious moment and reached for more.

She heard the tiny, inarticulate sounds issuing from her throat and the soft, answering groan from his as the kiss deepened, and his body moved against hers in a caress that made her gasp.

In the end, it was the precariously wobbling candle that

seemed to bring him back to himself. The fingers working their incredible magic on her nape slipped away, back down her arm to steady her hand. And slowly, very slowly, he detached his mouth from hers and raised his head a bare inch to look down into her face.

His breath was ragged, like hers, his desire surely as great as hers. But his self-control, clearly, was better, for he dropped his hand from the wall, cupped her cheek for an instant, long enough only for her to sink against his palm, and then he stepped away, releasing her candle-hand last, and ran downstairs into the darkness.

Kitty stared after him in bewilderment until she could no longer even make out his darker shape.

Throughout the whole incident, neither of them had said a word.

On trembling legs, she tottered on toward her bedchamber.

Somewhere on the journey, she began to smile. Because she *loved* him, and he had kissed her. Kissed her so…thoroughly, so…deliciously.

She had no idea what it meant, but it gave her bright, burning, thrilling *hope*. For *something*.

JOHNNY SLEPT LATE the following morning, not, as had once been a frequent occurrence, because of over-indulgence the night before, but because he had been awake most of the night wrestling with the twin demons of temptation and guilt. And desire so intense it made him feel like an adolescent boy. Which, God help him, he was not.

He had known, sitting beside her at the piano, watching her face light with pleasure in the simple game, that desire still flared between them. He had known he should not touch her and had quickly, deliberately, made things casual between them once more. And he had known that, for any number of reasons, he had to keep their relationship carefully between those boundaries.

But that was before he had gone to bed with visions of her smile in his head and torturing speculations as to what lay beneath her becoming new gowns. He recalled only too easily the feel of her in his arms at Maida, dancing, kissing him. He should never have kissed her. He had always liked naughty women, not sweet ones, so what the devil he had been thinking, he had no idea.

In his defense, of course, he hadn't been certain which she was until he began kissing her, and then the answer had knocked him sideways.

Both. A sweet and probably wonderful young woman, capable of very wicked passion. Even if she hadn't been Cousin Margaret's daughter—probably—that had been a warning to him.

He had heeded it, for the most part, allowing in only the affection and growing pleasure in her company as she had relaxed and come out of her shell. The inappropriate lust he had kept well-buried, until, by the piano, she had looked at him like *that*. And hadn't even known what was in her eyes.

That look had tormented him as he went to bed and he tossed and turned, longing to feel her beneath him, kissing him, moving with him… Until he realized bed was the wrong place for him when his entire being was full of her. And so, he had decided to go to the morning room, which was nice and cold, and either pace or read until he felt like an adult again.

It had been a good enough plan, if only it hadn't been thwarted by Kitty herself.

He groaned, now, dunking his head in the washing bowl. Why had he touched her? Why had he not stayed hidden or merely walked past with some jest about sleeping at night?

Because there was something between them. Something rare and warm.

Slowly, he dragged his face out of the bowl and reached for the towel.

Something of value. Something priceless.

This isn't impossible at all.

While he let his valet shave him and help him dress, his mind was busy on this stunning fact. And by the time he rose to go to breakfast, he was smiling and ready.

The others were all in the breakfast parlor, planning an outing to the park with all four children.

"Coming, Johnny?" Harry asked with more than a hint of mockery.

It was a pleasure to drawl, "Why not?" And see the startlement in Harry's eyes.

He was aware of Kitty's head turning toward him, daring to look at him for the first time since he had entered the room. So, he met her gaze and smiled. "It is a beautiful morning, is it not?"

"Very," she managed, blushing adorably while a shy, relieved smile dawned on her passionate lips, and he knew that, even if he didn't win, the chase would be worth the heartache.

Accordingly, accompanied as usual by two stout footmen, they walked to Hyde Park. It was hardly the occasion for dalliance—there were too many children to keep track of and play with—but her company was enough. In teams, they played hide-and-seek and tag, straying off the main paths.

They had all met up again, the footmen still following gamely, when Johnny noticed the struggle just ahead. Two men were wrestling with a solitary woman, trying to drag her off the path and into the trees.

The female appeared to be giving a good account of herself, making excellent use of her knee and elbow, but there was clearly no way she could win this fight. Johnny loped immediately to the rescue, calling back over his shoulder, "Harry, stay with them!"

It was only a few yards to reach the struggle.

"Back off!" one man warned, flashing a knife at him.

More annoyed than frightened, Johnny kicked his hand, sending the knife flying into the undergrowth. In the same movement, he spun and punched the astonished villain with all the force he'd gathered.

"You back off," he suggested to the man on his backside.

Harry and the others, including the footmen, were almost upon them now, too. The man holding on—just—to the furious woman clearly decided discretion was the better part of valor.

"Leg it," he growled at his confederate and shot off into the bushes, closely followed in a stumbling run by the man Johnny had punched.

"Well," the woman drawled, half-laughing despite her ordeal. "I always said you were my hero. How are you, Johnny?"

Johnny stared at her in total astonishment. *"Aline?"*

CHAPTER TWELVE

KITTY GLANCED FROM the woman who had been attacked to Johnny and felt her chest constrict. Although proud of his quick intervention on the lady's behalf and relieved he had emerged unscathed, something very like dread twisted through her feelings.

She had never seen that precise expression on his face before, and she didn't like it. Nor did she like the smile on the woman's lips, a flare of excitement, a pleasure that mirrored his own.

He is her lover.

Harry strolled forward, a baby in one arm, a small boy clinging to his other hand. "I am devastated. I thought I was your hero."

"Ah, but your heroics belong to your country and your lady wife, Captain Harry. How do you do, Lady Meg?" Her amused glance took in all the children. "Exhausted, I imagine."

Meg took both her hands, which seemed to take the strange lady by surprise. "How are you, more to the point? Are you hurt?"

"Only my pride. I dropped my umbrella and couldn't wield it to proper effect. I am very grateful you happened along." She spoke with a charming hint of a foreign accent, just enough to be intriguing.

"In the midst of another adventure, Aline?" the duke asked,

his eyes gleaming with laughter and clear admiration. And the blossoming hope in Kitty's heart began to shrivel.

"Sadly, yes, although I had hoped it was over." For the first time, she appeared to notice Kitty.

So did the duke. "I'm sorry," he said easily. "Where are my manners? Princess, allow me to present my cousin, Miss Rennie. Kitty, this is… Actually, I have no idea of your title."

"Princess was a good start," drawled the lady. "I gather you have been talking to the Sayles whom I met in Paris last year. Princess Hagerin, if we are being formal." The lady extended one languid hand. "Always delighted to meet another member of the Winter clan."

Kitty, who would have preferred to curtsey from a distance—a great distance—took the proffered hand and curtseyed. What did she call a princess? My lady? Your Highness? It didn't matter. It seemed the princess did not expect her to speak. She was awarded a swift, piercing appraisal half-hidden behind a smile, and then her fingers were released.

"And Prince Hagerin?" Meg asked.

"Alas, I am a widow once more."

"Really, this time?" Johnny asked inexplicably.

"Yes." She hesitated. "Which is, I fear, the reason behind the contretemps you just ended."

"Where are you staying?" Johnny asked abruptly.

"It doesn't matter. I will have to move, now, for they must have followed me from there."

"The trouble came to you, this time," the duke guessed, which did not seem to please the princess. She merely shrugged. Meg gazed steadily at her brother. An odd smile flickered over his face and vanished. "You had better come with us, Princess. Providing it will not bring your enemies down upon my family."

The princess appeared to consider. "It's me they wish to kill, and they wish to do it without being caught, so I believe you, your family, and your house would be safe."

"Will your son accompany you?" Meg asked.

"My son is safe in France."

"Then why aren't you?" Harry asked bluntly.

"Because I had a commission here. And Basil is no threat to them. Shall we go? I can hear people coming this way, and I really don't wish to discuss such matters out here."

The duke offered the princess his arm, which, stupidly, felt like another nail hammered into Kitty's heart. Ignoring it, she played with the boys as they walked back through the park. Only when the little boys had to be gathered to a more sedate walk in the street, did Kitty find herself beside Meg, carrying one of the babies.

"The princess is an old friend?" she asked carefully.

"Yes." Meg hesitated, then added, "She once helped me greatly, and she is, I think, the bravest woman I have ever met. But she is not at all what she seems."

Was that a warning? "And she has a son?"

"Yes, a sweet, lively little boy. Although I don't suppose he is so little now! It is four years since I have seen them."

"And His Grace also?"

"Well, I wouldn't know about that," Meg said evasively.

In front of them, the duke bent his head toward the princess, smiling at something she said. Something in the familiarity of the gesture, in the quality of that smile, confirmed what she didn't want to believe. That whatever they were to each other now, he had once been her lover.

Her fierce pang of jealousy took her by surprise. She had known he was a rake, that sooner or later she would come across one of his women. She just hadn't expected it to hurt so badly, when the sad truth was, there had never been any possibility that she would mean anything to the duke, not in the way the princess did. Even had Kitty been more beautiful, more charming, and more brave than Princess Hagerin, she could be neither mistress nor wife to the Duke of Dearham. The best she would ever be was a poor relation.

So why did he kiss me?

Because he suspects I am not his cousin after all? Or a mere slip after a glass of brandy too many. I was just...there.

The most wonderful moments of her life were reduced to ashes.

OVER LUNCHEON, ONCE the servants were dismissed, the princess told her story.

"So, tell us how you became a princess," Harry invited.

She sighed and shrugged. "I was tired. I needed a home for Basil and me, with a little wealth, respect, and security. The prince offered me that, and I took it."

"Were you happy?" Meg asked.

The princess's eyes turned mocking. "In connubial bliss like you, Lady Meg?"

"You were," Johnny said, his gaze on her face, though it told Kitty nothing. "What happened to him?"

"A *coup d'etat*," she replied carelessly. "I'm fairly sure he was poisoned. And then, behold, his brother, the general, stepped into the breach, and all liberal reform came to an end. I was pronounced an evil influence on the late prince and asked politely to leave the country."

"Which you clearly did," Johnny said, "so why are they attacking you here?"

The princess laid down her fork, and Kitty had the impression she didn't want to answer. Then, a too-bright smile lit her face, and she reached for her wine glass. "Because I played a bad card. I was reluctant to leave a comfortable home where Basil was happy, and where I had security, wealth, and friends. And so, I told the general I could not travel yet because I was with child."

"Are you?" Johnny asked steadily, and Kitty couldn't help wondering how much it mattered to him.

"No, as it happens," the princess replied.

"Then it was surely a very temporary solution," Johnny

pointed out.

She inclined her head with a return to mockery. "I have already agreed the card was poor. To be honest, I thought it would give me a few months' grace while everything settled down and returned to normal. I would pretend to lose the baby and be quietly forgotten about, living peacefully in my country house with Basil. I...misjudged. When my maid died from eating a meal I did not want, I took Basil and fled." She raised her glass to the company. "*Vive la révolution.*"

"And they followed you here?" Harry scowled. "Are you not entitled to some kind of protection from the British government?"

"That is part of my self-appointed commission. Along with offering my services once more. I lost everything when the prince died."

"And the men this morning?" Kitty asked. "They were from your husband's country?" *Leg it!* had not sounded particularly foreign.

The beautiful, unreadable eyes met hers for an instant. "They were certainly *paid* by my husband's country."

"Then we had better discover the go-between who arranged it," Johnny said briskly. "As it happens, we know a man who is excellent at finding people."

"Poor Dunne," Harry murmured. "Does he ever get the chance to sleep, I wonder?"

❯❯❯✕❮❮❮

DURING THE AFTERNOON, Kitty kept largely to herself and composed a letter to Uncle Bill and the boys. Since she then went to spend time in the nursery with Meg's children, she elected to have tea there rather than with the adults, a decision cheered flatteringly by the twins. Afterward, Nurse, Meg, and the housekeeper converged upon her to examine her injuries and advised her to leave off the rest of the bandages.

"I don't know which is worse," Kitty said lightly, examining the ugly new and healing skin of her palms and fingers.

"I'll give you some gloves when we go out," Meg said. "I don't think you need to worry here."

"No," Kitty agreed.

But there was no point in sulking because her ridiculous fantasies had been shown up for what they were by the return of the princess to Johnny's life. Instead, she resolved to make the most of reality, enjoy his friendship while she could, and hide her inconvenient feelings until they died from lack of nourishment.

Accordingly, she went early to the library in the hope of spending a few minutes alone with the duke before dinner. But although the fire blazed merrily, the room was empty, and she was reduced to reading the novel she had snatched up last night.

Curled up on one of the large armchairs, she found the novel to be delightful—a light-hearted and witty comedy of society manners, which she suspected was even funnier when one was actually part of the *haut ton*. She was laughing aloud when the library door opened, and she glanced round, her heart beating with expectation.

But it was the princess who entered, now wearing a charming evening gown of exquisite blue silk. Her baggage must have been brought over from wherever she had been staying before. She smiled. "Ah, good evening, Miss… Oh dear, do forgive me, I've forgotten your name."

"I'm not surprised," Kitty said generously. "You had just been attacked. It's Miss Rennie, but everyone calls me Kitty."

"How sweet," the princess remarked, smiling. She sat on a nearby chair. "What are you reading?"

Kitty passed it over, and the princess laughed. "Lady Meg's book! Isn't it wonderful? I laughed all the way through."

"Lady Meg's?" How could she know such a thing? It wasn't inscribed. "What makes you say so?"

"Oh, a little bird told me who the author was, and in fact, once you know her, it's quite clear she wrote it. Were you really in the dark or just defending your cousin's privacy?"

Kitty could feel herself blushing with awkwardness. She had no idea how to answer, so it was well the others joined them at that moment.

However, the princess was not inclined to let the matter drop. Holding up the book, she said, "I've given away your secret, Lady Meg. Your cousin is quite shocked to hear you wrote this."

A frown flickered on Meg's brow and vanished into a smile. "I suspect she's more surprised than shocked. Cousin Kitty has only recently come to live with us. But you shouldn't waste time on it, Kitty. It's not remotely improving!"

"Does she need improving?" inquired the princess guilelessly. The duke's gaze fell on her, his expression unreadable, and she smiled. "I feel we are all entitled to a little fun."

"Just so," he said in apparent agreement.

The pleasant informality of previous evenings seemed to have vanished. Sherry was offered by a footman from a silver tray, and afterward, the duke as host, escorted the highest-ranking lady— the princess—into the dining room.

And the conversation veered between the princess's adventures and the doings of various Winter family members and friends, whom Kitty had never met and sometimes never heard of. Kitty had nothing to contribute and found, in any case, that she didn't wish to, for she knew suddenly that her voice and her accent were still wrong for this society, and even the foreign princess had spotted it. Why else would she have said, *Does she need improving?* in that precise manner?

After dinner, although it was clearly the custom among this rank of society, the gentlemen did not linger over their wine but joined the ladies in the drawing room almost immediately, and the princess suggested a game of whist.

"That would leave one of us out," the duke protested.

"Let it be me," Kitty said brightly. "I don't mind."

"Don't you play?" the princess asked.

"Too well," Johnny answered for her, though he cast her the

quickest of winks in acknowledgment of her secret and less than respectable skills. Which somehow didn't make her happy either. "We'll take it in turns to sit out."

"There's no need," Kitty assured him. "I shall be happy just reading Cousin Meg's book."

She sat in one of the armchairs, the book open on her knee, while the others played, chatted, and laughed. And Kitty realized this was the only evening since the first when she had not felt part of the family. Kindness, she reflected, was very different from acceptance. She knew an urge to go home. Even on ball nights when she was left in the cottage by herself, she had never felt this lonely.

She pulled herself together, keeping an amiable expression on her face while she tried to concentrate. She really wished to go to bed but was afraid they would think she was sulking. So she served the tea in Meg's place and took cups to everyone at the card table. The duke cast her one of his quick, dazzling smiles, and that sustained her through the rest of the evening.

Only when the party finally decided to break up, she was so relieved, she left without Meg's novel.

And if she went back from her bedchamber to fetch it, would she run again into the duke?

She closed her eyes in sudden pain. When Jilly had unlaced her gown, she sent the maid away and huddled inside a shawl, looking out of the window at the gardens in the center of the square and the tall, gracious houses surrounding it. She missed the wide-open vistas from Maida Gardens.

Abruptly, she stood and picked up her candle. She would fetch the book because she didn't think she would sleep. And she had the feeling that even if she did meet the duke tonight, he would barely notice her. On her part, there would be no more...submitting to such treatment either. Whatever her birth, she was not a toy to be picked up and put down whenever his mood or his company changed.

She opened the door and glanced out to see the passage was

not yet in darkness. Instead, at the end of the passage, two people stood very close together. One of them, with his back to her, was undoubtedly the duke, his hair gleaming golden in the candle-light.

Elegant female arms were locked around his neck, and the unmistakably accented voice of the princess murmured, "Oh, I have missed you, Johnny."

"And I, you," he replied, his head bending toward her.

Kitty whisked herself back inside, being careful to close the door too softly to be heard by the couple further along. She leaned against the door, closing her eyes in misery. She didn't know why. It was no more than she suspected. She just hadn't known it would hurt quite so much more to see it confirmed.

CHAPTER THIRTEEN

OVER THE LAST four years, Johnny had expected uncomplicated delight in any reunion that should occur between him and Aline. Four years ago, her bravery, spirit, and generosity had won a little bit of his heart. That she was a passionate and inventive lover had not hurt either.

He was more than happy to have found her again and to be able to return the help she had once given to Meg, and, indeed, to the whole country. She was a rare and magnificent woman. She was also a highly perceptive one, so he did not care for her odd, mild jibes against Kitty, who seemed, in Aline's company, to lose all the self-confidence she had been gathering over the last week. In fact, Kitty had begun to shine in his environment as she had always done in her own, and he hated to see her light dimmed.

The exclusion of Kitty from the evening's card games had been unnecessarily petty and wouldn't have worked either if Kitty herself had not stated her preference. Perhaps the niece of Bill Renwick feared showing exactly how comfortable she was with the cards. Or maybe she was falling too easily into the role of the poor submissive relation, which wasn't what he wanted at all, even though it was, in effect, what he was asking her to become. She was, after all, the daughter of Cousin Margaret, who had been the unpaid companion of his grandmother.

As Kitty all but fled up to bed, his feelings began to crystalize.

Yes, he was pleased to see Aline, an old friend and lover. But the old, passionate intensity had…gone. He wasn't sure why, but he suspected it had something to do with kissing Kitty the night before.

Since he was trying not to think of that or any other difficult subject, he barely noticed that Aline was detaining him with reminiscences on the stairs, on the landing, and finally at her bedchamber door, where he had civilly escorted her at her request.

As she slowly released his arm, he smiled and said, "Good night, Aline."

She smiled back, sultry, inviting, and utterly desirable, working all her old magic with his wayward body, which remembered all too well the pleasures to be found in hers. "It doesn't have to be." In one graceful, tempting movement, she wound her arms around his neck. "Oh, I have missed you, Johnny."

He held her shoulders in a light grip. "And I, you," he said honestly, bending to kiss her cheek.

As though disappointed, a frown flickered across her face, still so close to his. "There was never anyone quite like you, you know," she said huskily. "Not even my prince."

"I can honestly say there was never anyone remotely like you either. It is sad, in a way, that time passes and changes. But I'll always be glad we had our moments. Good night, Aline."

Never, in all his erratic—and indeed erotic—fantasies of their reunion, had he envisioned himself voluntarily walking away from her clear invitation. His body wasn't entirely happy about it either, but he did it anyway.

He was, it seemed, finally learning self-control. The late duke, his father, would have been delighted. In his bedchamber, Johnny raised a last glass of brandy to the man he still thought of as His Grace before tipping the liquid down his throat and allowing his valet to prepare him for bed.

FOR KITTY, THE high point of the following day was to be the theatre in the evening. She just hoped she would not have to give up her place for the princess.

A note from her uncle cheered her somewhat. Receiving it from the butler on her way to breakfast, she slipped into the cold morning room to read it alone. Uncle Bill was not a great correspondent, but he did relay the facts, and that he had written at all reassured her of his affection. Apparently, the rebuilding of the fire-damaged part of the hotel had progressed apace, and there had been no further attacks or acts of sabotage. Rob and Dan, he wrote, were missing her, and several of the staff had sent affectionate messages demanding her return.

Foolish tears welled in her eyes, so she wiped them on her sleeve as she stood up and stuffed the letter inside her cuff.

"Not bad news, I hope?"

Johnny stood in the doorway of the morning room, gazing at her. Her heart performed its usual somersault, made all the worse by the fact she didn't know how to look at him anymore.

She smiled and shook her head. "No, nothing like that. All is well at Maida."

"And in Grosvenor Square?"

"What do you mean?"

"Is all well with you here?" he asked patiently.

"Of course." She walked a little blindly toward him, trusting courtesy to force him out of the way and let her past.

He didn't move. Instead, he stood still, blocking the door and gazing down at her. She felt his searching eyes even though she didn't look up.

"You miss them."

She shrugged. "Of course. Will you excuse me? I'm quite looking forward to breakfast, now."

"I will when you look at me," he said lightly.

She cast a fleeting glance upward and was caught. By his mesmeric eyes and a sense of longing she had no right to. And pain. But she was not submissive by nature. Refusing to appear overwhelmed, even though she felt exactly that, she tilted her chin and forced amusement, "Why? Are you afraid you've left crumbs on your face?"

"No, I wanted to see if there were tears on yours." Unbearably, he took her hand. "I don't want you to be unhappy here, Kitty."

"Then rest easy. Of course, I'm not." She would have drawn her hand free, but he was examining the skin of her palm and fingers.

"They've healed well," he observed. "Do they pain you still?"

She shook her head. "No, but they itch something terrible."

A smile glinted in his eyes that she almost answered.

"Nurse will have ointment for that," he said gravely. "She has ointment for everything." He stood back, letting her breathe once more and yet filling her with a silly sense of loss. "Breakfast?" He offered his arm, and she took it because it would have been rude not to and because she secretly loved any safe opportunity to touch him.

Inevitably, the princess was discovered in the breakfast room, drinking coffee and eating half a bread roll. Since, by accident or design, she sat in a beam of sunshine, her beauty was dazzling, breath-taking. And Kitty was bombarded with sudden visions of naked bodies entwined in just such golden light.

Shocked at herself, she all but bolted to the sideboard to help herself to breakfast. She wished Meg or Harry would come in because she really, *really* did not wish to be the gooseberry at this breakfast party.

However, the duke and the princess were clearly sophisticated enough to converse civilly across the table. He even asked her if she had slept well.

"Excellently, thank you," the princess replied, raising her coffee cup to regard him over the rim. "Did you?"

Surely there was a hint of malice in the question, but the duke only smiled. "Not as badly as I'd feared. What would you ladies like to do today?"

"I have an appointment," the princess announced. "At the Foreign Office."

"Then I shall accompany you," he said at once. "I and two stout footmen. And I'm assuming you wish to be part of our theatre party tonight?"

"Of course," the princess replied. "I would not miss it for the world."

⇥⟩⟩⟩⟨⟨⟨⇤

"YOU SHOULD WEAR the new Pomona evening gown," Meg advised as she left the nursery to change for dinner. "It will be just right for the theatre."

"Will there be room for me?" Kitty asked bluntly. Five was an impossible squash for any group of people in a carriage. For aristocrats in full evening attire, it wasn't to be thought of. And if anyone stayed behind, she didn't want it to be Meg, who needed a child-free outing.

"Of course," Meg said in surprise. "We'll take two carriages."

And so it proved. Inevitably, as the unmarried female who needed a chaperone—the Quality's rules could be ridiculous—Kitty traveled with Meg and Lord Harry, leaving the duke and the princess to travel alone together. But it was not a long journey, the most time-consuming spell for the carriages being the wait to stop close enough to the theatre to disgorge their well-dressed passengers.

The Duke of Dearham, naturally, kept a box all year round that commanded an excellent view of the stage and all the other boxes. Despite her companions mentioning several times that London was thin of company at this time of year, most of the boxes were occupied by richly dressed people, many of whom stared into the Dearham box, though few were acknowledged.

"They're wondering who you are, Cousin," Meg murmured, thus reminding her who she was meant to be.

Kitty, who thought it more likely they were ogling the princess, merely smiled distractedly, waiting for the curtain to go up.

"When the interval…" Meg began, then broke off to exclaim, "Good God, Peter, what are you doing here?"

"I was invited by His Grace," retorted the serious young man who had just entered. He looked vaguely familiar to Kitty.

"Well, either you or Johnny are clearly in trouble with the other," Harry observed, holding up an amiable hand to shake Peter's.

"Why?" Peter asked suspiciously, though he gripped the hand with friendly familiarity.

"If Johnny's reduced to 'His Grace,' you're either buttering him up or far too much on your own dignity," Meg said.

Peter frowned. "What do you expect me to call him? Fish?"

"Why *is* he called Fish?" Kitty asked.

"Loose fish," Meg said, "which is slang for—"

"It relates to his youthful misbehavior," Harry interrupted. "And his old courtesy title of Lord Fishguard, when the old duke was alive."

"Of course it does," Meg said hurriedly. "Peter, have you met our cousin Kitty yet? Miss Kitty Rennie. Kitty, this is my brother, Lord Peter Winter. Oh, and I should present you to Princess Hagerin, Peter, who you probably don't know either."

With the flurry of introductions accomplished, Lord Peter sat beside Kitty. "I don't believe we have met, and yet you do look familiar."

"It will be the family resemblance," the duke observed, looking up from his conversation with the princess.

Or the fact that Lord Peter had been with the duke's party at Maida Gardens.

Kitty did not hear what was said next, for her wandering gaze had settled on the pit of the theatre, from where the ordinary people watched the play. It was where she had sat when Uncle Bill had taken them. She and the boys had waved excitedly across the aisle to Mr. and Mrs. Harris and Vera and…

Toby.

Toby Harris stood at the end of the aisle gazing up at her box. He didn't wave, but he did grin, as though he knew the exact moment she had seen him. And then he sat down in his seat and faced the stage.

Kitty sat back, unreasonably disconcerted. Toby was quite entitled to come to the theatre, and as her old friend, he was certainly owed acknowledgment. But he had given her no chance. She didn't know if she was bothered by that oddity or just by the unexpected connection of what she had come to think of as her two separate worlds.

The curtain went up, instantly drawing her attention to the stage. Even that served to link her further to her "real" life, for a clever display of juggling opened the program. She decided she would be happy to hire them at Maida Gardens and then realized that very few people in the boxes were paying them any attention. Everyone was still chattering away, acknowledging friends, and generally behaving as if nothing was happening on the stage. At least the jugglers got a cheer from the pit as they departed, and a few minutes later, the curtain lifted on a farce.

The noise died down a little, though Kitty still had to strain to hear much of the dialogue. Nevertheless, with her gaze glued to the stage, she quickly lost herself in the silly story and laughed happily at the characters' jokes and antics.

The curtain came down, and Kitty sat back smiling to find everyone in the box was looking at her with varying degrees of amusement.

Heat seeped into her face. "What?"

"Delightfully *ingénue*," the princess murmured.

"Just delightful," the duke said. "I think we all enjoyed it far more, watching it with you."

"Why?" Kitty muttered to Meg as Lord Peter claimed his

brother's attention. "Did I do something wrong?"

"No, bless you," Meg said, giving her arm a quick squeeze. "But sadly, it is the fashion to be bored by the entertainments on offer, as if one has seen it all before. But it's a ridiculous affectation, as you have just shown us. Now brace yourself, Cousin Kitty, for I suspect we are about to be invaded."

The invasion was by people from other boxes calling to greet the duke and his sister and be introduced to the princess. Some were clearly also curious about Kitty, and she was introduced as His Grace's cousin, Miss Rennie, to a sea of faces she had no chance of remembering.

In a very short time, the box grew oppressively full and overheated with too many candles and bodies. Kitty, used to the open spaces of the Gardens and the well-aired pavilions, began to feel both dizzy and panicked.

"Are you quite well, Cousin?" Lord Peter asked quietly.

"Oh yes," she replied at once but, clearly, she was not convincing enough.

"Shall we find some cooler air?" he suggested, and she nodded gratefully.

Somehow, he carved a path for them between visitors, and they emerged at last into the cooler, drafty air of the passage. Of course, there were people out here, too, milling between boxes, but at least they were in smaller numbers and well spread out.

"Oh, thank goodness," Kitty murmured. "I could not breathe in there."

"No, I'm afraid all the other boxes emptied into ours. At this time of the year, Dearham has little competition, and I fear he is also subjected to a flood of toadies who would not normally get near him. Then there are the nosy, desperate to know who the unknown ladies are."

"How can he stand it?" she blurted.

Peter shrugged. "Better than we thought he would. It's no secret that when my father was alive, he leapt from scandal to scandal with charming insouciance. I think it was his way of dealing with… Well, being a duke's heir brings one a lot of supposed friends. Being the duke has made him grow up before he was ready."

"Does he resent it?"

Lord Peter thought about it. "I don't know," he said in vague surprise.

For so apparently open a man, the duke revealed very little.

"It would make no difference if he did," Lord Peter added. "There's nothing he can do about it."

Trapped in the life he was born to, as she had often felt trapped in hers.

"Why, Lord Peter!" came a voice from behind them. A group of people, led by a determined dowager, accosted them. "I thought I saw you earlier with His Grace. What a pleasant surprise to find you still in town. Are you fixed here for the winter?"

"No, ma'am, we shall go to Dearham Abbey soon for Christmas. Allow me to introduce my cousin, Miss Rennie…"

Another slew of instantly forgotten introductions followed, and then even more as another group of people joined the first. As soon as she civilly could, Kitty edged back to the fringes. And then was when she saw Toby lurking at the top of the stairwell.

Her attention was immediately distracted again by a gentleman making polite conversation, but when a pretty lady in white diverted him, Kitty slipped away and followed Toby into the shadowy stairwell.

"Toby? Is everything well?"

"That's what I came to ask you." He grinned, taking her arm and looking her up and down. "Don't you look a treat! You must be wearing a fortune."

"The duke will take it up with Uncle Bill," she said impatiently. "How are Vera and your parents?"

"Fine and proud of you. As I am, of course. So what have you got out of him so far? In coin, I mean, not fripperies, though they're sellable, of course."

She frowned at him, uncomprehending. "Toby, what is it you want?"

"To make plans with you. If you give me the coin, he can't take it back. And I'll salt it away until we can be married."

She stared. "What are you talking about?"

"Don't be coy, Kitty," he said drily. "We all know Bill Renwick wouldn't have let you do this without advantage to himself. So give him enough to keep him quiet, and we'll keep the rest. What do you say?"

Kitty was speechless. There were so many misunderstandings here she didn't know where to begin. More than that, she was disgusted. In the end, she simply brushed off Toby's hand, turned on her heels, and emerged back into the corridor—right beside Princess Hagerin, who stood by the wall, elegantly fanning herself.

Kitty stopped dead.

"Dear me," the princess drawled with a curl of her lip. "Dear, dear me."

Hysterical laughter surged in Kitty's throat. Only misery forced it back down.

"You have no idea," Kitty said and walked on to collect Lord Peter and return to their box.

CHAPTER FOURTEEN

THE LAYERS OF misunderstanding forming over Kitty's head began to weigh her down. Certainly, they prevented her from enjoying or even understanding the main play. The rest of the intervals were torture when she had to keep the smile plastered to her face while she longed simply to be away.

It doesn't matter, she told herself in the carriage, finally returning to Grosvenor Square. Toby's schemes were not hers. The duke already mistrusted Toby and would understand the truth. Still, it made her angry that the princess had eavesdropped and immediately jumped to the wrong conclusion about matters, which were nothing to do with her anyway.

Unless she marries Johnny, in which case she imagines we are stealing from her.

Either way, Kitty did not care to be on the back foot, as it were, with the duke and his family. And she knew instinctively that the princess would present what she had overheard in the worst light possible.

Perhaps, the best solution was for her to tell Johnny immediately. But he was alone with the princess at this moment, no doubt hearing everything from Aline Hagerin.

Damn Toby! Why does he even think *he can interfere with this?*

By the time she stepped out of the carriage, her head was pounding, and she could not face dealing with anything else tonight. If they thought the worst of her, she would simply go home to Maida. Whoever had attacked her and the hotel had probably fled the country by now. Or Uncle Bill had dealt with him in his own way, though she wasn't quite sure what that way might be.

She had no need to be here. Perhaps it was time to go home, whatever tomorrow brought.

It would be best, she thought miserably, if she just left and never saw Johnny again.

A cold hand seemed to squeeze about her heart. She was almost glad when the maid's knock sounded at the door. "Come in."

But it was not Jilly who entered, but the princess.

Kitty rose to her feet.

The princess closed the door and walked unhurriedly toward her. "I thought we should have a little talk in private. In fact, I shall come straight to the point. You are no more His Grace's cousin than I am."

"Probably not," Kitty agreed.

This lack of fight seemed to throw the princess. She peered at Kitty. "Your speech is common, your manners gauche. In short, you have no pretensions whatever to gentility. Whatever made you think you can get away with it?"

Kitty had had enough. "Whatever makes *you* think I could? Do you find His Grace foolish or childish?"

The princess's eyes narrowed. "No. But then he didn't hear what I did."

"Which was what?" Kitty said tiredly.

"You and your lover plotting to steal from him."

"I don't believe you heard me plotting anything."

"Then this *Toby*," the princess mocked, "is just some insane stranger who importuned you?"

"No," sighed Kitty. "He is a misguided old friend."

"Misguided by whom? Bill Renwick? Who appears to be both victim and villain."

"You don't know what you're talking about. I wish you would just go."

The princess smiled with icy amusement. "I'm sure you do. By chance, it's the same advice I was about to offer you. Just go and leave His Grace alone. I won't allow him to be let down."

Let down. Not fleeced. The word choice kept Kitty's retort in her throat. And perhaps seeing the hesitation, the princess said, "Don't misunderstand me, Miss – er… Rennie. You really are very good. The lost cousin plucked from her lowly background to take her rightful place among her noble relatives. Innocent, bewildered, grateful—and injured, too, just to gather a little extra pity. You really do excel at the role. Even I was fooled for a little, and I assure you I am sharper than most. I have had to be."

"Sadly, your edges must be blunted," Kitty retorted. "I'm sure it happens over time."

The princess's eyes widened, and then, unexpectedly, she laughed. "You have claws. What a pity. I almost like you. But I can't let you interfere with the duke."

"Why, because that's your job?" Kitty was almost enjoying herself now. Almost.

"Yes," the princess said frankly. "And Johnny and I have a long and pleasant history."

"And present. So I have gathered."

The princess, who was turning away, paused and glanced back, searching Kitty's face. "I thought you were there last night. How much did you see?"

"Enough."

"Then you know you have no chance. If your plan was to betray your confederates and simply marry the duke, know it will never happen. He is mine and has been for years. You cannot compete."

"I would not so demean myself."

The light from the lamp was dim, so Kitty might have been mistaken. But she thought a hint of color might be staining the other woman's cheeks.

"Quite right," the princess said, recovering. "Think of what I have said. Act on it. And I shall bid you good night."

Kitty did not answer her. Her throat felt too tight to speak.

❊

BY MORNING, KITTY had come to the decision that she would lay the whole matter before the duke, explain about Toby without even mentioning the princess. Accordingly, after breakfast, which she shared only with Lord Harry, who was about to dash off about some business or other, she plucked up her courage and asked a passing footman if the duke was yet up.

"I believe he's in the library, Miss."

"Thank you." She marched on to the library, trying to gather her courage, for the unwelcome thought she had been trying to avoid had finally forced itself to the front of her mind. *What if he sends me away?*

She had no objection to going home, with or without the danger of the arsonist. Only...the duke would not be there, and the very thought of never seeing him again left a great, empty hole in her life. Well, she could live with that. She could live with anything if she thought he was happy. Really, she could.

Drawing back her shoulders, she knocked on the closed door and went in.

The duke and the princess were standing together by the fireplace as though in the midst of a serious discussion. Both heads turned toward her.

The princess smiled. And Kitty knew she should have told the duke last night. She had been outplayed. Now he had his lover's version of events, and the unusual frown on his face told her he did not like it.

"Kitty?" he said with surprising mildness.

Helpless pain wrapped around her heart. But at least it came with a ragged surge of pride. She did not need to defend herself when she had done nothing wrong. She did not need to be here.

And if he could believe such ill of her, he was not worth her blind, foolish devotion.

"Nothing," she managed, already stepping back out of the room. "Forgive the intrusion."

Her decision made, she endeavored to squash her feelings with determined practicality. She was used to organizing and arranging. She went immediately to her chamber and wrote a brief note. This was the hardest part, and she wrestled quite hard with the wording.

My Lord Duke,

I have come to realize my presence here creates too many complications and misunderstandings. Whatever you might have heard, I never have and never would try to rob you or yours. On the contrary, I have ever been grateful for your kindness and for that of Lady Meg and Lord Harry. Please forgive my abrupt departure, but I hate farewells and would spare us both further distress.

The truth is that, whatever blood relationship may or may not exist between us and whatever fears my uncle harbored for my safety—now surely passed—my place is with him and my cousins. You have my undying gratitude for your help and friendship.

I cannot express the depth of my good wishes for your future happiness.

Yours,
Kitty Renwick.

A single tear dropped onto the paper. Hastily, she blotted it and decided it didn't interfere with the legibility of her letter. She set down the pen, then snatched it up again and all but scribbled a postscript.

Please also pass on my farewells to Lord and Lady Harry and their delightful children.

Having sanded the missive, she folded it and wrote the duke's name on the front. Then, leaving it on her desk, she left her chamber once more and hurried downstairs to the front hall. Somewhere in the house, she heard the children's laughter, the squawk of one of the babies, the chatter of the maids cleaning in the drawing room upstairs. Her throat tightened again. How had this place become so appealing, so *comfortable*, so quickly?

She had to be quick and brisk to make herself do this.

She marched up to the young footman lounging on the seat by the front door. Deep in dreams of his own, it took him a few moments to notice her approach. He sprang to his feet.

"Aidan, can you bring a hackney to the door in fifteen minutes?" she asked. The shorter the time, the less chance of anyone finding out.

"Of course, Miss. But His Grace will prefer you use the town carriage."

"No, others will need that this morning. A hackney is best." Since she knew they would not let her out alone to walk to the hackney stand, it made the most sense to have one brought here. Of course, no one would be happy about her entering it alone, but she thought she could probably dash in and be gone before anything could be done about it. "Also…" She lowered her voice. "It is a private matter, Aidan. I don't want His Grace or her ladyship bothered by this. That's very important." To prove it, she passed him a coin from the purse she had been given by the duke and never used.

Aidan hesitated.

She had thought he might, so she looked him straight in the eyes and lifted her eyebrows. "If you cannot do this for me, I shall merely find someone who can."

"Of course, I'll do it, Miss!" he said, properly aghast, which made her feel even more guilty.

"Excellent. Please be discreet."

He tugged his forelock, and she hurried to the staircase without looking back.

Returning to her room, she wrestled herself out of her morning gown with some difficulty and hung it back in the wardrobe. She took out her own autumn red dress and threw it on the bed while she removed her stays and changed out of her new chemise and stockings, replacing them with her own.

She fastened her gown as best she could and put all her new and borrowed things away in the wardrobe. She tied on her old bonnet and cloak and took one more coin from the purse before she left it on the dressing table. Then she threw her few things into her old carpetbag and picked up the letter from the desk.

Opening the bedchamber door a crack, she peered out. Lady Meg was talking to the housekeeper at the top of the stairs, so she waited impatiently, her heart drumming, until the two went their separate ways and the landing was quiet.

Then, with a last glance at the most luxurious chamber she would ever sleep in, she slipped out, closed the door, and walked swiftly along the passage, down the stairs, past the maid polishing the banister. They exchanged good mornings as she hurried on.

She had hoped Aidan would be about business elsewhere in the house by now, but as she crossed the empty hall, he appeared breathlessly through the front door and opened his mouth.

Please don't shout that the carriage awaits!

As though he heard her silent instruction, he closed his mouth again, giving her time to reach him.

"It's waiting for you, Miss," he told her. "Shall I come with you?"

"No, thank you, Aidan." She gave him the letter with her final coin. "I would like you to give this to His Grace an hour from now. If he is not at home, then give it to him when he returns."

"Miss, I really think I should…"

With a smile, she ducked under his arm and walked down the steps. "Maida Gardens, if you please," she said to the driver and stepped inside unaided, closing the door behind her.

⟫⟫⟩⟨⟨⟨

"ALINE, YOU KNOW nothing about her," Johnny said impatiently.

"Neither do you," Aline retorted.

"I know enough."

"To discount her alliance with the greedy young man?"

"I don't discount the greedy young man," Johnny allowed. "In fact, I'm fairly sure I know exactly who he is."

"Then why won't you see what *she* is?"

From the window, gazing down at the street, where a hackney had drawn up by the front gate, Johnny turned and met Aline's gaze.

"Why won't you?" he countered. "Look, I know you are sharp, smart, with survival instincts honed through all sorts of dangers I can only guess at to assess character at a glance. But do you really take me for a fool?"

She stared at him, for the first time looking uncertain, though whether of her position or how to answer him without offense was moot.

"Aline," he said softly, "I have not navigated my world badly over the years. I don't believe I need a nanny at this stage."

She blinked, suddenly appalled. "A *nanny*? Is that how you think of me?"

Johnny wanted to laugh and knew he shouldn't, so he dragged his gaze hastily back to the window. A female in a familiar old cloak and bonnet hurried from the front steps into the hackney. A jolt shocked through him, and he spun around and bolted from the room.

Aline, what have you done?

He flew along the landing and took the stairs in three bounds, leaping across the hall so fast that Aidan, the footman, who was just closing the front door, flattened himself against it in alarm.

"Where has Miss Rennie gone?" Johnny barked, reaching for the door and wrenching it open, propelling Henry across the floor

134

in the process.

"I d-don't know, Your Grace," Aidan stammered. "She begged my discretion and bade me give you this."

Johnny paused long enough to glance back at him.

"In an hour," Aidan said miserably.

Ignoring the letter, Johnny sprang down the steps and raced up the street after the hackney.

A maid cleaning the front steps gawped at him. Two gentlemen jumped out of his way, their expressions torn between astonishment and amusement. Johnny ignored them, intent only on catching up with the hackney, which was heading along the square in the direction of North Audley Street.

His vague plan was to reach the horses and force the driver to stop, but as he pounded along beside the carriage, he glanced in the window and saw the small, solitary figure of Kitty gazing straight ahead, quite unaware of him. He would have laughed, except he needed his breath for running, and, besides, her unguarded expression was so bereft he could not bear it. He lunged at the carriage door and wrenched it open.

Her head jerked around in pure shock. And just as he leapt for the carriage, it began to swerve around the corner into Brook Street. For a moment, he seemed to swing in the breeze, anchored to nothing except the door handle. He really was about to make a mess of the cobbles. And that was before Kitty hurled herself at him, her eyes wild as though she would push him out.

But she grasped the fabric of his coat in both hands and hauled, just as the carriage straightened, and he catapulted inside, releasing the handle just in the nick of time.

He bounced off the seat and somehow retained enough sense to reach back and pull the door closed. Then he sat back on the bench, panting, and gazed at Kitty.

Her eyes wide, her breast heaving, she stared at him from the floor of the carriage. Wordlessly, he stretched down his hand. She blinked at it, then grasped it and allowed herself to be helped onto the seat beside him.

"You are insane," she uttered.

And abruptly, he laughed with sheer elation. "It has been a long time," he gasped.

She looked at once wary and fascinated, and he sobered enough to say lightly. "In any case, you can talk, suborning my staff and fleeing from my house."

"I took only two shillings from the purse," she said defensively. "And I packed only my own things."

The last of his smile died on his lips. "I know that. But why did you go? And so secretively?"

She shrugged. "Because it was the only way I could. I explained it all in the letter I left with Aidan."

"I know. He tried to give it to me as I bore down upon him, probably to stave off the thrashing he could see coming his way."

Her eyes widened again like saucers. "You thrash your servants?"

"Not yet," he said grimly.

Relief flooded her gaze before she dropped it to her hands, and a pang pierced him that she still knew him so little that she could imagine he beat his dependents. No wonder she ran away.

"I thought you were comfortable with us, Cousin Kitty."

Her gaze came back to his. She swallowed. "I'm not your cousin, sir, not in any way that matters."

"Is that what Toby Harris told you last night?"

She didn't even flinch. She shook her head. "Toby looks on life as one big flim-flam. I suppose the princess told you."

"You do know that running away merely confirms her suspicions?"

"I am not running away," she said with dignity. "I am going home."

"I wish you would change your mind."

Color stained her cheeks, though she asked bluntly, "Why?"

"I would miss you," he said honestly.

She only smiled with blatant disbelief.

"Nothing has changed," he said, frowning. "There is no need

to break our agreement."

"I think there is. I would rather go home."

"Because of Aline?" he asked bluntly.

She was silent for a long moment, twisting the fabric of her gown between her fingers. "The princess is only looking out for you."

He stared at her. "You are generous. What makes you think so?"

"Because of something she said when she spoke to me last night. She did not say she wouldn't allow me to fleece you. She said she wouldn't allow me to *let you down*. I know she cares for you."

"So you let her warn you off? I thought you had more spirit."

She cast him an indignant glance but said nothing.

"You think I care for Aline and trifle with you?" he asked ruefully. "Or that I trifle with both of you?"

"The ways of the aristocracy are beyond me," she muttered. "And so, I'm going home to my own people."

He found he was drumming his fingers on his knee and forced them to be still. He worried for her safety, for her hurts, both emotional and physical. But more than that, he didn't want her to go.

"Then," he suggested at last, "allow me to come with you, since I appear to be half-way there already. We can spend the day at Maida, and then you can decide whether to return to town with me or stay with your uncle. Who, I'm sure, will have his own opinion."

She gave an unhappy smile at that, and he took her hand. It jumped in his and then was still.

She took a deep breath. "The princess will not like that."

"The princess," he said steadily, "is a good friend. But she is not my keeper. Nor yours."

Her thick, long eyelashes lifted, revealing a glimpse of intense emotion he couldn't read, and in any case, it was gone in an instant. But it was enough to thrill, to give him hope, though of what, he wasn't quite sure. His life seemed to be growing complicated in bizarre but undeniably fascinating ways, and he could only welcome it.

CHAPTER FIFTEEN

FOR KITTY, THE odd discussion in the carriage en route to Maida was conducted against the constant memory of him leaping into the moving carriage and swinging around the corner in midair. Such a foolish, reckless, and yet supremely casual act. And it thrilled her far beyond what it should, simply because it gave her a glimpse of the wild, fearless boy he must have been and what it cost the man to be the duke.

And then, of course, there was the fact he had done it in pursuit of *her*. She wasn't quite sure why, and part of her was appalled. But only part. Most of her was ecstatic at the prospect of spending several hours with him at Maida or anywhere else.

Even here, he handed her out of the carriage as though she were a lady. And the only witness, Susie at the ticket kiosk, gawped appreciatively, then greeted her with surprised pleasure.

"Lawks, Kitty, it's you!"

"It is," Kitty agreed. "How are you and the Gardens?"

"My mum's got a cold, and the Gardens are quiet." She was wrapped up in layers and wearing warm, woolen gloves with the tips of the fingers cut off. "Glad of the winter hours!"

"My best to your mother. Is my uncle around today?"

"I ain't seen him leave." Susie blushed and fluttered her eyelashes as the duke raised his hat to her.

It seemed very strange to be walking up the familiar path, on the arm of the Duke of Dearham, odder still when Dan caught sight of her and dropped the spade and bucket he was carrying to rush over and hug her, whirling her right off her feet.

"Goodness," she laughed. "Have you missed me?"

Dan grinned and released her. "No one else has your way with pastry. Or scrambled eggs. Or tea, come to that." He nodded warily at the duke, as though he knew perfectly well who it was he had ordered tied up during the smuggled delivery and would never, ever admit it.

The duke nodded gravely back, although Kitty was sure she caught a glint of amusement in his eyes.

"I wouldn't go to the house," Dan said. "We still haven't found Franks or Smith, but Dad's worried someone might still be watching us. From where, I don't know. But it's you he's worried about. I'll tell him and Rob you're here. We'll find you."

Because she didn't know what else to do, Kitty took the duke on a tour of the Gardens, recalling stories as she went about the creation of various areas or amusing events that had happened there. He asked questions, smiled, and even laughed. If he was merely being polite, he gave no sign.

Only when they reached the building site, where the hotel was further along than before, did his eyes grow bleak and cold. Kitty shivered in the silence, and then his arm came around her, hugging her hard to his side.

"I hate that you suffered here," he whispered.

"So do I," she said wryly, and a breath of laughter stirred her hair. Something soft and warm touched her head—surely not his lips?—and then he released her, merely drawing her hand through his arm instead.

Luke appeared, grinning, and gave her an enthusiastic report on the building's progress. "Despite the setback, I really think we might be ready to open at Christmas. Or at least New Year. Barring any more accidents, of course."

"Good news, indeed," Kitty agreed. "Tell Vera I'll write."

As they walked on, she told the duke about Vera and Luke

and how the Harrises were reluctant to let them marry.

"What will they do?"

"Vera says she will marry him with or without their consent. After all, she is one-and-twenty. She will do it, too."

"Vera is the same age as you?"

"Yes, there are only a few weeks between her birthday and mine. Which is one reason Sal offered to bring us up together."

For some reason, the duke seemed to think about that quite deeply. Then the small coffee marquee, where he had first told her of his belief she was his lost cousin, came in sight, and they sat sheltered from the sharp breeze, with a beam of autumnal sunshine to warm them.

Here, Uncle Bill came to join them, with Rob and Dan. Uncle Bill kissed the top of her head, as casually as if she was back after an hour at the market, and yet she felt his intense pleasure across the table as he sat down.

"Any news?" he asked the duke.

"None. You?"

Uncle Bill shook his head gloomily. "We're still looking. So is Mr. Dunne, but Albert Franks seems to have vanished into the mist, along with Alf Smith."

"Maybe he got hurt in the fire, too," Kitty said suddenly, and they all stared at her.

"Actually, that's a very good point," the duke murmured. "And one Dunne might have overlooked. Tea, gentlemen?"

For the next half hour, they talked of other things. It was curious, Kitty thought, as her uncle and cousins departed about their business, that somehow, they had been beguiled into talking to the duke as equals. He did not hold himself high in the instep but accepted people with respect, from the princess to Uncle Bill and everyone who worked for him. It was an endearing trait and one she imagined more intensely afterward as he told her amusing tales from his childhood running wild at Dearham Abbey and the neighboring land, which belonged to Lord Harry's family. A lot of his stories involved his own siblings and the de

Veres, but there were also a blacksmith's daughter and farmer's sons, shepherds, and laborer's families.

"Is it the same with all these friends, now you are the duke?" she asked curiously.

His smile was crooked. "It wasn't the same *before* I was the duke. How could it be? We all grew up. Our people had to work, while Harry went off to be a soldier, and Robert and I went to Oxford. I became *my lord*, not Johnny."

"And you miss it."

He shrugged. "Someone has to be the duke. And I wouldn't swap. It's better than working for my living."

"But you do work," she said shrewdly. "I've seen you poring over reports in the library, sending off bags full of instructions, meeting with all those men of business. And I have only been with you for a couple of weeks."

"Is that all?" he said in vague surprise.

"I expect the time drags," she said with mock sympathy, and he grinned.

"You know it doesn't. Will you come to Dearham Abbey for Christmas?"

"Who will be there?" she asked warily.

"Just a gaggle of Winters. I think Meg and Harry will be gone by then, but my other sister, Martha, will come with her husband and children. And Peter. My mother, of course. Great-Aunt Augusta, inevitably. Possibly a few friends."

Like the princess. "Sir, I will not fit in with these people," Kitty protested.

"Why not? You appear to fit perfectly with Meg and Harry and their tribe."

"But this is different, isn't it?" She took a deep breath. "Even if I were your cousin, I would have little enough right to be there. As it is, I have none. I am Bill Renwick's niece, and you will be ashamed of me."

He looked startled. "Of course, I will not."

"Be reasonable. I have the wrong accent, the wrong conversation, no knowledge of the aristocracy or the ton. I will use the wrong fork, be clumsy and gauche. Your guests and I will despise each other, and I shall be miserable."

He blinked and smiled. She wished his smile didn't melt her in quite this fashion. "Don't be silly. I shall make sure you are not."

"How?" she challenged.

He considered. "Because I think you are a little like me. You don't simply like or dislike someone just because of their place in the world. My family—and my friends—will respect that, some of them, probably, without quite knowing why."

She walked on silently beside him. Then she said, "I will still feel a fraud."

"Because you don't *feel* yourself to be my cousin?"

"Something like that."

Somehow, they were climbing the steps to the lily pond. It was different in daylight, and at this precise moment, the sun shone directly on the water. The boulders around it were warmed, and they sat side by side in silence for a while.

His presence seemed to seep into her along with his physical warmth. Just for a little, she let her pleasure in his company wash through her, enjoying the sweet edge of excitement.

He said casually, "I am not Aline Hagerin's lover."

Oh, don't spoil it, don't lie to me. "Why would you even trouble to say that? It is none of my business."

"Isn't it? I may have been out of order to kiss you as I did on the stairs that night, but it is probably hurtful to imagine I could go straight from that delight to her arms."

"*Lies* would be hurtful."

He turned his face toward her. The sun dappled across his hair and his skin. "Why would I lie?" he asked curiously.

She picked a dying leaf off a nearby hedge and began to shred it in her lap. "I saw you."

"The night she arrived. In the passage."

It wasn't a question, but she nodded anyway.

"When I first met Aline," he said conversationally, "it was four years ago. She was pretending to be married to a Bonapartist spy in order to discover the chain of his contacts. In spite of all that, she took the time to help my sisters. I had never met anyone like her. Actually, I still haven't. But I used to wonder, when I was lonely, what it would be like to meet her again."

"What *was* it like?" She tried not to care.

"Different. We had grown, changed. Or I had. I suppose she will always have a little piece of my heart—a pleasant piece, but one I don't really need. I recognized it that first day. And at her door that evening, I kissed her cheek and left her."

She raised her eyes from the shredded leaf to his face. "Why are you telling me this?"

"I don't know. Because we are friends. Because although I shouldn't have, I *did* kiss you."

And not on the cheek.

His hand closed over hers. Without meaning to, she threaded her fingers through his and listened to the urgent, insistent beat of her heart. When they spoke after that, it was about little things, funny things that did not matter. It was *he* who mattered, whose being seemed to seep into her soul and wrap around her heart. She made no effort to disentangle their hands, and neither did he, until the sun moved, and the cold began to penetrate her warm cloak. Then, as one, they stood, and he handed her down the stone steps. For a while, they walked hand in hand, and nothing had ever felt so sweet. But on the public path, he offered her his arm more properly, and they walked down to the gate to climb into the solitary waiting hackney.

They were half-way home before she realized he had not asked again if she would come back with him to Grosvenor Square. In the end, neither of them had doubted it.

She re-entered the house in something of a glow from the day of pure happiness she had spent with him. More than that, she felt she had drawn back a couple of layers from the invisible mask he habitually wore. Though this made her want to know more, her growing understanding deepened her contentment. It did not even seem wrong to have been holding hands with him for so long, for there was a special pleasure in that. Of course, she had no real idea what it signified now or what it meant for the future. But as they stepped into the house, she did not care about those things. She was living for the moment.

The duke came to a sudden halt. The footman closed the door behind them, and Kitty followed Johnny's gaze to the top of the staircase, where a regal, middle-aged lady stood. She was too far away for Kitty to read her expression, but her posture declared barely contained outrage.

"Mama," Johnny said amiably. "What a pleasant surprise. I was not expecting to see you until next month at Dearham Abbey."

"So I perceive," uttered the lady.

Unhurriedly, the duke unfastened Kitty's cloak and, as she shrugged it off and passed it to Aidan with her old bonnet, Johnny winked at her.

"Her bark is worse than her bite," he murmured and offered Kitty his arm to ascend the stairs.

The duchess sailed ahead of them into the suddenly daunting formality of the drawing room, where she turned, stony-faced and silent.

Johnny sighed. "Mama, allow me to present Miss Kitty Renwick, who is Cousin Margaret's long-lost daughter. Cousin Kitty, my mother, the Dowager Duchess of Dearham.

Kitty curtseyed as Meg had taught her. Though Kitty felt rather pleased with the grace of her gesture, the duchess did not acknowledge it, merely transferred her cold gaze from Kitty's face to her son's.

"You are ridiculous," she stated. "Whoever this female is, she is not Margaret's daughter."

"Your Grace is mistaken," the duke said evenly. "Ludovic Dunne—who, as you know, is responsible for having Dominic Gorse's wrongful conviction quashed *and* discovering the truth about the Cornish embezzlement—has traced Margaret's last days to the room in which Kitty was born."

"I don't care if he traced the very bed. Margaret's daughter was not named Kitty or Katherine or anything remotely similar."

Johnny seemed about to dispute it when the full meaning of her words hit him. "Mother? How do you know what Margaret's daughter was called?"

"Because I corresponded with her," the duchess admitted, looking slightly shamefaced. "It seemed too harsh of your grandfather to banish her altogether, for she had been close to your grandmother for some years. I could give her no material help, of course, but I tried to keep in touch with her." Her gaze, contemptuous once more, swept over Kitty. "Her last letter was to tell me she had given birth to a daughter, whom she had named Isabel."

Isabel... The name sounded strange to Kitty, alien as applied to her. She could not be *Isabel*. Could she?

"That may well be true," Johnny said evenly. "We don't know her real name. Mr. Renwick, who rescued her as a baby and adopted her, renamed her Kitty."

That seemed to throw the duchess off her stride, for she frowned.

"We can find out what I used to be called," Kitty volunteered, speaking for the first time. "If my uncle doesn't know, Sal Harris will."

The duchess's eyes narrowed. "Why would you offer that? So that you can prime them in advance?"

"No," Kitty said bluntly. "Believe it or not, my origins are of at least as much interest to me as to Your Grace."

"Don't be difficult, Mama," the duke said. "You must know I haven't plucked some stranger off the street—or from the opera house. I believe Kitty *is* our cousin, but the main reason for her being here is to keep her safe after an attack at her home. You will know this if you have spoken to Meg. But whether or not she turns out to be related to the Winters, she is a welcome guest in my house."

It was subtly done, the gentlest of reminders that not the dowager's word but her son's was law here. Curiously, Kitty had no doubt that Johnny would win that battle and any others. But it gave her an unpleasant hint of the hostility she would face for her intrusion.

LATE THE FOLLOWING morning, Kitty sought refuge in the small, formal garden at the back of the house, beyond the kitchen garden. Although there was a hint of fog in the air along with the inevitable if faint smells of the city, the outdoors gave Kitty a few moments to think.

She had written to Vera, suggesting they meet in the Green Park tomorrow, and asking her to find out from her mother what Kitty's name had been at birth. If it was Isabel, then it was likelier than ever that Kitty was related to the Winters. If it was not Isabel, then this had all been a mistake.

And Kitty no longer knew how she felt about that. She had no doubt that the duke and his family would continue to keep her safe in such circumstances, but her position would be altered, subtly or otherwise. Without being of Winter blood, she had no pretensions to being a lady. And no excuse to be with Johnny except in a somewhat scandalous relationship.

The uncertainty kept her on edge. But the tension between them was strangely sweet, and she was aware she would not easily give up his company, which would put her firmly in that scandalous relationship category.

Could I really become his mistress? Would he even want me to? The man who had apologized for kissing her and yet held her hand at Maida Gardens as though they were a youthful, ordinary courting couple.

He is a flirt. That was undeniably true. He had always been a flirt, and it was more than likely that's all he wanted of her, to enliven a few weeks of boredom. And yet that didn't sound like him either. He was not so silly or so unfeeling.

In fact, they were friends. And although a few kisses had confused the matter, that was all they would ever be, whether or not she was a lady by blood. He was too honorable for anything else. So why did that not make her happy either?

"A penny for them, Miss Kitty."

From where she stood still in the middle of the garden, facing the back wall, she jerked her head around to see Princess Hagerin, who looked as beautiful as always. Like Kitty, she wore no bonnet, but unlike Kitty, she had remembered to wrap herself in a shawl before venturing into the cold.

"For your thoughts," the princess clarified, moving past her to examine a blooming Christmas rose bush.

"They are not worth as much as a penny," Kitty said. Something beyond the princess's head caught her attention. With a jolt, she realized someone was sitting astride the wall which separated the garden from the mews. He was largely screened by the young apple tree, which grew just in front of him and had not yet lost all its leaves.

She was about to seize the princess by the arm and drag her inside when it entered her head that it was probably one of the Dearham grooms or stable boys, perhaps even one who had been instructed to watch for their safety, even in the back garden. So, she used her sudden movement merely to step nearer the princess, and with her foot, she idly disturbed the earth in the nearby flower bed until her toe came across a decent sized stone.

"You are modest," the princess said, presumably still discussing her thoughts. "And you are still here."

"Do you expect me to run away because you tell me to?" Kitty asked. She bent and picked up the stone before straightening and hiding it among her skirts.

"Actually, yes. Because I can't imagine what you think you are achieving by being here. Her Grace does not believe your claim, indeed can hardly bring herself to look at you, let alone speak to you. And Johnny will never marry you, though he might ruin you."

How could she understand him so little? "His Grace would never ruin me. I am in his house, under his protection."

And as she stepped away, the man on the wall moved out of the concealing apple tree. She only saw it out of the corner of her eye, and the princess's focus seemed to be entirely on the flowers.

"You have made him a hero," the princess observed, turning more toward her. She glanced up with a faintly rueful smile. "I can understand that. I suppose I have done the same. Laughter and love are a heady combination. But the truth is, he is not for innocent little girls."

"Then why," Kitty asked, tracing with her eyes the angle between the princess and the watcher on the wall, "are you so eager for me to go?"

The man on the wall raised his hand and drew it back, and something glinted in the low, autumnal sun.

The princess said, "Because—"

"*Run!*" Kitty commanded and hurled her stone with all her might.

Some instinct or the sheer force of Kitty's voice made the princess jump back on the path, but she did not run. At the same time, the stone connected audibly with the man on the wall, accompanied by a ludicrously surprised cry as he fell backward off the wall. The glinting weapon he had thrown must have lost its aim just in time, for it landed on the lawn, several feet short of its mark.

"What the...?" the princess uttered.

But Kitty did not stay to hear the rest. She flew across the garden and leapt, using one foot to spring from the lowest branch of the apple tree, and grasp the top of the wall with both hands. They were still tender and didn't much like to be scraped, but at least she managed to haul herself onto the wall, from where she could see the attacker bolting down the muse.

A stable boy and the under-coachman had emerged from the Dearham carriage house and were gawping between the running man and Kitty on the wall.

She pointed desperately after the attacker. "Catch him! He tried to kill us!"

It was enough to inspire a stream of men from the mews buildings, all shouting and haring after their quarry.

The princess exclaimed, "Oh, excellently done! I didn't even see him! Come down from there before the wrong people see you."

Kitty slipped down, and the princess caught and steadied her. Their arms dropped from each other, and Kitty said, "He was aiming at you."

The princess's lips quirked into a rueful, unexpectedly deprecating smile. "You see why I need to retire. My instincts are no longer what they were. Without yours, I would probably be dead."

"It seemed…wrong for him to be there, but I didn't know if he was friend or foe until I saw the blade."

"Well, you are either a damned fine shot—if you'll pardon my language—or a lucky one. Either way, you have my undying gratitude."

Kitty shrugged with embarrassment. "Childhood games with my male cousins, who were obsessed with hitting things with other things."

"I'll wager you beat them all to flinders."

"Sometimes," Kitty agreed, returning the princess's smile with a quick, shy one of her own.

The princess took her arm and set off for the house. "I think we need to find His Grace before his servants haul that miscreant before him. And I don't know about you, but I feel the need of a very large brandy."

It wasn't really funny, but a breath of laughter escaped Kitty's lips.

CHAPTER SIXTEEN

H IS GRACE, HOWEVER, was not at home, though he entered the library some twenty minutes later and came to an abrupt halt at the sight of the princess and Kitty swigging brandy together on the sofa. His face was white, his eyes desperately angry and anxious and full of some pain she could not read. Then he stretched out one hand and gripped the nearest table as though to steady himself.

"Thank God. I thought one of you had been injured or worse."

"Oh, no," the princess said with enthusiasm. "Kitty saved the day using a stone wielded with terrifying accuracy. I owe her my life. Did your people catch the perpetrator?"

The duke's eyes had found Kitty's gaze and were staring at her. It seemed to take an effort to drag his attention away. "What? Yes. He's one of the men who attacked you in the park, though he either doesn't know or won't say who hired him. The stable boys in pursuit apparently yelled instructions ahead, and our would-be assassin ran into a strategically opened stable door. We'll haul him off to Bow Street and let the magistrate's fellows have a go at him."

"You might want to send this, too," the princess said, picking up the blade from the table. "He was about to throw it when Kitty's stone took him between the eyes."

Wordlessly, the duke took it and strode back to the door. They heard him shouting to someone, and a few moments later, he returned, walking quickly, and threw himself into the armchair closest to them. A trace of anger still lurked in his eyes, but to Kitty, there was an air of rare uncertainty about him, as if he had no idea what to say or do next.

Kitty put down her glass, from which she had taken only a couple of steadying sips. But the princess raised hers to their host. "Join us? For medicinal purposes, of course."

His hand gripped the arm of his chair. "It seems I can't protect you sober. I really don't fancy my chances if I start drinking brandy in the middle of the day. I think we need to go early to Dearham Abbey."

"We could be followed there, too," the princess pointed out.

"But anyone who did would stand out as a stranger." He closed his eyes. "One man, sitting on the garden wall with a knife, barely yards from my own staff... Only a miracle prevented murder."

"Well, I think we are agreed Kitty is all the miracle we need," the princess drawled. "In which case, it does not matter where we go."

"And the duchess has only just arrived," Kitty reminded him. "She won't thank you either to abandon her or drag her off on another journey. Besides, if the assassin gives away any details, we might get to the princess's true enemy."

The duke looked from one to the other, his tension slowly dying into a wry but definite smile. "The pair of you put me to shame. You are a formidable alliance. And I'm glad to see it."

With that, he rose and strode out, leaving the women looking at each other in bafflement.

IN TRUTH, JOHNNY was thoroughly rattled by the assassination attempt, and not just by how close disaster had come. There had been a terrifying few moments when his people were all talking at once, when all he had heard was Kitty's name, and the blood had roared in his ears at the unendurable thought that she was dead. That the sweet, spirited presence that had become so necessary to his contentment was simply wiped out, horrifically, tragically, before she had truly lived.

And then he had realized that his servants were far too triumphant for anyone to be dead. Collins mercifully had murmured, "In the library, Your Grace," and Johnny had abandoned them all, taking the stairs three and four at a time, to burst into the library and find her side by side with Aline, cozily drinking brandy. There was no sign of injury, although her dress showed a streak of mud. And Aline, when he could drag his gaze to her, was as composed as ever.

He had not been able to deal with it then, but gradually, as he understood exactly what had happened, his heart swelled in pride.

"I always knew you were remarkable," he said to Kitty the next day as they walked to the Green Park, trailed by two footmen.

He constantly scanned the street and the windows on both sides of the road for any signs of threat. His heart felt torn in two, for although he had wanted her to stay at home out of danger, he could not help rejoicing in her nearness.

"Because I can throw stones?" she said deprecatingly. "It is not a ladylike accomplishment, but I'm glad it was useful in the end."

"There is that," he allowed, "but also…you are taking the incident very much in your stride."

Her eyes were distant, and he wondered if she were thinking about the fire.

She said, "I feel for her. For Aline."

Johnny noticed the two women were now on Christian name terms, but he said nothing. If there was a danger to his hopes from Aline's growing closeness with Kitty, it was outweighed by the care they could clearly take of each other.

Kitty said, "After the fire…when I was safe…it was not so much the physical pain that bothered me as the fact that this had been done deliberately to *me*. So, I feel for Aline, not so much for myself. It is important but doesn't…*shatter* me. Does that make sense?"

He nodded, and after a few moments, changed the subject. "Are you sure Vera will come?"

"I haven't heard from her, but I know she will make every effort."

"Whether or not you are Margaret's daughter," he said carefully, "you are still our friend and under our protection."

Her eyes teased him. "If by ours you mean yours and your mother's, I think you might want to confer with Her Grace first. I suppose no one has found Mr. Franks or discovered whether or not he is really the Alf Smith I was taken from?"

He shook his head. "Dunne thinks he may have fled the city."

"He might," she reflected. "But it's also possible he's merely hiding in Seven Dials. No one there will answer his questions or anyone else's. You can hide in there as if you were dead."

He hoped she was wrong, though he suspected otherwise. "Did Toby Harris tell you that?"

"No. Uncle Bill."

He wondered whether to tell her that Toby was probably indirectly responsible for the fire at Maida. That, according to what Dunne had learned, Toby had been running off at the mouth about how he and his sweetheart were about to fleece an amorous duke they had induced to believe was her long-lost cousin. He had thrown Bill Renwick's name around, too, in a proud sort of way, but not in a manner Renwick would thank him for.

They found Vera Harris sitting alone on a bench in the autumnal sunshine, eating an apple, which she threw away with an exclamation in order to throw herself to her feet and into Kitty's arms. Then she pushed her friend back and looked her anxiously up and down.

"You look better than the last time I saw you. But lawks, aren't you fine!" Over Kitty's shoulder, her gaze connected with Johnny's, and she released her friend, curtseying low with what he could only describe as an impudent grin. "My lord duke."

"Miss Harris," he returned, bowing elaborately. "How do you do?"

"Lord, I'm fine," she said impatiently, dragging Kitty down on the bench with her.

Johnny leaned negligently against the nearest tree and scoured the surrounding parkland for possible threats. At least it was quiet at this hour, with only a few children out with their nurses and governesses. He kept looking while the girls chattered.

"How are your hands?" Vera demanded, seizing Kitty's wrists.

"Healed," Kitty said hastily. "How is everyone? I saw Luke at Maida the other day, and he thinks you're making progress with your mother at least."

Vera nodded. "I think she's been on our side for a while."

"Because you threatened to marry without their permission?"

Vera appeared to consider. "Not really. I think she wants me to be happy. She didn't really know Luke at first, assumed I'd throw him over as soon as someone richer and more obviously charming turned up. But she knows him better now, can see how wonderful he is. And she understands that I love him and will never love anyone else."

In spite of his usual disinterest in girlish talk of love and romance, Johnny couldn't help glancing at Vera. Her brazen brown eyes had softened, and he recognized she spoke the simple truth. It struck an alarming chord for him, as it apparently had for her mother.

He went back to studying the horizon and the paths. At a discreet distance, the footmen were observing the ground behind him.

"She hasn't said so, of course," Vera went on, "but even before the ball at Maida, I heard her dropping hints to Dad. She'll bring him round, too."

"I'm glad," Kitty said warmly.

"I spoke to her about your mother as well," Vera said in a rush. "Asked her what Maggie had named you when you were born. She said Isabel."

Kitty's breath caught, and her gaze flew up to Johnny's. For an instant, he wondered why he didn't feel more triumphant. Then it came to him that he didn't actually *care* what her name was or whether she was his cousin or not. She was *Kitty*. And that was the simple cause of the happiness suddenly rushing at him.

He must have been smiling like a loon, for Kitty blushed a bright red, causing Vera to glance from her friend to him with some interest. He took control of his features.

"As I thought," he said smoothly. "But the news will calm my mother's suspicions."

"Then she knew your cousin's baby had the same name?" Vera said with interest. She regarded Kitty with slightly more awe. "Blimey. Will you really still speak to us, now you're a nob?"

Kitty pushed her shoulder. "Don't be so daft."

"Good. I'm glad it's the right news because I've got a more difficult confession, too."

"You have?" Kitty said in surprise. "What?"

Vera drew in her breath and glanced up at Johnny again before returning to Kitty. "I don't know if your uncle told you. But I think Toby might have been responsible for informing the world about the connection between you and the duke. He had too much drink in some low tavern and blabbed about it. He seemed to think he and Mr. Renwick could easily persuade you to fleece His Grace and that you'd all be rich."

"Except me, presumably," Johnny murmured.

Vera grinned with more than a trace of relief. "I'm glad you're not angry, for it was all in Toby's cup-shot mind. He's made some sort of hero out of Mr. Renwick, or out of Mr. Renwick's mythical past, imagines him as some sort of commander of criminals, which I doubt he ever was and certainly isn't now. More to the point, you'll never meet anyone more straight and honest than Kitty."

"I know that," Johnny said mildly, feeling Kitty's gaze on his face.

"As for Toby, I'm sorry," Vera said determinedly. "He's my brother, but he's got a big mouth, and he's been brought up to think he can get whatever he wants, whether that's fancy clothes and jewels and lots of money or Kitty. I told him months ago she wasn't interested, but he never seems to take the hint."

"I've more than hinted," Kitty said frankly.

"Well, don't worry about it," Vera advised. "Dad has put him right and is dragging him off to apologize to your Uncle Bill, so I don't think he'll be making *either* of those mistakes again."

Johnny, returning to his observations while the women's conversation moved on, found he was glad of Vera's honesty and that of the people Kitty regarded as friends and family. In between times, his mind reeled, thrilled, blissful, and anxious about what he should do next. There were many things being a duke simply didn't help with.

Although, on the other hand, one had to use the advantages one had been given...

When it got too cold, the two young women embraced and parted with promises to meet again soon, and Johnny pushed himself off the tree to bow once more to Vera and thank her before offering his arm to Kitty and walking back toward the gate.

As the footmen fell in behind, he heard a snort of feminine laughter in the distance.

"Lord, Kitty," Vera's delighted voice crowed after them. "You've even got fart-catchers!"

Kitty gave a very strange hiccough, and he felt the tremble of laughter through her before she glanced up at him surreptitiously to see if he had heard.

"It could not have been Miss Harris," he said gravely. "But I'll tip them in case they overheard."

She grinned openly. "Sorry." Then she sobered. "You weren't surprised about Toby, were you? You already knew."

"Dunne had discovered something similar."

"Why didn't you tell me?"

"There seemed no point. The damage was done, and whatever Toby's idiocy, he certainly didn't mean anyone to hurt you or your uncle."

She accepted that, even squeezed his arm as though he had been doing her a favor. Perhaps he had been trying to. And it was certainly worth it to have his arm hugged to her breast.

"So, this Alf Smith was drinking in the tavern with Toby," she mused. "Or just overheard him."

Johnny shrugged. "Or even picked up the rumor later. Either way, such talk might well have reminded him of old grudges and dropped a particularly nasty means of revenge into his lap. So, he applied to his old neighbor, Jimmie Harris, who probably wouldn't recognize him after nigh twenty years, under a false name, and got himself sent out to work at Maida." Johnny gestured with one deprecating hand. "Possibly. Until we can lay hands on him, we won't know for sure."

She walked on in silence for a while, which was fine with Johnny. He liked the sense of her movement beside him, her light, familiar touch on his arm. Then she said lightly, "Since it seems I probably *am* your cousin now, will the duchess be happier or unhappier to see me?"

"Who knows?" Johnny said ruefully. "She is not unkind, you know. But since my father's death, she has grown more distant, more conscious of the family dignity, which is unfortunate since of all her children, only Peter ever had much dignity about him."

She considered. "Lord Peter is unsure, which makes him a little stiff. But even surrounded by children and bone-tired, Lady Meg has her own grace."

He glanced at her, pleased and not a little surprised by her insight into his siblings. "True."

"So do you," she added.

He laughed. "My dear girl—"

"It's natural," she interrupted, although color seeped into her face. "You don't look down your nose at people or strut about puffed up with your own importance. You don't throw orders around just because you can. But when you speak, even though you never raise your voice, people listen and obey. They notice you, and they like you. But no one would ever mistake you for less than you are."

Speechless, and not a little touched, he gazed down at her. "I'm not sure I recognize myself," he managed at last. "But thank you. My father was the one with presence and power. I have neither the aptitude nor the interest."

"But you do. They're just not the same as his. You lend your name, your time, and your money to many charitable causes."

He must have looked startled again, for she cast him a quick smile. "Lady Meg," she said apologetically, by way of explanation. "And I know that although you don't sit much in the House of Lords, you do vote on some issues and have even been known to rally support for it. You could, if you wished, exert more of such power toward the social causes you value."

He regarded her, no longer quite amused but not angry either. Rather, it was as if...as if she was showing him a way forward, a way to wield his position for good in a more structured and useful way that his occasional, erratic espousal of causes that just happened to catch his attention. A purpose to his casual, hedonistic life.

Something in him leapt, though whether to embrace this notion or simply its lovely proponent, he would need time to think about.

In the meantime, he was happy to announce, over luncheon, that Kitty had been born Isabel and that therefore there was really very little doubt left that she was indeed Cousin Margaret's daughter.

Meg and Harry, and even Aline smiled with relief and pleasure. His mother, to whom he gave most of his attention, gazed at

Kitty until her eyes glazed over.

"Then there is only one thing to do," the duchess pronounced at last.

"What?" Meg asked suspiciously.

"Teach the girl to dance," said the duchess.

CHAPTER SEVENTEEN

Although the duchess's sally was greeted with relieved laughter, she was not joking. And there was rather more than one thing on her list. But it did mean that Kitty's "education" suddenly became much more intensive.

Meg's vague instruction had consisted largely of letting her observe the customs and manners of the house, how to address servants and equals, and pointing out any words or actions that were wrong in the world of the Quality.

Now, Kitty was bidden daily to the duchess, who took her speech in hand. Kitty knew that simply by being among the duke's family, her accent had moderated and improved. Even Vera had noticed, though she had said nothing, merely cast the odd half-amused glance at her as they talked.

But this was not enough for the duchess, who had her reading aloud and corrected every tiny "mistake" by constant repetition. It was boring and infuriating, and even slightly humiliating, which, with unexpected shrewdness, Her Grace picked up on.

"I know it's maddening, but if you wish to pass muster among our guests by Christmas, you will be much more comfortable speaking as they do."

Kitty almost snapped back that it was the duchess who would be more comfortable, but basic honesty shut her mouth. Not just the duchess but the whole family and their guests would be more comfortable if she spoke and behaved as they did. And in truth, Kitty herself *would* be more comfortable if she did not embarrass herself or her hosts by speaking like the orphan of Seven Dials. Or even like the waitress from Maida Gardens, who entertained Bill Renwick's friends with displays of card tricks and sharp practice.

"No one will be rude to you," the duchess went on, rubbing it in. "But you're smart enough to notice the pity or the amusement, the laughing conversations that stop as soon as you approach. Is that what you want?"

Kitty shook her head. She almost said she would rather go home to Maida, where she was loved however she spoke. But God help her, Johnny would not be at Maida but at Dearham Abbey.

Of course, there was more than speech involved in the duchess's teaching. There were lessons in posture and manners, although the duchess allowed her curtseys to be good enough.

"At least you are intelligent and educated," Her Grace allowed once, "although you could do with more accomplishments. A knowledge of French or Italian would help, as would some skill on the pianoforte or with watercolors. But we have no time for that now."

The duchess regarded her so closely that Kitty began to fidget.

"What do you know of your mother?" the dowager asked abruptly.

"Very little," Kitty confessed. "I wasn't even two when Uncle Bill took me in, so I don't remember her. He told me she was good and kind, but he was always vague as to who she actually was. I grew up assuming she had been his late sister, and no one disputed it."

"She *was* good and kind," the duchess said shortly. "She was the poor relation who kept my mother-in-law, the old duchess, company, but she was good and kind to me."

Kitty's heart beat quickened. Without reason or logic, she was suddenly desperate to absorb every scrap about her mother.

"I was not always the staid person you see before you," the duchess murmured, so quietly that Kitty had to lean closer to hear. "I was a little wild, a little…immoderate. The old duke and duchess disapproved of me. It was Margaret who explained family matters I needed to know, and even covered up my mistakes, frequently getting me out of trouble with Her Grace. We were friends. And yet when she was in trouble, I did not help."

Kitty drew in her breath. "His Grace told me she ran away with an unsuitable man, someone her family forbade her from marrying."

The duchess nodded. "I think it was selfishness on their part. My mother-in-law just wanted her at her beck and call, not married with a home of her own, however modest."

It was, Kitty reflected, just possible that her mother-in-law had been right. "Who was this man? It was not…Alfred Smith?"

The duchess blinked. "Alfred Smith?" she repeated contemptuously. "Who is Alfred Smith?"

"I think he was a thief," Kitty offered. "And possibly a builder by trade."

"Don't be silly. Margaret would have had nothing to do with such a man. She would never even have *met* such a man. No, her husband was a respectable, middling sort of a man, a clerk of some kind. Reginald Penrose."

"My father?" Kitty blurted.

The duchess nodded.

"What…what happened to him?"

"He died before the baby was born. I begged Their Graces to take Margaret back, but they would not. I went to see her, secretly, but she had already moved out of their little house and left no word where she had gone. I only heard from her once more, when you were born, but she never told me where she was."

"Why not?" Kitty asked, not so much of the duchess as of the world.

"I don't know. Pride, perhaps. Or perhaps she was still looking after *me*, because I would have got in trouble for helping her." Her Grace's gaze refocused on Kitty's face. "Do you really know nothing about her?"

Kitty looked at her hands. "I think her life went…downhill. She died in poverty." More, she thought, it would be unkind to tell a lady clearly remorseful for something she could not change.

"And the man who took you in," the duchess said, rallying. "He is a good person?"

"He has always been good to us—to his stepsons and me."

"It might be better if you don't see him again."

"No," Kitty said firmly, "it would not."

To her surprise, the duchess did not argue, merely said, "That will be all for today. You are improving."

The more fun part of her education was the dancing. This took place in the elegant ballroom at the back of the house. The dowager duchess sat at the piano and played merry tunes that echoed in the empty space while she was taught several country dances and the quadrille. Meg, Harry, Johnny, Peter, and Aline were rounded up for these lessons, though they often were not enough to demonstrate the various dances. Chairs were set up to represent other couples in the set, and everyone danced around them, often with much hilarity.

Kitty thoroughly enjoyed these lessons and the exhilaration of dancing. Even Peter unbent, and it was all conducted with great good humor and a sense of fun.

"Then, there is the waltz," the duchess pronounced. "Everyone waltzes these days."

"Oh, that is the one dance I *do* know," Kitty said. "At the Maida balls, there is nothing but waltzes."

"You would be well advised to keep such knowledge to yourself," the duchess observed. "And you had better show me."

"Allow me," the duke said, bowing elaborately to Kitty.

And stupidly, Kitty's heart somersaulted. He had taken his turn partnering her in the lessons, and she had secretly treasured every touch. But the waltz was so much more intimate, and, besides, her memory flooded inconveniently with memories of their previous dances at Maida. He must have understood the blush she could not hide, for a look of wicked teasing entered his eyes and deprived her of breath.

And yet when the duchess played her introduction, and he bowed once more, he took her very sedately into his arm. His clasp on her fingers was light, his hand barely resting on her back at all. When he began to dance, it was much more *formally*, and so far away from her that for the first few moments, she found it harder to follow him.

"Not quite Maida, is it?" he murmured.

"I should have known."

"It can still be fun," he assured her, his thumb softly circling the skin of her hand. At the same time, he spun her and walked her backward and turned again, and she laughed as she followed him.

"Better," the duchess commented. "But don't make me give you lessons, too, Dearham."

She only called him by his title when he displeased her in some way.

"Sorry, Mama," he said humbly, although his grin suggested another emotion entirely.

THE DAY BEFORE Meg and Harry departed for his new posting, Ludovic Dunne called to speak to Kitty and the duke.

"I'm going down to Kent next week," he said without preamble, "and won't be back until January. I still have people with their eyes and ears open for traces of Alf Smith, and if they find him, I shall, of course, let you know."

"Then you've still found no sign of him?" the duke asked.

"We were close," Mr. Dunne said ruefully. "We found a local so-called nurse who had treated a man with burns to his hands and body. He hadn't paid her, so she was willing to tell me where he lived. Unfortunately, he'd gone by that time, but he was using the name Alf Smith, not Franks."

"So he did burn himself that night!" Kitty exclaimed with a shiver.

"Managed to set fire to his own clothes," Mr. Dunne said. "But put out the flames before they had done him too much damage. It may also be why the hotel wasn't burned to the ground. He had to stop before he'd set all the fires he meant to. Or maybe he got a fright when the other builders and the Renwicks woke too quickly. In any case, Smith has vanished again. I'm sorry, Miss Kitty."

"If nothing else, it's an excuse to keep her with us for longer," the duke said lightly. "We're going down to Dearham Abbey at the beginning of December."

It was a party Kitty no longer dreaded. Indeed, she looked forward to seeing the duke on his ancestral acres, and if there was a twinge of dread concerning his guests and the Christmas entertainments, it was outweighed by excitement.

WHEN DUNNE HAD left, Johnny went in search of Aline, whom he found playing with Meg's boys in one of the salons. She was always at her best in such situations, without artifice or guile, and he knew she was missing her own son, whom she would not go near while this danger lurked over her head.

After joining in the game and falling dead with enough drama to entertain his bloodthirsty nephews, Johnny surrendered them to their nurse.

"Walk with me," he invited Aline.

If she felt flattered by the invitation, she gave no sign of it, merely walked at his side into the garden where they both scanned the walls for signs of intruders. And he wondered how best to approach this. Aline was a woman of sophistication and a survivor, but she had already offered herself to him and been refused, and in the light of that, it was difficult to suggest her continued refuge with his family in a manner she could accept. He had no wish to hurt her or to raise expectations he would not meet.

She glanced at him, waiting with exaggerated patience.

Oh well, honesty had always served him before, though he was prepared for a slapped face.

"The man we captured," he began, "is giving away no links to this Count Ledel we suspect of instigating the attacks against you. Or to anyone else from your country. But as you know, neither the emperor nor his ambassador in London is happy with the death of Prince Hagerin. At least the ambassador has engaged to keep Ledel in London for the next two months. Despite receiving your letter, neither of my friends in the British government will admit to me that you ever worked for them, let alone that they have a duty to protect you. But I believe they will watch Ledel and add pressure on the ambassador to keep him within reach. Which should stop him from arranging any more blatant assassination attempts but does nothing to stop those already in motion. I think it would be best if you came with us to Dearham Abbey."

A strange little smile flickered on her lips. "Goodness, that was a long speech to justify an invitation. Even so, I would once have been delighted to say yes."

"I hope you still are."

She met his gaze squarely. "No, you don't, Johnny. You are kind, but your mind and your heart are elsewhere."

"Aren't yours?" he asked evenly.

"Oh, I don't have a heart."

"Did you not even love your prince?"

She shook her head. "Not really. I am not capable of the kind of love you mean. If I were, he would have come closest. And you."

"I can't work out if I'm flattered or disappointed."

She laughed. "Yes, you can."

He smiled back. "Our time is past, but we are still friends. Martha will like to see you again."

"There will be talk, Johnny. The world thinks you fought a duel over me. And against my worse nature, I have no desire to hurt your Kitty."

"Don't," he said quickly, without quite knowing what he was forbidding. But where Kitty was concerned, he possessed a tender spot he could not bear to be prodded.

"She loves you," Aline said flatly. "One of you should face up to that."

He felt more than prodded. He felt pierced by something sharp and breathtaking, something equal parts pleasure and pain. Aline, damn her, was nothing if not perceptive. But he strove to keep to the point. "I will face up to everything if you come to Dearham as my friend. After all, with Meg gone, Kitty will need you."

Aline sighed and appeared to think about it. "I thought my only male friend was Lord Harry," she grumbled. "I liked it that way."

"I am not too proud to substitute for Harry," Johnny said meekly and let her punch his arm just a little too hard. He supposed he deserved it, though he wasn't quite sure why. Until, as she turned away, he caught the faintest glitter in her eyes that might just have been unshed tears.

THE FOLLOWING DAY, Lord and Lady Harry set off to join his regiment at their headquarters in the north. Apart from curtailing dancing lessons, their departure also left the house feeling empty and quiet without crying babies and over-exuberant children.

Kitty felt a little lost when they had gone, a little unsure. Not least, because as she had embraced her brother, Meg had murmured something in his ear, something that had startled him and sent his gaze flying straight to Kitty. It had been an odd look, one she could not identify but which made her suddenly afraid.

Had Meg—kind but practical Meg—warned him against her? Did Kitty take up too much of his time? Or had Meg guessed that Kitty adored her brother and realized it would not do?

It wouldn't, of course, but maybe a few more weeks—just a few more—would give her the strength to leave.

"Shall we pack up and go to Dearham?" the duke said abruptly, over dinner. "How long will you need, Mama?"

"A day," the duchess replied dismissively. "I no longer travel with my favorite furniture, paintings, and dinner services."

"Goodness," Kitty said, awed. "I wish I had seen you travel before. It must have been quite a caravan."

"It was," the duchess agreed modestly. "It certainly got me noticed." She appeared to pull herself together. "Two trunks and my maid now suffice."

"Then I propose we leave the day after tomorrow," the duke said restlessly. "Will that suit, Aline? Kitty?"

"Of course," Aline said at once.

Kitty laid down her spoon. "I would like to go to Maida before we leave."

"I'll take you," the duke promised.

"There is no need. You will be busy—"

"I won't be busy. I have an army of servants who are quite used to my sudden starts."

Kitty opened her mouth to argue and unexpectedly caught Aline's eye.

"Say 'thank you, my lord duke,'" Aline drawled.

Confused, Kitty repeated, "Thank you, my lord duke."

CHAPTER EIGHTEEN

DEARHAM ABBEY WAS massive. It made the London house look like a cottage. An impressive stone pile formed of three wings, surrounded by rings of formal gardens, parkland, forest, and farms, it dominated the countryside as it had clearly done for centuries. An original medieval great hall, now used as a formal dining room, dominated the east wing, while much of the rest was clearly much newer, added in the previous century.

"I will get lost," Kitty said in awe, following the duke and Aline from the great hall and back into the marble entrance hall, from which a sweeping staircase curved up to a long gallery.

"No, you won't," the duke assured her. "At least, not after the first day or so! Until then, servants will always point you in the right direction."

Kitty gazed up at the painted ceiling and the great windows shedding light down the staircase. "It must have been a great place to play as children."

"It was. On rainy days, at least. Mostly, I remember being outdoors. Ah, here is Mrs. Brown, our housekeeper, who will help with anything you need."

Mrs. Brown, a plump woman of middle years, with a vast array of ancient keys dangling from her belt, smiled and curtseyed. "Tea will be served in the small drawing room." She pointed along the gallery. "Third door on the right along there."

She nodded and went serenely on her way.

Kitty followed the duke and Aline along the gallery and up another grand staircase, still gazing about her with awe. The house was on a completely different scale to any building she had ever seen before. "I thought it would be like Uncle Bill's hotel," she said.

Johnny cast her a crooked smile. "My ancestors built on a grand scale. Especially the first duke, who is responsible for the massive expansion. Here is your room, Aline." He threw open a door on his left for the princess. "Your baggage should already be there. Kitty, you are just a little further along the passage…"

Kitty followed obediently.

Johnny lowered his voice, "Her Grace has put you on the edge of the family wing which, in case you had doubts, is acceptance. In fact," he added, opening a door almost at the corner of the passage, "I think she likes you. These were Cousin Margaret's rooms."

Uncertainly, Kitty walked into a fine, comfortable sitting room, off which were two doors. One led to a well-appointed dressing room with a truckle bed, perhaps for a maid. The other gave on to a large bedchamber with heavy, dark blue hangings.

"All for me?" she said, backing once more into the sitting room to find the duke still leaning in the open doorway to the passage.

"Of course. Your things should already be put away for you. And the maid should be up shortly with hot water for you to change and join us for tea. Afterward, I'll show you more of the house or the grounds if it's light enough."

"Thank you," she replied, feeling very small and over-whelmed, with a sneaking longing for the simple coziness of the cottage at Maida. Reminded, she turned back to the duke, just as he pushed his shoulder off the door jamb and stepped back. "Sir?"

"Madam?"

"What were you talking about so earnestly with my uncle? The day before we left London."

"Investing in his hotel," the duke said unexpectedly. "With the extra money, he should be able to get the internal work done in time to open early in the new year, perhaps even for Twelfth Night."

A surge of warmth caused her to take a step nearer. "You didn't need to do that."

"No, I didn't. But I'm hoping to make a fortune out of it, so never imagine it's philanthropy."

"I would never so insult you."

He grinned and sauntered off, leaving her alone in her overwhelming rooms.

SHE WOKE TO the warmth of the sun on her face and remembered she had left open the bed curtains and the shutters because the country view had reminded her of Maida.

She stretched in her grand bed, then slid out of the covers to peer out the window. The sky was clear and blue, the trees and the hedges and the ground sparkling with frost. The outdoor beauty called to her, urging her to explore.

So, she washed and dressed hastily in front of the fire— already lit by some unseen hand while she had slept—wrapped herself in shawls and her old cloak and boots, and then sallied forth.

She could hear the movement and chatter of servants around the house, but she doubted anyone else was up yet. Just in case, she made no noise as she crept downstairs, though she exchanged cheerful good mornings with the maid mopping the entrance hall floor.

Outside, it was one of those mornings that made one glad just to be alive—sharp and bright and smelling of clean, cold air. She inhaled it as her boots crunched across the gravel drive toward the gardens.

They were pretty, she decided, and extraordinarily well kept, but without any of the fantasy or silliness of Maida. Briskly, she crossed a large lawn away from the house and headed toward the woods, enjoying the singing of the birds and the distant calls of sheep and cattle and horses. All around her was open farmland and meadow. True countryside rather than a park tagged on to the edge of London.

As she breathed in, she imagined herself growing with the land and laughed at her own foolishness. Still, she could be content here… Maybe.

She wandered with her head so far in the clouds that she lost her sense of direction. In the distance, she could hear soft footsteps so muffled by the spongy ground that she couldn't work out if it was two humans or a horse. Either way, she felt a sudden longing for the open sky and turned toward the sun. Which should, she thought doubtfully, bring her back out facing the house.

It didn't. But as she emerged onto a meadow, she was still glad to be in the open once more, under the benign, wintry sun. If she skirted the wood, now, it should bring her home, only a little later than she had intended.

And then, as she walked briskly through the meadow, a horseman emerged from the wood just ahead of her. Her stomach tightened, for after the fire, it seemed she had learned to be afraid of strangers. Had Alf Smith followed her here? Or was it another assassin about to mistake her for the princess?

The rider took off his hat, which was, she thought, too polite for anyone who meant her mischief. The sun glinted on his dark blond hair, turning it golden, and she smiled with relief because it was the duke. Looking casually splendid as only he could.

"Lost?" he teased.

"Exploring," she said with dignity. "It's such a beautiful day to be outside, and there is so much *space!*"

"Come, I'll show you some more." He bent from the waist, stretching down his hand.

She glanced nervously at the head of the horse, who snorted and stamped his feet. "You know I can't ride."

"Trust me," he said. "Up you come."

And somehow, she was hauled up in front of him, almost sitting in his lap, hemmed in by his powerful thighs and his arm at her waist. She sat side-saddle like a lady, though her skirts spread over his legs, and she grasped his coat with both hands.

"Dear God, how do women actually stay on, let alone ride like this?" she demanded.

"With a proper lady's saddle, of course. I'll keep you safe for now."

She swallowed. "It's a long way to the ground."

"Then look ahead. Prince here is much too polite to even try to throw us."

"He doesn't *seem* very polite," she said doubtfully, remembering his impatient head-tossing and stamping.

"That's because he wants to run. Like you. But he'll be good until I let him. Look, my favorite view of the house is from this hill…"

Gradually, as he pointed out various landmarks and farms and villages, she began to relax. Most places came with funny stories that made her laugh. He pointed to a gracious house in the distance, Alvern Park, one of the Marquess of Staunton's estates, and where Lord Harry had been brought up.

"We're invited to dinner there tomorrow night," he said casually, "and Staunton and his family will no doubt be around Dearham a good deal, too."

She saw the town of Dearham, but only from a distance. "Since we don't want to shock the good townspeople," he explained wryly, reminding her, just when she had relaxed, of the improper closeness of their ride.

"What about shocking your lady mother?" she retorted. "I knew I should not allow—"

"Are you uncomfortable?" he interrupted.

In truth, she had never been more comfortable in her life.

Alone within his arms—and his legs—and absorbing the heat of his body even though the cold weather and the thickness of their winter clothes, her whole being sang with secret pleasure.

Incurably honest, she shook her head, though she could not look at him.

"Good. Then let's add a little excitement." And his leg moved against hers, sending a jolt of unexpected pleasure through her. However, there was nothing amorous about the action, he was merely urging the trotting horse into a canter which made her gasp and then to a gallop across open country.

She clung to him again in mingled terror and delight at the sheer speed. Her stomach seemed to have been left yards behind, but still, she laughed aloud with pure joy because she wanted the wild motion to go on forever.

At last, with Dearham Abbey once more in view, he slowed the horse with his voice and the surprisingly gentle tug of the reins.

"Oh, my goodness," she uttered in breathless wonder, smiling up at him. "That was…overwhelming! Will you teach me to ride, Johnny?"

Only from the triumphant gleam in his eyes did she realize she had used his Christian name. She blushed and was glad he wouldn't notice because of her already wind-blown cheeks.

"Yes, I'll teach you to ride." The amused crowing faded from his eyes as they stared into hers. And suddenly, her excitement had nothing to do with the horse or speed but only with the man holding her. Her heart seemed to dive among the butterflies already playing in her stomach, and when his gaze dropped to her lips, everything seemed to plunge even lower.

"I'll choose you a horse," he murmured, his voice low and distracted. "We can begin this afternoon if you like."

"Thank you," she whispered, afraid to breathe because his head had dipped as though he would kiss her.

It had happened before like this, as if he was giving her time to avoid his kiss if she wished. She didn't. Nor did she have any intention of evading him, for she longed with every fiber of her being to feel his mouth on hers once more. She parted her lips from sheer instinct.

And then his breath rushed against her mouth, and he drew back. "We'll be seen. Come, we'll get down and walk the rest of the way."

Still stunned, she was vaguely aware of his leg sweeping over the horse's back. Then he jumped to the ground, and he held up his arms. She jumped into them and was lowered to the ground. She might have imagined that he held her against him for the merest instant before he released her and stepped back.

Confused and not a little disappointed, she walked blindly along beside him as he led the horse toward the stables at the back of the house. He spoke about various things, and she knew she answered, but what she chiefly noticed was the soft smile in his eyes when they regarded her.

It made breathing difficult, and yet nothing in the world had ever been so exciting or so wonderful.

※

FROM THAT MOMENT, their relationship was subtly altered. Or so it seemed to Kitty. It wasn't that the duke's manner became suddenly loverlike or even over-attentive. Indeed, he was busy a great deal of the time about estate business, and when he wasn't, he still teased and bantered with his guests as though they were his sisters.

But every day, Kitty found herself alone with him at some point—a walk, a riding lesson, a long talk in the magnificent library when she went there ostensibly to read, a visit to a tenant. For her part, she looked forward to these casual moments with fierce longing and treasured them with all her heart because she felt she was truly getting to know the man who had always made her pulse race. And there was always something new to discover, such as his surprisingly deep knowledge of the classics, history, and various sciences.

"He is actually very clever, isn't he?" she blurted to his sister, Lady Calvert—Meg's twin, who was still known at Dearham as Lady Martha—who had arrived that day with her husband and children.

"Johnny?" Martha glanced at her with unexpected interest as they walked among the gardens once the rain had gone off. "Yes, he is, surprisingly enough. He got a first at Oxford, but no one ever talks of it, least of all Johnny. Cleverness is never what people remember about him because he is so entertaining, or a walking scandal, or simply a duke. But no one has ever called him a fool. Except my father, of course, but even he didn't mean it. He was just afraid that Johnny would never settle down and take up the duties of the dukedom. It never entered his head that one could be done without the other. But Johnny goes his own way."

Kitty smiled and discovered Martha's gaze on her once more.

"You like him," Martha observed.

"Of course," Kitty said lightly. "Who does not?"

The trouble was, the liking that had always been there had become almost an obsession. And with her physical attraction to him only growing stronger every moment she was near him, his every casual touch threatening to dissolve her, she began to fear her hopeless devotion would be on display to the world.

And oddly, although they were in the country, the world seemed suddenly larger.

They went to Alvern Park for dinner, and she was introduced to the Marquess of Staunton, Lord Harry's brother, and the rest of his family, which included small children and various adult siblings, all of whom dropped into Dearham Abbey thereafter with the ease of old friendship.

The local vicar and his wife called, as did the squire and other nearby landowners, and anyone else with a pretense to gentility. In company with the duchess or Martha, she called on various neighboring worthies in the town and surrounding countryside, including old governesses and maiden ladies ousted from grander homes by the next generations.

To everyone, she was introduced as "our cousin," and was treated with appropriate respect. On some level, this still felt vaguely fraudulent, but it also gave her a pleasant taste of life as a member of the Winter family.

And she liked it.

Other members of the extended family began to arrive, including the famous Great-Aunt Augusta. She had traveled to Dearham Abbey with the duke's long-suffering first cousins, who seemed delighted to have her diluted.

Kitty rather liked her. She was hard-of-hearing, forgetful, mostly amiable, and, just occasionally, hilariously caustic.

"Margaret's daughter, eh?" She peered at Kitty. "You don't look like her, so far as I can recall, but that's probably all to the good. Pretty little creature, isn't she?" she added to the duchess. "You must be glad to have her back."

Only as Kitty was summoned to the other side of the room by Martha, she heard Great-Aunt Augusta's clearly audible stage whisper, "How the devil did you find her?"

"Dearham did, Aunt," the duchess said patiently, "with the aid of Mr. Dunne, who is exceptionally good in such matters."

With the cousins came more children and more excuses for games outside when the weather allowed. Kitty rather enjoyed those since they gave her opportunity to run off some of the excess energy that built in her around the duke—and waiting to be around him.

So it was that one day, a game of tag with the children led to Kitty pelting through the less formal part of the garden in zigzags and dodging around trees in order to avoid being tagged by Cousin Charles's eldest son. As she swerved to double back within the "boundaries" of the game, she realized she'd forgotten about the wretched plain tree, which it was surely too late to avoid.

She tried to pull to the side, caught her foot on a root, and hurtled forward to her doom. Only at the last possible instant, a hand jerked her to the right, and instead of the tree, she slammed into the large, lean body of the duke.

"Phew!" she gasped, laughing up at him in gratitude, and suddenly she couldn't breathe. Every inch of her was aware of his length pressed against her from her shoulder to her knees. The responsive smile still lurking on his lips was dying in his eyes, drowned in a warmer, much more exciting blaze that she suddenly recognized as physical desire.

He wants me.

The knowledge exploded inside her, paralyzing, triumphant, delicious. The world seemed to stop, blotting out everyone but him.

And then a cheerful male voice said, "Typical! Put her down, Fish, we've arrived to keep you in order."

Mercifully, perhaps, young Charles, son of Cousin Charles, chose that moment to leap out and grab her arm. "Tag!" he yelled, and she managed to pull free.

"Wretch!" she called, rushing after the boy, while on the periphery, she was aware of Johnny shaking hands enthusiastically with three young men, all clapping him on the back.

"Kitty," he called a few moments later. "Come and meet these reprobates!"

Considering the original greeting, Kitty approached somewhat warily. Although she trusted in the duke to protect her, she knew there were many ways to insult while appearing to speak with respect.

"Cousin Kitty, allow me to present my old friends Lord Calton, Sir Keith Harborough, and Mr. Dornan. Gentlemen, my cousin, Miss Rennie."

Since they were his friends, she felt obliged to offer them her hand, and each gentleman bowed over it with perfect courtesy, murmuring delight in the acquaintance. Lord Calton was tall and languid, with a jaded look behind his amiability. Sir Keith was stockier, with pleasing laughter lines and dancing eyes. Mr.

Dornan was darker, slighter, and so handsome, in a refined kind of a way, that had she not already been besotted by the duke, Kitty would undoubtedly have stared.

"And please do forgive my earlier remark," Lord Calton said disarmingly. "My only excuse is that the sun was in my eyes, but I humbly apologize for speaking so before a lady."

"And children," Mr. Dornan reminded him helpfully.

"And children," Calton agreed.

"You are forgiven, sir," Kitty said hastily. "But I will not be if I don't return to the game. I'm still it." And she lunged after young Charles and his squealing sister, leaving the newcomers to make of that what they would.

Dinner and evenings in the drawing room became much livelier affairs, even without company from outside. Two of the duke's bachelor friends were inveterate flirts, inspiring Dearham's young lady cousins to compete of an evening to show off their accomplishments. Mr. Dornan, of a much quieter nature, observed with a faint smile.

"Will you not play, Miss Kitty?" he asked once, catching her gaze upon him.

"Oh, no, I can't," Kitty said frankly. "Though I would like to learn one day."

The two young lady cousins laughed at the very idea of someone so old learning an accomplishment.

Aline said vaguely, "It's never too late to learn. In fact, one should never stop."

The cousins stopped laughing, though they didn't seem very sure why.

Lord Calton said, "And what have you learned recently, Princess?"

Aline smiled, the smile that could, Kitty imagined with a frustrating mixture of amusement and jealousy, devour men whole before breakfast. "The value of friendship, for one."

Mr. Dornan's steady, dark gaze was on her face, and for some reason, Kitty thought Aline knew it.

And then Calton changed position to sit beside the princess. "Tell me more," he murmured.

Mr. Dornan's gaze shifted away. He was an interesting man. Kitty noticed him at all sorts of odd times, sketching scenes or people. Sometimes, his cravat was askew and his hair on end, which made him look eighteen years old instead of the ten years older school friendship with the others would make him in reality.

Once, she found him gazing at her a lot while he drew, and when he began to put his notebook away, she said blatantly, "May I see?"

He hesitated, then opened the book again. Several people closed in on him to look before Kitty got there and saw a pencil sketch of a lady who was unmistakably herself, a smile in her eyes and either just forming or just dying on her lips. It was Kitty, and yet not. The girl in the picture was too elegant, too refined, and yet he had caught an air of mischief that she suspected *was* her.

"Goodness, you are clever," Martha said, clearly impressed.

"Will you do one of me?" one of the cousins demanded.

"I can't do them to order," Mr. Dornan said hastily. "But maybe."

"No one is to importune him," Martha declared. "But perhaps...would you consider laying out all the sketches you are happy with, to let us see them on, say, Christmas Day?"

Off the immediate hook, Mr. Dornan looked relieved. "I can probably do that."

That night, it began to snow.

CHAPTER NINETEEN

S UDDENLY, EVERYTHING SHIFTED outdoors. The children were out building snowmen before breakfast and only paused for the swiftest sustenance before haring back out for snowball fights. Naturally, the younger gentlemen joined in, and so did Kitty and the flirtatious cousins.

Inevitably, they split into teams, with the duke and Aline claiming Kitty after her deadly accuracy against the princess's would-be assassin. She thoroughly enjoyed herself, knocking hats off at will and striking Sir Keith in the chest so that he clutched his heart and fell so dramatically that all the small children fell on him with delight.

If she felt a pang, wondering if Uncle Bill and the boys were also playing snowball fights with each other or with the smaller guests at Maida Gardens, she was able to thrust it aside with the general "missing" feeling and enjoy the carefree moments to the full.

It snowed all that day, and by the next, the ornamental pond had frozen over sufficiently for skating. Kitty had skated before on homemade wooden blades tied to her boots, a skill she demonstrated to the duke after their curtailed riding lesson. And she found yet a new joy in skating around the pond hand in hand with him, her heart hammering and bursting with emotion. Until the others arrived, and she smilingly made way for them.

Much of her time in that week before Christmas was spent under the dowager duchess's command, preparing baskets of provisions for the duke's tenants, which were to be Christmas gifts. Since the snow slowed traveling down so much, the task of delivering the baskets was divided into three. The duchess, escorted by Lord Peter in the carriage, took those nearest the Abbey. Lady Martha and her husband rode out to those further afield, with baskets dangling from their saddles, while the duke himself hitched a stunning, ornate sleigh to two of his best carriage horses.

All the children clamored to accompany him on this magnificent vehicle, and he seemed prepared to take as many as could fit in. It was Martha who put the hems on it.

"Don't be silly, Johnny, you can't be out all day with them, they'll freeze," she said prosaically, and to the children, "If you're good, His Grace may take you for a drive in the sleigh tomorrow."

"Then I shall be lonely," the duke mourned.

"Take Kitty," Martha said casually. "It's time she met the tenants anyway."

It was so much what Kitty wanted to do that she blushed. Johnny merely held out his hand to help her mount the sleigh. And since she was already wrapped up against the cold in the new sable-lined cloak and Martha's second best but pleasantly matching fur hat, she merely took his hand and stepped up beside him.

Casually, he tucked a soft blanket over her knees and his, raised his whip in salute, and they set off while everyone waved, and the children ran beside the sleigh in great excitement.

The scene was repeated nearly everywhere they went. People ran out of their cottages to the sound of the sleigh bells to shout greetings and wave. Children dashed toward them from various snow games, shouting in delight. And when they swept up before the various farms and cottages they were supposed to visit, they were always welcomed with laughter as well as open arms.

As mere cousin and companion, Kitty had plenty of leisure to observe. She was interested to see the *friendliness* of the Dearham tenants. Very few of them seemed remotely overawed by their duke, and some even offered him their hands before he did. These latter, she thought, were his old childhood friends. And somehow, that friendship was sustained, despite the difference of their status in adulthood. Johnny had somehow seen to that. He delivered their gifts quite casually and relaxed in their homes, accepted cups of mulled ale and conversed with the same interest and humor he did with his friends.

Of course, it wasn't *quite* the same as the way he bantered with Calton and Sir Keith—he kept things subtly more respectful than with his peers—but it was close enough to assure he kept his people devoted. The best antidote to revolution, Kitty thought cynically. Although if that was part of was his motive, it was so mixed with his natural amiability that she doubted even he would ever know.

At last, with the final basket delivered, the tired horses set off for home. As they sped over the fields, a kind of lazy contentment spread through Kitty. With all the stops and visits indoors, she was not even cold beyond the pleasant sharpness of the air against her cheeks. She could just breathe in the fresh air, admire the white beauty of the scenery, and enjoy the closeness of the man she loved.

As though he heard her sigh of contentment, he smiled down at her. "You sound happy."

"I am."

His gaze held hers, and somehow, she got lost in his blue, compelling eyes. His smiling lips parted, and she knew he was going to say something important, something vital. But he never got the chance.

Without warning, or instruction, the horses swerved, and the back end of the sleigh swung into the snowdrift at the field wall. They should not have been that close to it, but neither of them had been paying much attention, and now they were about to pay, for as the horses neighed in fury and tugged, the sleigh was dragged through the drift on one side, struck an obstruction of some kind and overturned, throwing both Kitty and the duke face-first into the freezing wet snow.

For an instant, the cold drove all other thoughts from her mind.

She rolled, gasping, onto her back. "Johnny?" she cried out in panic, an instant before he collided into her, his expression one of such astonishment that laughter bubbled up. Then he shifted abruptly, craning his neck, and she followed his gaze to where the horses stood perfectly still, snorting and shaking their heads.

"They did that deliberately," Johnny said, flopping down beside her.

By then, she was trying to wipe the snow off her face with her arm and stop the hysterical laughter which shook her from head to toe.

"Dear God," he whispered, looming suddenly above her, tugging her arm off her face. "Kitty, are you hurt?"

She gasped and made a choking sound before the laughter flooded out, and his whole face shone with relief.

"Why, you little baggage, how dare you laugh before me?"

That only made her laugh harder, until, without warning, his body sank on top of hers and he kissed her.

All at once, the laughter vanished. Even though she could feel the smiling shape of his lips on hers. She lay so stunned by the thrilling weight of his body against her breasts, her stomach, her hips that it took a moment to realize he was kissing her at the same time.

Her mouth opened under his, although whether to speak or to kiss, she had no idea, and after he groaned and sank his mouth deeper, she could only respond. Her arms closed around him, clinging to his back, his shoulders, his nape, while his gloved hand knocked off her hat to drive into her hair. An instant later, he must have torn off his glove, for it was his cool fingertips she felt caressing her cheek, the corner of her mouth, her neck.

His tongue caressed its way along hers. His hand swept down the side of her body, from shoulder to hip and back up to her breast, and she arched up into him from pure instinct, and between her legs she felt the hard ridge of his arousal. She made a small, desperate sound of need into his mouth.

His lips left hers. But she couldn't bear that. She was lost in him, in love, and in pure, wild lust. She followed his mouth and took it back with her own. In the end, it was several devouring kisses later before he grasped her hands in the snow above her head and raised his head enough to say breathlessly, "Will you marry me, Kitty Renwick?"

In a haze of blissful desire, bombarded by new, overwhelming emotions, it took a moment for his words to penetrate. She was more concerned with wriggling her body beneath his to make him caress her again. She wanted his hands, his...

She blinked up at his clouded face and went suddenly still. His eyes may have been thrillingly hot, turbulent as she has never seen them, but they were also serious. The sensual lips that had reduced her to a mere bundle of trembling hunger were closed and firm. He was waiting for an answer. To a question she was sure she couldn't have heard aright.

"Wh-what did you say?"

"I asked you to marry me."

Somewhere she registered the unsteadiness of the fingers caressing her jaw. He was overwrought (*Dear God and I am not?*), which was astonishing enough, but this put the duty of common sense squarely on her shoulders.

"Don't be silly," she managed shakily. "You're the Duke of Dearham. You can't marry Bill Renwick's niece."

He eased off her, and her body cried out in loss. Inevitably, they had sunk deeper into the snowdrift and were in danger of being buried. Johnny stood and took her arm at the elbow to haul her to her feet. "We probably shouldn't debate the matter while freezing to death. You may be Bill Renwick's niece, but you're also part of my extended family, and as such, a lady by blood as well as nature. The funny thing is none of that matters. Do you think you could go to the horses' heads and stop them rushing off while I see if I can right the sleigh?"

Kitty closed her mouth, realizing for the first time that she was wet and icy-cold. She shivered as she ploughed through the snow to soothe the horses.

The sleigh, fortunately, was not completely overturned, just at an angle sharp enough to have tipped them out when it hit the obstruction. Now its side lay at a forty-five-degree angle against the snowdrift, and Johnny put his back into heaving it upright once more.

Somehow, he persuaded it, and in two more minutes, they were back in the sleigh and speeding for home. This time he kept his attention on the horses and the ground ahead.

Kitty, shivering with cold and shock, began to think she'd imagined everything from the moment she'd landed face-first in the snow. Perhaps she'd lost consciousness and dreamed.

Johnny transferred the reins to one hand and threw his arm about her shoulders, drawing her close into him. "You're wet and freezing. We have to get you home quickly and out of those things."

She rested her cheek against his cold, snowy shoulder and breathed in his distinctive male scent once more. That seemed to ease the tumult.

He said, "I'm sorry for tipping you out and for the appalling timing of my proposal. It just…slipped out."

It might have been the cold that drove the blood from her face. "Don't worry. I won't hold you to it."

A quick glance flickered in her direction, warm and wicked, stirring her to her bones, chasing off the chill. "I know. But *I* am still holding *you* to an answer. It doesn't have to be now, but soon, please, for the sake of my sanity."

"Johnny, you could have anyone!"

"I don't want anyone. I want you."

"Why?" she demanded.

A hiss of laughter escaped him. "Oh God, where do I start? Because you don't care for my rank or my title or my wealth. Because you are beautiful and funny and intelligent. Because you make my blood sing, and you kiss me as if I'm all you'll ever want. Because you're all *I'll* ever want. Because you give me purpose and meaning, and somehow, I'm not complete without you. Because I love you."

His words battered her with wonder as the sleigh glided and bumped them over the gentle hill behind the house and down toward the stables.

"Please don't ask me why I love you," he added. "Because I don't know the answer. I just do." Slowing, he removed his arm from her shoulders. "I know *this* life—" He waved his free hand toward the house. "...is new to you, but you *fit* here, you know, and I want more than anything for you to share it with me. Will you think about it?"

She nodded dumbly, unable to speak or to take her eyes off his face. Never had it entered her head he would speak such words to her. Vaguely, she wondered what it was she was supposed to think about.

Inevitably, the sleigh bells brought everyone running, from servants to children, and almost as soon as he had lifted her down, they were separated, and she realized vaguely that he was giving orders for hot baths, and Martha was leading her hastily into the house, castigating her brother over her shoulder as she went.

Some time later, as she soaked in a steaming hot bath, it finally entered Kitty's head that her abstraction and lack of speech were worrying everyone. They thought she was ill from her tumble into the snowdrift, not completely flabbergasted by what had happened after.

I let him go without telling him I loved him...

The marriage issue was considerably more terrifying. How could she, Kitty Renwick, become Duchess of Dearham? It was ridiculous, laughable. But she knew she would do that, too, and try her very best to make him proud of her.

She exerted herself to smile at the maid and to ask for the towel. Wrapped in it, she walked through to the bedchamber, where she found Martha and a tray of tea and scones.

"Nurse is making you a posset," Lady Martha said anxiously. "It will taste nasty but usually helps stave off chills and worse. Now, into bed with you and drink your tea in the warmth."

"Oh, I don't want to go to bed," Kitty assured her. "I'm fine now I'm warm. I'd just like to sit before the fire. Is Joh—Is His Grace well?"

"Alarmingly." Martha sat in the armchair and, when Kitty had knelt comfortably before the fire, handed her the cup of tea. "Did he tip you out deliberately?"

Kitty blinked. "Oh, no. Why would he do such a thing? He just wasn't paying attention."

Martha stayed talking to her until she had finished the tea, then nodded as though satisfied and left her to the maid, who brushed out the tangle of her hair to dry before the fire and went to fuss with clothes for her to wear to dinner.

Only then did it occur to Kitty that she would have to face him in front of everyone else, with his kisses and his offer of marriage between them. His unanswered offer of marriage. Her cheeks began to glow. She had to speak to him before dinner, in a moment of privacy, or she felt she would burst.

"YOU ARE AN idiot, Johnny," Martha scolded him. "What were you thinking about to upend her in the snow?"

"I wasn't thinking of anything," Johnny replied ruefully. His sister had caught him lurking in the gallery waiting to catch Kitty and dragged him into the small drawing room which was still empty of guests. "Which is why I upended us both in the snow. I just didn't pay attention."

"That's what she says." Martha hesitated, then said, "You will be careful of her, Johnny? She doesn't understand the restriction of her position, and she isn't one of your ton women who deal in flirtation. And more."

"What do you take me for?" he said with rare irritability.

"I take you for a rake and a libertine," replied his sister. "But you're never knowingly unkind, so for God's sake, think about Kitty."

I think of little else.

"You could hurt her, Johnny," Martha said, scowling at him. "Without trying. Just by paying her attention."

Johnny glanced at her, his annoyance fading as fast as it had come. Martha was looking out for his Kitty, and he approved of that. But before he could say anything, Calton and Dornan came in, arguing over something, and the time for private discussion had passed in favor of pre-prandial sherry.

As he circulated among his guests, he edged closer to the door, still hoping to catch Kitty before she entered the social fray. But Great-Aunt Augusta caught him, and while he patiently decoded and answered her rambling question, he felt rather than saw Kitty enter.

When he was able to disengage from Augusta with any degree of politeness, he found her between Calton and Keith Harborough, gamely holding her own. She looked, to his relief, none the worse for her adventures. In fact, wearing one of Meg's altered evening gowns in a pretty shade of dark green, her beauty as well as her new-found poise closed up his throat.

He had not taught her that poise. She had always had it in her old world, had merely, finally, transferred it to his. To theirs. She did not need him to defend her from Calton or anyone else. She did not need to marry him. God knew she could receive many offers.

If she wished it, he would dower her and let her take her pick, which had always been his intention—to leave his courting until the new year, to let her meet other gentlemen first, better men than he, whom she might like better.

But God help him, he had never wanted her to like anyone better. He still didn't. If Calton laid a finger on her, he'd kill him. If she *wanted* him to, he would…

She doesn't. For some reason, I'm the one who moves her. If nothing else, the sleigh incident had proved that to his sweet satisfaction.

With a laugh, she extricated herself from Calton and Harborough, leaving the field free for his young cousins, and sat down by his aunt instead. As though she felt his gaze on her, she flushed rosily but did not look up. It almost felt like a battle of wills, and that felt good, too, in a strange, predatory kind of way.

And then it was time for dinner, and they all trooped into the Great Hall, where, in winter, the fire blazed all day in the massive hearth. Thanks to the alterations his father had made, it was no longer cold or drafty, though his mother had seated Kitty so far away from him, it might as well have been.

He passed the time between conversations trying to catch her eye and knew by the ebbing and flowing of color in her skin that she was aware of it. But only twice did he manage to trap her gaze. The first time, over the fish, she had immediately turned to speak to Calvert on her far side. The second time, she held his gaze for an instant, a small fugitive smile flickering across her lips before she again looked away.

Johnny breathed a sigh of relief. From that one gesture, he knew that the hours following their sleigh adventure had not brought her sensible counsel. She was still on the verge of being his, and now he simply had to wait for her decision.

Restored to happiness and the constant thrum of bodily excitement, he relaxed into his role of genial host, and even, once the ladies had withdrawn, a rather more rollicking friend. As a result, when he rose to relieve himself, he may not have been foxed or even a trifle disguised, but neither was he as sober as when he had sat down.

He hummed to himself as he strode across the outer hall

toward the cloakroom, and almost didn't hear the hiss from the anteroom on his left. He spared it a vaguely curious glance, and then the hum died in his throat.

Kitty stood in the doorway, urgently beckoning to him.

He didn't hesitate but swerved back the way he had come and brushed past her into the room. To his surprise, she shut the door. Inappropriately, his body stirred.

She leaned against the door, clearly ready to say something, and then seemed to get stuck.

"What is it?" he asked urgently. "Is something wrong?"

She shook her head and swallowed. "What you said earlier, did you mean it?"

Pain pierced his heart that she could even think anyone would say such things to her and not mean them, that she could imagine him capable of such cruel deception. And for what reason? To get her into his bed? Well, God knew he looked for such an outcome in the end, and his body was screaming at him that the sooner, the better.

Words deserted him, and he acted purely on instinct, stepping forward and taking her into his arms.

"Every word. Every action. Except throwing you out of the sleigh," he said and kissed her thoroughly enough, he hoped, to remove all doubt. She tried to speak and then simply melted into his arms as before and kissed him back.

"Then you do love me?" he whispered against her lips while his heart thundered with desire and with rare fear of rejection.

A breath of laughter kissed his mouth. "Oh, you idiot, I have always loved you, from the first moment you smiled at me, even though you promptly forgot about me. There was no reason in it. There still isn't, for you should have some beautiful, witty heiress to be your duchess."

"I want you," he broke in. "Will you have me?"

She stared deep into his eyes, her fingers convulsing around the hair at his nape. "Oh God, yes," she whispered and kissed him as though she would never stop.

But she did, eventually, slipping out of his arms just as he was contemplating the possibilities of the wooden table in the middle of the room since one shouldn't really take a virgin against the wall…

Her breathing was ragged, though not as erratic as his own. But it was her smile that slayed him all over again, just before she whisked herself out of the anteroom and fled across the hall and round the corner toward the drawing room.

She had come to find him.

And he, poor fool, had not thought to look. Laughing softly, he recalled his original mission and walked slowly and slightly awkwardly toward the cloakroom.

CHAPTER TWENTY

CHRISTMAS EVE WAS a day of merriment and joy, particularly for Kitty as she hugged to herself the astonishing joy of the duke's love. Johnny's love. The idea of being a duchess, the highest possible rank of British noblewoman outside the royal family, would take rather more getting used to. But it wasn't the rank or the riches she wanted. It had always been Johnny.

And since he seemed to have stopped pretending, so did she. As the younger people all stamped out into the snow that morning and split up to collect greenery and berries with which to decorate the house for Christmas, Johnny simply took her hand and led her off with him. Not that he tried to hide from the others, merely he seemed to crave her company as much as she needed his.

It was not easy to find greenery under the snow, but Johnny knew where the right plants were to be found. He shook various trees and bushes and began to pile holly, ivy, and mistletoe into her arms and the waiting wheelbarrow. Then, collecting a huge bundle under his arm, he pushed the barrow as they returned to the house. Another successful forage by all concerned, and the duchess declared they had enough to decorate as they wished.

While the ladies and an army of footmen were set to ornamenting the great hall, both drawing rooms, the entrance hallway, and the ballroom, the men were sent off to the woods to find the traditional Yule log.

Chatting and laughing as everyone worked together to transform the main public areas of the house, Kitty felt a wave of contentment slide over her. This was her family now, novel, rich, and just a little eccentric, but they no longer seemed so strange. For Martha, as for Meg, she already felt a certain affection. Also, for Peter and even the duchess now that she had unbent. The flirtatious cousins she found were actually pleasant company when not trying too hard to be grown-up, And the duke himself... She had never imagined the profound pleasure of simply loving and being loved in return.

She did not even need to be alone with him to be happy, though she was delighted to be on his arm as they walked into the Great hall for dinner. In all its festive greenery hanging from the walls and ceiling, sprigs of holly ornamenting pictures and mirrors, there was a timeless element to the ancient room. Kitty imagined it looking very similar at Christmases spanning back hundreds of years, especially with the huge hunk of tree lying barbarically across the hearth, wound in ivy and holly. She enjoyed this feeling almost as much as sitting beside Johnny for once as they ate, exchanging banter and short, private conversation.

"I'll tell my mother tomorrow morning," he murmured. "And announce our engagement formally before the ball, so that I have a reason for monopolizing your waltzes."

A cold dash of reality struck at her. "Your family won't like it. They will want better for you."

"My mother can't help being worldly, but she will come around. So will Peter, and my sisters only want me to be happy." His lips quirked. "But none of that really matters. Sometimes, it's good to be the head of the family."

She glanced up from her plate. "And Aline?"

"Aline already knows the direction of the wind."

Glancing around the table to discover several pairs of eyes surreptitiously observing them, Kitty murmured, "I doubt she is the only one."

"So, are we walking down to the village to church tonight?" Martha asked later as the duchess stood to lead the women from the dining room.

"Through the snow?" the duchess said acidly. "Hardly."

"I think it's thawing." Martha was eternally optimistic. "And we are expecting everyone to trudge through the snow for our ball tomorrow evening."

"That's for fun, my dear, not church," Aline drawled, to a burst of laughter, both shocked and appreciative.

"We have a chapel," Johnny said mildly. "And a newly ordained clergyman amongst us. I vote we all squeeze into the chapel and allow Cousin George to take his first service."

That was greeted with cheers and much back-slapping of Cousin George, who blushed fiery red and grinned.

The evening was spent in a quiet, pleasant mixture of music, talk, and card games. To avoid being roped into the latter and inevitably giving away her excessive facility with the cards, Kitty slipped out of the drawing room to fetch another shawl, which she would need in the cold chapel.

Returning, she saw from the staircase that the drawing room door was ajar. Leaning against the wall was Johnny, looking so handsome as he laughed at something within the room that Kitty's heart turned over.

He will be my husband, she thought in awe, just as he glanced out the door and saw her.

At once, he eased off the wall and walked out the door, moving toward the foot of the stairs to meet her.

"At last," he said, seizing her by the waist and swinging her down the last three steps to land scandalously close against his person. Smiling, she raised her face to receive his kiss, which was long and deep and melted her bones.

"I believe you are improper, sir," she said breathlessly when she could say anything at all.

"Not in the slightest," he argued, pointing upward at a sprig of mistletoe that dangled from the arch over their heads. "The servants tell me it's bad luck *not* to kiss when you meet beneath the mistletoe."

"Oh," she said, thoughtfully. "Then you had better do it again, for we'll need all the luck we can muster when the duchess—" The rest was lost in his mouth as he obliged, his arms closing more tightly around her.

"Dearham!" snapped an all too familiar voice in shocked fury, causing Kitty to gasp and jump. "Have you *no* decorum?"

The duke, who had kept an arm firmly around her when she had leapt away from him, now swept her with him into the center of the hall to face his mother—and most of the other curious guests spilling out of the drawing room to discover what mischief Johnny was about now.

"How could you?" the duchess demanded bitterly. "This child is under our protection!"

"More so than you think, Mama," Johnny said calmly. "Kitty has just agreed to marry me."

And that was when the pandemonium really started. Johnny's friends surged forward to shake his hand but were still behind Martha, who hurled herself at her brother and then at Kitty before they even reached him. Even Peter was slapping him on the back, the flirtatious cousins fluttering around Kitty with a hundred delighted questions.

In the midst of the vocal crowd, the duchess stood rigid, her emotions impossible to read. And on the edge, curiously alone, Aline caught Kitty's eye and raised her glass to her.

Kitty's throat closed up, and then, without any recollection of how she got there, she found herself standing beside Johnny before the duchess.

"Your blessing, Mama, would mean a lot," he said steadily.

The duchess, whose gaze had been boring into Kitty's face, shifted her attention to her son, and, perhaps, read everything she was supposed to. Her blessing did mean a lot. But it was not everything, for the duke was head of his family and would marry whoever he chose with impunity. The warning was there, and it hurt Kitty that it was necessary.

Or was it?

A single tear escaped the duchess's eye. "It is fitting," she said unsteadily, "for Margaret's daughter and my son."

Kitty couldn't help herself. For the first time, she embraced the duchess, who, taken by surprise, patted her back and then hugged her once, convulsively, before releasing her.

"Well!" commanded Her Grace. "A toast to my son and my future daughter-in-law, I think. And then it will be time for church!"

Accordingly, it was a merry crowd who, after a toast to the betrothed couple, made their way into the tiny, beautiful chapel, squashed into the four pews, and lined the walls. Cousin George made no attempt to preach or sermonize, merely welcomed the time of Christ's birth, prayed for everyone to be better in His honor, and led them all in several Christmas carols.

Johnny threaded his fingers through hers as they sang, and Kitty wondered if one really could explode from happiness.

To Kitty's surprise, the duchess herself came to inspect her toilette as she prepared for the Christmas day ball. By the time Her Grace arrived, Kitty's hair had been dressed in a soft, simple style threaded with Martha's pearls, and her new ball gown was being thrown over her head.

Catching sight of the duchess, Kitty immediately and somewhat nervously curtseyed. The duchess looked her up and down and, even before the gown was laced up, nodded once. "You will do."

"Of course she will," Martha said stoutly. "She and Meg chose the gown in London."

"Then I am pleasantly surprised by Meg's improved taste."

"You always mistook disinterest for lack of taste," Martha observed. "But this delightful chestnut red is definitely Kitty's color." She grinned at Kitty. "Johnny will be fighting for his dances."

"Jewelry?" the duchess inquired. "You need something *here*." She ran her fingers across her own skin, from clavicle to clavicle.

Kitty picked up her favorite of the two necklaces she owned. The duchess, Martha, and the maid all exchanged glances.

"It will match Lady Martha's pearls in my hair," Kitty said defiantly.

"The pearls will do nicely in your hair," the duchess allowed. "For that gown, though, you need…emeralds. Martha, bring me—"

A knock at the door interrupted her, and she scowled as the maid opened it to reveal the duke with a posy of Christmas roses in one hand and a flat leather box in the other.

"What are you doing here?" demanded Her Grace, scandalized.

"Bringing these poor offerings to Cousin Kitty, in honor of her first ball," the duke said, seeking and finding Kitty's startled gaze through the throng. "And considering how well chaperoned she is, I really don't think it's too outrageous of me to present them myself."

Kitty, blushing furiously, accepted the posy with shy thanks and a smile she could not prevent. "This, too?" she asked in surprise as he continued to hold out the leather box.

"Yes," he said with a faint quirk of his lips. "If you like them."

Kitty opened the box and found, nestled among the velvet lining, a gold necklace of seven dazzling emeralds. Her eyes widened. Speechless, she stared at the necklace and finally managed to say hoarsely, "For *me*?"

"You know, she really is too sweet for you, Johnny," Martha observed. "You will have to let her go."

"Yes to you, Kitty, and no to you, Martha," Johnny said wryly.

"But they're...*beautiful*," Kitty said in awe.

While Johnny's eyes laughed appreciatively, making her blush even harder, the duchess said tartly, "Well, he would hardly give his betrothed something ugly, would he? In fact, they're just the thing." She reached for the necklace still clutched reverently in Kitty's hands, but Johnny was quicker, lifting it, and clasping it about Kitty's throat, where it lay, gleaming against her skin.

Everyone gazed at Kitty in the glass. She touched one of the stones, then impulsively turned and seized Johnny's hand and, in front of his mother and sister, kissed his knuckles.

"Thank you," she whispered.

"Go away, Johnny," Martha ordered. "You're making her cry."

Still, he lingered a moment longer, a faint frown tugging at his brow as he gazed down at her. "You are...content?" he asked.

"Oh, more than content," she said fervently. "I've never been so happy in my life."

The smile came back to his eyes before he closed one lid very briefly and sauntered out of the room.

SEVERAL GUESTS HAD already arrived at the house from some distance, for the Dearham Christmas ball was the most sought-after event in the county. These guests would stay overnight, while those who lived nearer by would go home. At least the snow was thawing, and none of the roads were impassable.

As her first "genteel" ball, it had loomed large in Kitty's list of fears because she was so afraid of breaking one of the many rules of polite society. However, she quickly realized it was merely a better-behaved version of the masked balls at Maida Gardens. The surroundings were grander, but the musicians were not as good, although there was greater variety of dances, and the wine was of much better quality.

In the beginning, she stayed close to Martha and was introduced as "my cousin, Miss Rennie." She was asked to dance at once by a young man whose name she had already forgotten and was so delighted to remember the steps that she relaxed and thoroughly enjoyed herself. It helped that with every step, she was aware of Johnny's gift lying across her chest, and his posy tied to her wrist.

Next, she danced with Lord Staunton and the vicar's son, and, at last, the orchestra introduced a waltz.

Kitty stood bemused as she was besieged by invitations to dance. She could not remember who had asked first and suddenly it wasn't funny anymore. Was she about to make one of those ridiculous social mistakes that would cast her forever beyond the pale?

And then the duke was there, carelessly handsome in his evening finery and yet somehow more distinguished than all the other men put together. Her little court objected with good-natured raillery as he walked straight toward Kitty.

"Oh, the devil, he's pulling rank," someone said.

"Don't be a spoilsport, Fish."

"Flee with me now, Miss Kitty."

Although it was noticeable that they also got out of his way.

"Shame on you, gentlemen," Johnny said, his voice amiable enough, though there was a glint of unexpected irritation in his eyes that was almost steely. "Let the poor lady breathe. Kitty?"

He offered his arm, and Kitty gratefully laid her hand on it. She remembered to smile apologetically at her now slightly shame-faced court.

"Thank goodness," she said to the duke with relief. "I was terrified of choosing the wrong one, but they all looked the same."

"Well, they should know better than to crowd you like a pack of dogs. I'm sorry. I would rather have been with you, but I had to do the pretty with our guests." He took her into his arms and smiled as he spun her around. "I've been looking forward to this all evening."

"Oh, so have I," she confessed fervently.

His eyes heated, although he asked, "Have you not been enjoying yourself?"

"Oh, yes," she said blithely. "Everyone has been so kind—and interesting. Do you know the vicar's son does not wish to follow in his father's footsteps but become a physician instead? He wishes to study at Edinburgh, but his father is set on Cambridge and then the church."

"No, I didn't know that," the duke confessed.

"I think he should be allowed to follow his own wishes, don't you?"

"Yes." His eyes gleamed. "Very well, I will give the vicar the best of my unwanted advice, but it really isn't my place to interfere."

She knew an urge to lean closer and rest her cheek on his chest. Hastily, she cast a glance around, almost afraid her scandalous impulse had been somehow seen by the arbiters of propriety in the ballroom.

She made a different discovery instead and turned her attention back to her partner. "Lots of people are watching us!"

"I know," Johnny said gravely.

"Because you are the duke?"

"Because word has clearly got around about our engagement. They want to see how we are with each other, if it is a love match or if I've snapped you up for some other reason, such as a massive dowry."

Kitty laughed. "Why would they even imagine I have a dowry?"

"Mystery. No one knows what happened to Cousin Margaret because no one talked about it. She could have married a nabob."

She thought for a moment. "Is that why these men all wanted to dance with me?"

Johnny hesitated, perhaps not wanting to hurt her, so she scowled, for there had to be truth between them.

"Perhaps one or two of them," he said steadily. "In every society, there are people who will use you to get what they want. And there are others who are intrigued by looks, talk, curiosity, and fashion. And those happy to take advantage of a young lady's innocence."

"And ignorance," she added ruefully.

"That, too. I imagine you were swamped by the entire gamut. But if it's any consolation, they are also accusing me of using my position to take advantage of your innocence and wealth."

"It's no consolation at all!" she said indignantly.

He smiled so warmly her heart turned over. "Sweetheart, we both have real friends, too."

She tightened her grip on his fingers. "That's what you've put up with all your life, isn't it? People pretending to be your friend because of the dukedom."

For the first time, she realized the magnitude of the Dearham miracle, that he had emerged the warm, kind, fun-loving person he was. He may not have been quite so guileless and open as the face he showed the world, but somehow, he had retained his essence. Even his reputation as a rake was understandable. He had taken love where he had found it and understood whatever form it had taken. And he remained unswervingly loyal to those who were true from childhood friends on the estate to Aline.

"I do love you," she whispered.

His brow twitched. A flicker of uncertainty, almost fear, flashed in his eyes and vanished. "A moment alone," he murmured and swished her suddenly through the curtain and out of the French door onto the terrace beyond.

The door had been opened earlier in the evening to allow the flow of fresh air into the ballroom, but the terrace was not lit, the weather being much too cold to entice any but the hardiest souls outside.

In the darkness, he took her face in his hands. "You take me as I am. And yet, with you, I want to be so much more than a frippery fellow."

"You are."

He kissed her, perhaps to stop her talking, perhaps just because he wanted to. Either was fine with Kitty, who immediately slipped her arms around him and yielded her mouth with pleasure.

The kiss was long and sweet. And when it ended, he drew her close into his body and began another. He filled her senses until she was lost in the taste of him, the masculine scent of him mingling with the outdoor smells of earth and pine and a hint of frost.

And, closer, an alarming odor of stale onion, beer, and tobacco.

With a gasp, she threw herself against him, shoving him closer to the house, just as something whipped through the air exactly where they had been. The faint light filtering through the curtain crack glinted on steel and on the unkempt, brutal face of a man she was sure she had seen before.

She had definitely smelled him before, too. In the darkness of the half-built hotel, an instant before she had been knocked senseless to the ground.

"It's him!" she got out as Johnny thrust her behind him. "It's Alf Smith."

The man lashed out again with his blade as Johnny lunged at him. Johnny swayed back enough to dodge the knife—at least Kitty thought he did—but at the same time grabbed the man's wrist and hauled. Smith threw his whole body against Johnny, enough to upset his balance, and pulled free. Clearly giving up, he bolted, vaulting over the terrace wall.

"Go back inside," Johnny commanded, already running after him. "Tell Peter and Robert Staunton."

Her every instinct was to follow him, to keep him safe, but God knew she could not. With a sound like a sob echoing her terror, she flew back inside the ballroom, blinking in the sudden brightness.

"Kitty?" It was Peter, mercifully, with a group of other young men. "Is everything…?"

She seized his arm, tugging him away from his friends. "Johnny's gone after the man who attacked me at Maida, and he's got a knife," she said urgently, if not entirely coherently. "You have to help him!"

"Which way did he go?" Peter reached up and snatched a candle from the sconce above his head.

"Straight across the lawn toward the wood."

"Tell Staunton and Calvert. But Kitty?" She stared at him, and a crooked smile twisted his lips. "Be discreet. It's family business."

Somewhere among the tangle of guilt—Alf Smith was here because of *her*—and fear, she felt a steadying buzz of warmth, because to Peter, she was family. It gave her the strength to walk, not run, toward Lord Staunton, who was making conversation with two dowagers. Through the curtains, she noticed a flaring, fast-moving light, as though Peter had lit a torch from his filched candle and was moving after his brother apace.

CHAPTER TWENTY-ONE

JOHNNY HAD NO light, and the idea of blundering about in almost total darkness, even on his own familiar terrain, in pursuit of an aggressive villain with a knife, was not appealing. But before he had more than thought of swerving around to the stables for lanterns and support, he saw a glinting light from the wood suddenly appear and wobble wildly.

The man, clearly, had left a covered lantern at the edge of the wood for his escape. Which meant that Johnny could see him, but he wouldn't necessarily see Johnny until it was too late. A risky strategy, but he was damned if he would lose the murderous scoundrel at this stage.

And then, just as he entered the wood, he was surrounded by other lights and four threatening males. All of whom, fortunately, recognized him before they could knock him to the ground.

"Your Grace! We thought you were an intruder!"

"He's in there," Johnny said grimly. "The question is, how did he get this close?"

"We don't know," came the miserable reply. "But we just found he's been sleeping in the home hayloft for at least a couple of nights."

Johnny let that one go for later. Snow, it seemed, made idiots of everyone. "Go back and get *everyone*. I want the home woods surrounded—and then move in. Lord Peter and Lord Staunton and possibly some others will help." He was already moving away from them, following the faint, bobbing light.

His quarry was no countryman. Johnny could hear him blundering in the undergrowth, cursing and tripping, even with his lantern to light the way. Inevitably, Johnny did his share of bumping into tree branches and tripping over roots, but he had no idea if Smith heard him or if the man even knew where he was going. Perhaps he intended to stay out here all night. Johnny wouldn't weep for the bastard if he froze to death, as he well might since the partial thaw was icing up again in the night. But he really wanted answers.

And then, just when Johnny was drawing closer to his quarry, the much more flaring light of a torch waved straight ahead. Peter? Or Smith's allies? It was too soon, surely to be the servants en masse...

At any rate, Smith saw it, too, for he stopped dead in his tracks, the light swinging in front of him and revealing his indecision. Johnny stepped into the cover of an old oak tree and waited. Smith swung around, that long, wicked blade still clutched before him. As the man peered in all directions, Johnny made one of his own impulsive decisions, grasped the branch above his head, and swung himself up into the tree.

Unfortunately, negotiating the slippery surfaces took him longer than usual, and Smith blundered past him, back the way he had come, before he was in position. Johnny almost dropped back to the ground, but surely that was another, fainter glow from the direction of the house?

He kept going, hauling himself onto a sturdy branch, well above the track, from where he watched Smith halt again. By then, the faint glow had separated into several lanterns, spreading out along the line of the woods. Smith turned, facing the torchlight, which, as one light, must have seemed preferable to many, even though it was closer. Especially since in that direction, there was much more space with no light at all.

Smith ran back, swerving the other way around the far side of

Johnny's tree.

Damnation! But Johnny had had enough of waiting around, and his hands were growing numb with the cold. Although he couldn't drop from straight above as he had meant to, he launched himself in a flying leap.

He was so relieved to crash into Smith rather than the ground that he barely noticed the pain of the first impact or the second. Shocked and winded, Smith had fortunately let go of the knife, which Johnny hastily swept out of his reach before he sat on his victim's back and wrenched up the man's arm until he screamed.

More shouts followed as a blaze of light came at them from all directions.

"I've a bone to pick with you," Johnny said unpleasantly, and as the man beneath him began to buck in earnest, he wrenched his arm harder and reached for the other.

"Johnny?" Peter panted, holding up the torch.

"Good grief, Fish," Lord Calton complained. "What did you get us all out here for when you clearly have everything under control?"

"WHAT'S GOING ON?" Martha asked beneath her breath as Lord Calvert and Lord Staunton vanished through the terrace door. At the same time, Lord Calton, Mr. Dornan, and Sir Keith walked out of the ballroom in the opposite direction. Suddenly, all the footmen seemed to be going that way, too. "I've seen this happen before. Where is Aline?"

Aline, in fact, was flirting with the vicar, although her gaze strayed occasionally beyond him, obviously aware of the movement and perhaps wondering if her assassin was on the premises. As one, Kitty and Martha moved toward her.

"Remind you of anything?" Martha asked as Aline excused herself from the vicar to join them.

"A little," Aline said, closing her fan.

"It isn't your enemy, it's mine," Kitty blurted. "He appeared on the terrace and…" She swallowed. "Well, Johnny's gone after him, and now so has Lord Peter and Lord Calvert and—"

"I can see who has gone," Aline interrupted. "And the servants along with them. The outdoor staff will be there, too, so I don't believe we need to worry."

You didn't see his eyes… Kitty pressed one hand to her throat, clutching the necklace Johnny had given her. Her other arm crept across her stomach. "Why is he doing this? Why is it so important to kill me that he even followed me here?"

"Because Mr. Renwick is prepared for him?" Martha suggested.

"So was Johnny," Aline noted. "And yet, here he is. I imagine you will find out everything now." She considered. "Unless they kill him."

A gurgle of shocking, hysterical laughter tried to escape Kitty. She swallowed it back, but not before Aline had seen her.

"Well, I suggest we walk casually toward the window," she suggested. "And make occasional forays on to the terrace. We may see nothing, of course, but at least Lady Martha and I can amuse you with the story of the last time we attended a ball together…"

At last, it seemed, she was to hear the story of Johnny's deadly duel four years ago. And at any other time, Kitty would have drunk it in avidly. Now, her fear for Johnny was so real that the words barely penetrated.

"I suppose Johnny was not *quite* the hero of that story," Aline finished judiciously, "but he did take the blame."

"So did you," Martha reminded her.

"Ah, but I am a scandalous foreigner and therefore not subject to the same rules. Look."

Kitty had already seen the torchlit crowd emerging from the wood and crossing the lawn in the direction of the stables. She bolted across the terrace, and would have run across the lawn after them, had Aline not suddenly seized her arm in a strong grip.

"You'll ruin your dancing slippers and fall in the slush," she said mildly. "Besides, our heroes are coming this way."

Trying to shake her off, Kitty peered at the approaching figures. She could hear their laughter, which was surely a good thing. They wouldn't laugh if someone was hurt or worse... Would they?

But one of the men was most definitely Johnny, for his long, casual stride was strangely distinctive, and the lantern light played across his golden hair and his thoughtful face. He wasn't laughing, but that he didn't appear to be hurt almost made her weep with relief.

"I might have known," Lord Peter said, catching sight of them. "Go back inside before you bring everyone out behind you."

"Don't be bossy," Martha retorted. "We just came to see that you were unhurt, though I've no idea why we bothered."

Kitty barely heard that interchange either, for though she didn't remember moving, or even Aline releasing her, she fell suddenly into Johnny's arms and was crushed to him, his lips on her hair.

"Did you find him?" Aline asked prosaically.

"Closed in on him from all sides," Lord Calvert said cheerfully. "Just as Johnny brought him down."

"Flew through the air like a dashed monkey," Sir Keith said proudly. "Felled him to the ground like a stone and made him squeal. Just as soon as he could breathe again."

"Is he dead?" Aline inquired.

Johnny raised his head. "No. But he's tied and on his way to Dearham gaol."

"My compliments," Aline drawled and strolled back inside the ballroom.

Kitty pulled herself together, resolutely drawing away from Johnny's solid comfort. "Mine, too," she said lightly. She looked him up and down. "I believe you will have to go and change before your mother sees you."

"The story of my life," Johnny remarked with a grin that was much more like himself. "But I'll be back for the next waltz."

He kissed her hand before he walked away.

In the end, it was after supper before she saw him, for a mud splatter had transferred itself from the duke to Kitty's gown, and Martha whisked her off the deal with it. By the time they returned, they had missed the supper dance, and Kitty's worry had been replaced by urgent curiosity.

She had to wait through supper, seated with the duchess and the dowagers, and return to the ballroom before she saw the duke, at last, standing with a group of friends, who he was entertaining with some story or other. Although he caught her eye and immediately smiled, he stayed among his friends until she couldn't stand it anymore.

She stood abruptly, excused herself to the duchess, and walked straight across the floor to Johnny.

"Ah, our dance," he said as she blatantly took his arm to drag her away. "Quite right."

She knew from the way his eyes laughed and from the amusement of his companions that she had broken some minor rule or other, but no one seemed to care, least of all Johnny, for he excused himself to the group and swept her off. As they passed the orchestra above them in the gallery, he exchanged some kind of signal with the musicians, who were tuning up after their break.

"Johnny!" she exclaimed. "What is so bad that you won't tell me?"

"Nothing," he said in apparent surprise. "It's just more convenient talk while waltzing than dancing some Scottish reel."

She blinked. "You made them change the dance? Won't Her Grace be angry?"

"Why should she be?" Johnny took her hand as the orchestra did indeed strike up a waltz and led her onto the floor.

Waltzing with Johnny would always distract her from anything else, and for some time, she allowed it, simply letting his nearness and the pleasure of the dance wash over her, mentally calming and yet physically exciting.

Then, because she had to know, she asked, "Was it indeed Alf Smith, the man who lived with my mother?"

"It was indeed Alf Smith," he replied, "and I think he's probably a little mad. To be honest, I couldn't persuade him to say very much, but I'm pretty sure he told the truth when he maintained he acted alone. For one thing, there was clearly no one but him camping in the nearest hayloft."

Her eyes widened. "He was sleeping in the hayloft?"

"He must have made it out from London before the bad weather closed in, and then, of course, the snow kept everyone from moving around." He scowled. "And from doing what they were instructed. Clearly, I did not keep you as safe as I promised."

"But I'm fine, and you captured Smith," she said warmly. Then, "But I don't understand why he was so determined to hurt me. Just to get at Uncle Bill?"

"Mainly. Your continued existence seems to offend him. I suspect he feels it unjust that you are returned to your wealthy family while he has nothing—which is entirely his fault since he appears to have been drinking himself out of work for twenty years."

Johnny's thumb stroked her fingers. "Kitty, don't be distressed. He was a vile man who beat Maggie *and* you. And stole from your uncle, though I suggest we don't inquire too closely into the true ownership of the objects in question. I won't even bring up what he has tried to do in the last two months."

She shivered, and Johnny drew her a fraction closer, concern in his gaze.

"I'm not distressed," she assured him. "I'm entirely glad and grateful he is captured and locked up. It just makes no sense to me."

"Nor to me," Johnny agreed. "I suspect it was simply bad luck that brought you and Renwick to his notice again. Without hearing your names, he'd probably have just gone on quietly drinking and starving himself to death."

He gave her a moment, then danced her more exuberantly backward and around so that her skirts swished against her legs. "Forget him. He's done with. Dance with me and plan our wedding. You had better write to your uncle tomorrow."

Her stomach twisted with a sense of loss. For every happiness, there was a price. "If I am to be a duchess, things will never be the same at Maida."

He smiled ruefully. "Things rarely stay the same. Whoever you had married, you would have gone away, lost something of the old closeness. But there will be no question that you see them whenever you wish, however you wish."

"And if word gets out that I was brought up by Bill Renwick?"

"A man of property," Johnny said at once. "Trade, of course, but everyone knows Margaret was banished because of an unsuitable man. The important thing is, you have Winter blood and are therefore a gentlewoman." He leaned closer, causing her breath to catch, *"My gentlewoman."*

⋙⋘

DESPITE THE EXCITEMENT in the middle, at the end of the ball, Johnny found Kitty tired but happy. As he escorted her on her slow, sleepy way to bed, they discussed banns and special licenses, and an awed look spread across her face, as though becoming his bride, his duchess, suddenly became very close, very real.

Johnny wanted it done quickly with a desperation fed by tonight's events. He wanted her beyond question, beyond her doubts or anyone else's. And that was quite beside the lust thrumming through his body. And the little devil sitting on his shoulder who said quite suddenly in his ear, *You don't need to wait.*

She was his, she would marry him, in no more than three

weeks—less, if he could possibly arrange it—and anything that would bind her to him now was desirable, necessary.

She held his arm as they climbed the stairs, and as the rest of the family and guests separated to find their own couches, he held back just a little so that they found themselves alone, turning into the passage that led to her chamber.

He covered her hand with his, and the faint trembling of her fingers, her clear awareness of him and the possibilities ahead, fed his lust like wind to a wildfire.

Johnny had always enjoyed his desires—and their satisfaction—with uncomplicated pleasure. But this, this was different. It had always been different because *she* was. In a way not even Aline had been. From the beginning, something in Kitty had spoken to something in him, melded with him until she was part of him. But there was little spiritual about the effect of her nearness, the curve of her jaw, the slightly parted lips, which had given him such a sweet taste of what passion would be like with her.

While she walked beside him, her breathing quickened, he let his gaze sweep down over her slender neck to the swell of her breasts. He felt something very like a growl form deep in his throat and deliberately dropped his gaze further down the elegant line of her gown over slender waist and hips, imagining the length and softness of her legs…

Even so, he might have fought the fire and let her go, had she not halted at her door and turned to him, lifting her face to his with those luscious lips already parted for his kiss.

And so, he stared down at her for two, maybe three beats of his heart, and then he bent and took her mouth voraciously. He held nothing back, showing her in that one deep, utterly sensual kiss what he wanted of her and how badly. And how sweet and pleasurable it would be.

And when, gasping, she came up for air, he kissed her again, sweeping his hand down her back to her hips and hauling her closer against his hardness. With his free hand, he opened her bedchamber door, and he walked her inside, his mouth fused still to hers.

"No good nights," he whispered against her lips, kicking the door shut behind him. "Not this night…"

By the lamplight, her eyes had clouded with passion. Her mouth was eager beneath his, her body responsive to his every touch. The softness of her breasts, the delicious curves of her waist and hip drove him on. And when her hands found their way under his shirt to caress his shoulders and back, his whole being rippled in response.

He unlaced her with practiced ease, let her stays fall to the ground, and nudged her gown and her chemise together off her shoulders with his lips. And now he could worship her breasts with his eyes and hands and mouth.

She clung to him, breathing wildly, her body adorably flushed and willing.

"My bride," he whispered, between kisses. "My wife…"

"I'm not yet," she gasped, her fingers in his hair as he straightened to lift her out of the gown and carry her to bed.

He smiled, "Not quite yet, but you are mine. Tonight, I'm making you mine." And kissed her mouth again while his own words repeated in his ears. *You are mine. I'm making you mine.*

She loved him, he was sure, but she was *not* yet his before the law or God.

What he was doing was taking advantage, taking away her choice, by means of his own much greater experience of fleshly pleasures. He was rushing something that should be perfect for her. This was no light, impulsive, one night of dalliance. She was under his protection and his mother's, and he was deliberately seducing her to bind her…

He tore his mouth free and hugged her to his galloping heart.

"What am I doing?" he whispered.

"Making love to me," she said unsteadily.

He squeezed his eyes shut, slowly forcing back the beast of his lust. It wasn't exactly contained, but at least his mind was clearer. "I want to. Very badly."

"I want you, too," she whispered. Her lips whispered against his throat, threatening his newfound control.

He drew in a shuddering breath. "I will make it perfect for you. Not tumble you when you are too weary to enjoy it, and I am too tired and desperate to do it as you deserve. Forgive me." He kissed her forehead and her stunned lips and slowly forced himself to release her.

Then, feeling her hurt, abandoned gaze boring into his back, he walked a little stiffly to the door and left her alone.

MANY THINGS BOTHERED Kitty as she lay sleeplessly in bed, gazing up at the ceiling. The sudden, flaring passion between her and the duke, his decision—not hers—to leave unfinished what he had begun. And yet he had begun it with the full intention of taking her to bed. She knew that from every kiss and caress, which had been different from anything that had come before. There had been definite, predatory intent, and God knew she had gloried in it.

And they were to be married quickly.

So why had he stopped? The rake who had known so many beautiful and experienced women. When it came to the point, was she not desirable enough? Not pleasing enough? Or had he really just decided that she was special enough to wait for? She didn't mind that. In fact, she quite liked lying in bed, remembering the intimate feel of his hands and lips. But it was a poor second to his actual presence.

Although her aroused body still hummed with frustrated desire, at least she could smile into the pillow and long for the night, surely not so far away, when he truly would make her his.

Her mind drifted back to the ball and to the other matter that bothered her. The capture of Alf Smith. Which, of course, was a huge burden off her mind, and the fact that it had been accomplished without harm to Johnny was a relief that still made her stomach dizzy. And part of her wished she had seen the flying leap from the trees that had brought him down.

She smiled again, remembering that despite his claiming of the next dance after that, she had been the one to approach him, to ask the questions she needed answered. And she remembered now that he had not wanted to talk about it.

Well, they were at a ball celebrating Christmas, and dancing together had its own attractive distractions. But now she remembered again the faint worry that had flickered and died at the time, that he was keeping something from her.

"Was it indeed Alf Smith, the man who lived with my mother?" she had asked.

And he had replied, *"It was indeed Alf Smith."*

And then, a little later, he had said of Smith, *"He was a vile man who beat Maggie and you."*

He hadn't said, "It was indeed Alf Smith *who lived with your mother."*

And he had called her mother Maggie. Not *Cousin Margaret.*

Tiny things, unimportant things, so why they stuck in her tired, overwhelmed mind, she did not know.

But they did.

Her stomach began to tighten, the constant butterflies no longer pleasant. Because in an *unpleasant* way, everything would fit together, if Alf had told him something he did not want to pass on to her. Something that had, in the end, reminded him not to bed her when he had so clearly wanted to. When she had so clearly wanted to be with him.

She sat up against the pillows. *Dear God, there will be no sleep now...*

But she was being foolish, her exhausted, over-excited mind playing tricks, reading false interpretations into things that were perfectly harmless and could easily mean exactly what she had first assumed.

He did not want to talk about Alf because the man was unrelievedly vile. And why should he not call her mother Maggie when that was how Alf had known her? He had not taken her to bed because he refused to rush her, because they would have the rest of their lives. She was making a fuss about nothing.

And yet still, she did not sleep.

With the first light of morning, she knew what she had to do. She had to speak to Alf herself. Just to be sure.

CHAPTER TWENTY-TWO

THE HOUSEHOLD WOULD sleep late today because of the ball, so all was still quiet when Kitty rose, shivering, washed, and threw on her old gown for ease of fastenings. She wrapped her hair into its old, simple style, put on her boots, shawl, and cloak, and walked out of the house into the rain.

In the stables, she found only one sleepy groom, yawning prodigiously, though when she asked him, he hastily went to wake the under-coachman and prepare the horses. In just a few minutes, they were bowling down the drive and along the slushy, grubby-looking road to the town of Dearham.

A blast of fresh, cold rain had done wonders for her perspective. She went now to set her own mind at rest, not to find out the imaginary secrets her betrothed had kept from her. All the same, she did not want the duke's staff to know where she was going. So, she bade the coachman to let her down in the town square, which was quiet because it was early still and because it was Boxing Day.

Still, she found a housewife to tell her where the town gaol was and walked into the front office.

A sleepy watchman leapt to his feet. "Ma'am! What can I do for you?"

"I understand a prisoner was brought to you last night from Dearham Abbey," she said calmly. "I would like to speak to him."

The watchman scratched his head. "Not sure I can allow that, ma'am. 'Specially as he's violent. Or was last night. Trust me, you wouldn't want to go near him. I certainly don't."

"I don't want to hold his hand," Kitty said dryly. "I want to speak to him, preferably at a safe distance. I am," she added, "a guest of the duchess."

The watchman regarded her doubtfully, running one hand over his unshaven face.

"Well," he said dubiously, at last, "seeing as there's only him in there—I loosed the singing drunks go an hour ago—I suppose you can talk to him through the bars of his cell. You're not to go near him, though."

"I would not dream of it," she assured him.

The watchman sighed, picked up an unfeasibly large ring of keys, and led her through a locked door at the back and down the steps leading to a passage, one side of which was made up of cells, divided from each other by stone walls, and with spars at the front like cages for wild beasts.

The watchman indicated the passage. "Second cell along. Keep to the wall on the right. I'll just be waiting here." And he sat down on the bottom step.

Kitty took a breath for courage, not quite sure what she would find, and then walked briskly into the passage, past the first, empty cell, and paused opposite the second. At first, she could see nothing but a vague, still shape on the pallet against one wall. She glanced back at the watchman, glad, for some reason, that she could still see him.

She cleared her throat and addressed the cell. "Mr. Smith."

With alarming suddenness, the shape flew up, resolving into the figure of a big man standing, gazing at her. His lips curled into what might have been a snarl or a smile, revealing bad teeth and a few blank spaces between.

"Well, well, well, look what the cat dragged in. Her High and Mightiness."

She ignored that. "Why did you try to kill me?"

"I never liked you," Alf Smith said with the same sort of casualness he might have said, "I don't care for oranges."

She frowned. "How can you dislike a baby?"

He stared at her as if she were stupid. "They squawk and cry constantly, demand *everyone's* attention…"

"Meaning my mother's attention," she said flatly, beginning to understand. "She couldn't run around after you because she was too busy looking after me."

"You made her ill," Alf sneered. "And then there was no running after anybody."

"And that inspired you to—" She broke off. "What did you say?" *And then there was no running after anybody.* "You knew her when I was born? Before I was born?"

"Course I did," he said disgustedly.

"But…but what happened to Reginald Penrose?"

"Who's he?"

"My mother's husband," she said dryly. "Did you never meet?"

He laughed. It wasn't a pleasant sound—hoarse and raw and without real amusement. "No, and not surprising, neither. *I* was as close as poor old Maggie ever got to marriage. Though I suppose I was her husband by common law."

The blood had begun singing in Kitty's ears. "Wait a minute. How long did you know Maggie?"

He shrugged. "All her life, more or less. We grew up in Seven Dials together."

No, no, no, that is not right! It can't be right, not now! She tried desperately to fight down the panic. "Then you are saying… Oh, no, *you* are not my father! You would not try to kill your own child!"

He studied her, head on one side. "Truth is, I never cared much whether you were or weren't. I told everyone you weren't mine just to annoy Maggie."

The world seemed to be falling about her ears while she desperately looked for the holes, the lies in what he was telling her. "What did Maggie call me?" she asked in a small voice.

He didn't even think about it, though he said it as a sneer. "Sarah. Sarah this, Sarah that. Bloody Sarah."

"Not…Isabel?"

He regarded her as though she were stupid. "Isabel?" he mimicked. "Who told you that?"

"Vera." She pulled herself together. "Sal. Sal Harris told me."

"Sal, who? Oh, that cow who lived across the landing? I thought she'd taken you, you know, that day I woke up with my head and my bones aching and all my worldly goods gone. But I never heard you cry anymore, so I suppose she didn't. Mind you," he added resentfully, "I got evicted the day after. *That* was your fault, too."

"Why would you think Sal had taken me in?" Kitty asked, trying and failing to make sense of any of this. "Because she and Maggie were friends?"

"Sal was always taking other people's kids. Couldn't have any of her own."

"She has two," Kitty said flatly.

"Not hers," Alf insisted. "But who cares? She still knows you, don't she? You and her boy are pulling some trick on a duke. His nibs up the road there who thinks he's a monkey."

"That's what bothers you," she said slowly, "my connection to the Duke of Dearham. Why?"

"Why do you think?"

"Because you don't want me to be wealthy?"

"Actually, I want you dead—more to spite Bill, you understand. I don't want him to be rich because it's off the back of what he stole from me. *I* should be the rich one."

"Except you drank everything you ever owned," Kitty retorted.

"Not so much that I didn't keep my eye on Bill Renwick and rejoice when he was going under. That stupid Garden of his was never going to make any money, and even he knew it in the end, so he started building a bloody hotel! And all sorts of rich bastards start giving him money for it, and the word is it'll make them all even richer. Especially when this high fallutin' duke enters the picture, wanting to adopt you and give Bill even more of the readies."

"So, you tried to chase the duke away by setting fire to the hotel," she said slowly, "making it an unsafe investment. Only then the duke took me away with him, and he still invested. You meant to kill us both last night."

Without warning, Alf flung himself at the spars of his cells. Kitty jumped, flattening herself against the wall, and he laughed. "I still will, eventually."

"You're insane," she accused.

"Then why are you standing there asking me stupid questions?"

Relief flooded her so hard her knees went weak. She wanted to laugh at herself for being so gullible. "You're lying to me. Making things up."

He bared his teeth again. "Why would I do that?"

"To punish me, to punish Bill Renwick. But I know you're lying because Maggie gave a valuable locket to Sal Harris, a locket I'm very sure did not come from you."

And he did pause, frowning. "What locket?"

"It had my hair inside it. And on the front was a miniature painting of the old Duchess of Dearham."

He was staring at her and then began to grin. "Oh, this is priceless! You're not flim-flamming the duke, are you? You *really* think you're related to him! Because of a lock of baby hair in a necklace, clutched in Sal Harris's greedy hands! That bloody locket was mine—or was after Maggie died because *Sal* gave it to *her*. Only then the stupid cow gave it back to Sal so I wouldn't get it, and Sal never did hand it over. Of course, she and Jimmie were always very thick with Bill Renwick."

Kitty felt her skin turn cold. "No. The locket was Maggie's. She gave it to Sal for her kindness."

"Rubbish, Sal gave it to Maggie to keep her mouth shut."

"About what?"

Alf laughed because he could see she already knew.

SOMEHOW, SHE GOT herself out of there. She wanted to sit down in the street and cry. She wanted to run back to the duke and never let him speak to Alf Smith…except he already *had* spoken to him. What Johnny had said, and didn't say, made sense now. As did his sudden withdrawal from her bedchamber last night.

The duke was a good man. He loved her and had offered her marriage. But neither of them was so naïve as to imagine Alf Smith's daughter could marry him and be his duchess. He would go through with it, though, if he had to. Only he wouldn't make it necessary by risking the conception of a child.

In her heart, her whole being, black despair was spreading like some insidious disease. But it could not drown her love of the duke. She ached for him because he did love her, and Johnny, more than anyone she had ever met, deserved to be happy. But he would not be so with her, not now.

Something dripped off her chin, and she realized she was weeping while stumbling away from the goal, and from the town square where she had left the carriage. She dashed the back of her hand across her face and deliberately straightened her back, trying to pull herself together.

What to do? Where to go?

Back to Uncle Bill, of course, where she belonged.

Tears threatened afresh because she had missed him and the boys so much…and she could not even begin to imagine how much she would miss the duke, who had come to mean so much so quickly.

Coming to a deserted alley, she ducked around the corner and flattened herself against the wall, gasping.

She had money in her reticule. Money the duke had expected

her to spend, only she never had, apart from the couple of shillings she had used to bribe poor Aidan the footman to fetch her a hackney in London. Right across the road from her now was the Black Bull Inn, from where she knew the mail coaches went up to London.

Her misery formed into tasks and those she could deal with.

Straight-backed, she walked out of the alley and across the road to the inn. A mail coach was due to leave in an hour, and she was lucky that someone had just canceled their ticket, so she could have a place inside. She handed over the required coin and went into the coffee room, where she asked for coffee and writing implements, and refused the offer of breakfast that she would never be able to eat.

Having drunk her coffee and written her letter, she left the inn and hurried back to the square where the carriage still waited for her. The rain had gone off, and the under-coachman was standing at the horses' heads, gossiping with a couple of fellows who had probably spilled out of the tavern on the corner.

Seeing her, he immediately sprang around to the carriage door.

"No, I'm not going back just yet," she told him. "I find I have more to do. But I would like you to return to Dearham Abbey now and see that this is given to His Grace." She handed over her letter.

He took it, frowning. "I'm to leave you here? But how will you get back?"

"His Grace will give you any further orders," she said pleasantly. "Thank you, Jeremy." And she spun away before she choked, hastening back the way she had come, to the inn and the mail coach that would take her home.

JOHNNY WAS A little surprised that Kitty had not risen to join the family in bidding farewell to the guests who had stayed after the ball. He supposed she was exhausted after her busy day and traumatic evening. And he had hardly helped by all but assaulting her in her own bedchamber. He had let his hunger, his need to possess her, overcome his patience and good sense, at least for a little. Although he knew why, that didn't excuse his behavior, and he was eager to see Kitty, to assure himself he hadn't frightened or hurt her.

And, in truth, he just wanted to be with her.

He wondered if he could just sneak up to her rooms without anyone noticing. But then, perhaps that wasn't such a good idea either. So he sent Martha.

"Will you go up and see if Kitty is awake?" he asked her casually.

She snorted. "Oh, I wish Meg was here to see this."

"To see what?" he asked with what dignity he could muster.

"Our brother chained to propriety by love. At last!"

He hurled a cushion at her head, which she easily intercepted before tossing it back and sweeping, laughing, from the room.

Johnny let the smile die on his lips, realizing that his sister had a point. He had always known he would have to marry one day to produce heirs, and one of the things that had always bothered him about the whole matter was whether or not his wife would expect him to remain faithful. And if she did, whether he could, for he had become so used to following his desires wherever they led. Somehow, it had never entered his head that he would *want* to be faithful. He had not truly imagined himself capable of that kind of love. But Kitty…

The smile returned to his lips, a different kind of smile that was totally involuntary. Kitty was everything.

Martha sauntered back into the room. "She is awake, for she's not in bed. She must have gone for a walk. I expect it would clear your head, too."

"I expect it would," he said amiably, rising and strolling to the door. "If I had a thick head, which I don't.

"Celibate *and* sober," Martha marveled. "You are clearly an imposter, sir. What have you done with my brother?"

"I left him crying over his beer for the good old days."

Martha's laughter followed him from the room. He was still smiling as he reached the front hall, shrugging into his greatcoat, and noticed the letter on the silver salver. Picking it up, since it was addressed to him, he unfolded it and stopped in his tracks.

My dear Johnny,

I hope you will permit me to address you so one more time in parting, as part we both know we must. I have spoken to Alf Smith, and I know I am not the child of your Cousin Margaret. In no way am I fit to be your duchess. I suspect you knew this, too, when we spoke last night, and I thank you for trying to spare me. You are too kind and too honorable to bid me go, and so I have taken matters into my own hands.

Your family has shown me nothing but kindness, so it is with heavy heart that I ask you to pass my farewells and my humble gratitude to the duchess, your mother, to Lord Peter, Lord and Lady Harry, and Lord and Lady Calvert. I am honored to have met your family and friends, especially Princess Hagerin.

For Your Grace, I have no words. Only the love I will ever bear you and the cause of your happiness could have made me leave you. I step out now upon another course and wish you only the best in yours.

Your servant,
Kitty Renwick.

He stared at the letter, feeling a surge of something very like irritation among the panic.

"Daniel!" he called to the footman by the front door. "Where did this letter come from?"

"Jeremy, the under-coachman brought it."

"Did he, by God?" Without further discussion, Johnny strode from the house, barely giving Daniel time to wrench open the door for him.

He all but ran to the stables, and Jeremy clearly saw him coming, for he detached himself from the carriage he was washing down and walked toward him with the sort of reluctance that grasped he was in for the dressing-down of a lifetime.

Johnny had no time for that. "Where did you take her?"

Jeremy didn't pretend to misunderstand. "To Dearham. I waited for her in the square as she asked, for about an hour, until she came back, gave me a letter to be delivered to you, and sent me home."

And you went? But of course he did. And Johnny would not waste time in unjust and unproductive scolding. "Do you know where she went then?"

Jeremy shook his head.

"When was this? Are you just returned?"

"Only ten minutes or so. By the time I left her in Dearham, it must have been heading for eleven."

"And the London mail leaves when?"

"Eleven," Jeremy replied, with the knowledge of the man who had frequently been sent with all speed to catch it arriving or departing.

"Then I've missed her," he said flatly. But he knew where she was going. He just hoped he would be fast enough to catch her at the coaching inn in London. His curricle would be fastest...only he needed a chaperone for Kitty, and the curricle would only accommodate one passenger.

"The light traveling coach," he said abruptly, already striding back to the house. "In ten minutes."

"You're going *now*?" In the morning room, his mother stared at him in clear consternation. "When the house is full of your guests?"

Johnny shrugged impatiently. "There is only Calton, Harborough, and Dornan, and they'll be gone soon enough. The rest are family."

"But where are you going?" she asked, bewildered.

Johnny drew in his breath, but he couldn't not tell them. Not when he needed Martha to come with him. His sister and Aline sat gazing at him from the sofa while Calvert leaned one shoulder against the mantelpiece, and Peter gazed out the window.

"London," Johnny said briskly. "Because Kitty has bolted there."

"Oh God," Martha said resignedly. "I knew it was too good to be true. What did you do to her?"

Johnny kicked at the chair leg in front of him. "I kept from her something I should have told her immediately. And now she has probably misconstrued my reasons." He drew in a breath, and for the first time ever, he felt like his father glaring around his family. "You should know Kitty is not who we believed she was. She is not Margaret's daughter, after all, but I will still marry her. Do I have your support?"

"If she's not Margaret's daughter, who on earth is she?" the duchess demanded, bewildered.

"No one," Johnny said on a slightly shaky laugh. "Everyone. And it does not matter who she is. Do I have your support?"

"Yes," Martha said. "And I speak for Meg, too. Peter? You have to agree—admit you've never seen him so…complete."

Peter—stern, upright Peter, who really should have been the duke—scowled. "We have to consider what is owed to the family."

Johnny's smile was twisted. "Am I not family?"

Peter's eyes widened, and a rueful smile touched his lips. "I have never seen you so…un-restless, so settled. What do you mean to do?"

"I have no time to explain it. But nothing that will bring disgrace either to Kitty or the rest of us. I'll make sure of that."

"Then go and bring her home," Peter said and stalked out of

the room.

"Who'd have thought it?" Martha murmured. "Mama?"

"I wanted Margaret's daughter," her mother whispered. "But I like your Kitty."

"It's the best we can do," Johnny said gently. "Martha, will you come and play propriety for me?"

"I'll come," Aline said, rising from the sofa. "Lady Martha has children to care for, and Her Grace needs family support with her guests."

Johnny frowned. "But you can't come to London. I've received no word that you are no longer in danger."

Deliberately, Aline ran her hand over her flat stomach. "Have you ever seen a woman looking *less* with child at seven months at least? *This* is my safety, and the sooner I spread the word, the better. People might talk, of course, but I don't care if you don't. I am still a chaperone to your cousin for as long as you need me to be."

Johnny smiled at her. There was no one like Aline, and he was privileged to have her friendship. "Five minutes?"

"Four," she said, already gliding through the door.

CHAPTER TWENTY-THREE

FROM THE COACHING inn, Kitty walked to Seven Dials. Which, since darkness had fallen some time ago, might not have been wise. Seven Dials, once built for the wealthy to rival the beauty of Covent Garden, had never had the chance. The ornate buildings had never been sold as intended, and in no time, they were occupied by the scaff and raff of London, the poor and the criminal, penniless immigrants and desperate folk with nowhere else to go.

Not for the first time, she wondered why the Harrises chose to keep living here now that Jimmie ran a successful business. Perhaps here they could be the big fish in a little pond, and certainly, the criminal elements seemed to leave the family alone. All the same, it hardly seemed safe for Vera to wander these streets without protection.

Or Kitty. She walked down the middle of the roads as much as she could, caught no one's eye, and ignored all remarks flung at her from doorways, most of which were ribald rather than threatening. She wondered if Bill Renwick's name would still be enough to get her out of trouble.

In the end, she didn't need to try it out. She arrived unhurt at the Harris's building and banged on the door until it opened a crack and then wide.

"Kitty! What are you doing here on your own? Come in,

come in!" Sal dragged her inside by the arm, closed, and locked the door before leading her to the stairs. "I thought you were in the country with your duke."

"I was. I had to come back."

"Have you just got here, then? Because Jimmie's taken Vera and Luke up to Maida."

"Oh. That was bad luck. But actually, Mrs. Harris, it was you I wanted to talk to."

Sal took her into the big parlor, where a fire blazed in the grate. "Sit here, and I'll get you something to eat. You look as if you haven't slept for days."

"I slept a little on the coach," Kitty said vaguely. But she sat and took off her hat and cloak and gazed into the flames until Sal reappeared with a plate of sandwiches and a glass of milk. "Thank you," she said with surprisingly sincere gratitude. "I've just realized how hungry I am."

"Does your uncle know you're here?"

Kitty shook her head. "Not yet."

"Well, eat up and warm up, and then I'll walk you to the hackney stand."

Kitty nodded and swallowed the rest of her sandwich. "Mrs. Harris, do you still have Maggie's locket?"

"'Course I do, love."

Kitty met her gaze. "It was never Maggie's, was it? It was yours. Who really gave it to you?"

Sal's gaze fell. She was silent a moment. "I did give it to Maggie once. And she gave it back to me to keep it from her old man, so I didn't lie to you or your duke."

"Not quite. I don't really care about that, though. Where did you get it, Mrs. Harris? For I'm pretty sure *you* are not the duke's Cousin Margaret."

Sal collapsed on a stool before the fire and dropped her head into her hands. "Oh God, Kitty, how did you find out?"

"Alf Smith. He told me you couldn't have children, but he's a nasty, lying creature, and I'd like to know the truth from you."

Sal sighed. "He didn't lie about that. I suppose for once the truth let him serve up pain enough. No, I can't have children. Broke my heart and Jimmie's. But we took my niece's baby, Toby, when she couldn't look after him and brought him up as our own." She paused. "And then there was Mrs. Penrose."

"Cousin Margaret," Kitty murmured.

"I cleaned her little house for her. She was a nice lady and good to me. So even when she couldn't afford to pay me anymore, I went round to see her. She was devastated when her husband died, leaving her with a child, but them fancy relations she hinted about never came near her. And she wouldn't ask them to help, though I begged her to. But she didn't live long after her man."

Sal swallowed and swiped at her eyes. "She came here to die. Stayed with Jimmie and me, asked us to take her little Isabel when she'd gone. And she gave me her last piece of jewelry to pay for the child's keep or to give to her when she grew up, perhaps. She didn't really make it clear. And in any case, I gave it to Maggie to stop her telling anyone that the child was Mrs. Penrose's."

"And you changed the child's name," Kitty said, "to Vera."

Sal nodded once. "We loved her to distraction. Always did. Always will. I couldn't bear her to be taken away, even by her own people, even to make her rich. By the time that Dunne came poking around here, Vera only wanted Luke. And I didn't mind doing *you* the favor... And Maggie had the right name, which helped." She smiled faintly. "Did you know Maggie even called you Sarah after me?"

"I guessed."

"I was touched," Sal admitted. She raised her eyes to Kitty. "But why are you here? Didn't it work out with your duke?"

"No." Kitty swallowed. "It could never have worked out. It was based on a lie, and you must have known I could not flim-flam him into marriage."

There was a long silence, during which Kitty consumed another sandwich and drank her milk.

Sal stood up. "Come on. I'll go with you back to Maida. It's time I told the truth to your Uncle Bill."

⮞⮞⮞✳⮜⮜⮜

THE GARDENS WERE eerily dark. The hackney dropped them at the back entrance, nearest to the cottage, and Sal knocked Kitty's hand away as she tried to pay. Kitty let her and moved up the path toward the cottage.

Although the lantern hanging by the front door was lit, there was no glow from within the house.

"They must have gone up to the pavilion for a private party," Sal said behind her.

"I expect so. Who else were they expecting?"

"I'm not sure. Your cousin, Pete, I think, and his parents. A few old friends."

"Why didn't you go?" Kitty asked curiously. She unhooked the lantern and used it to light their way to the main drive.

Sal's smile was twisted. "Jimmie and me have been fighting. He thinks I shouldn't have let this masquerade go so far, that it's no wonder Toby lies. And I told him he only wants Vera to be a duke's cousin."

"Does he?" Kitty asked evenly, while every part of her that could hurt did.

"I don't know," Sal said. "I don't think he does. Mostly he doesn't want her to throw herself away on Luke."

"And now he has ammunition…"

"If he tells Bill the truth and persuades Bill to tell your duke."

"That would be best," Kitty agreed, while her insides seemed to crumble.

"Would it?" Sal's gaze was on her face. "I rather got the impression that you were in love with the duke. And that he was sweet on you. He might not marry Maggie's brat."

"He won't," Kitty said with certainty. "But that has nothing to do now with what you do or don't tell Uncle Bill."

The upper part of the pavilion, which actually had a fireplace and a chimney, was lit up like the Dearham Abbey ballroom, although there was no music. As they drew nearer, talk and laughter drifted down to them, along with the clink of glasses and the smell of wine and beer and food.

"Just like a ball night," Kitty said lightly. Except no one as much as glanced out of the upper windows.

Entering the pavilion, she blew out the lantern and left it at the foot of the lit staircase. She hung her cloak and hat over the back of a chair. Sal dropped hers on top. Then they went up together, and in spite of everything, Kitty's throat ached to be back with her family. Her true family. Not the Dearhams, and certainly not Alf Bloody Smith.

The old familiarity hit her like a battering ram. Various friends and family members were scattered across the various tables, everyone nibbling and drinking as they caught up with news and jokes. There was a tiny instant when everyone stopped talking, and then a cheer erupted.

"Kitty!"

A chair fell over as Uncle Bill sprang up from the corner table and charged across the room to fold her in his strong arms.

It was too much. The tears spilled, silently down her cheeks onto his coat as she hugged him fiercely, and he murmured her name over and over into her hair. And then, laughing and crying at once, she could embrace Rob and Dan and wave to the entire room. Until, over Dan's shoulder, she saw the man standing half-hidden among the shadows by the corner table, where Uncle Bill had been sitting. Where Jimmie and Vera and Luke still sat.

The man was tall, seemed ridiculously well-dressed for this place. She had to blink several times because he looked so like the Duke of Dearham. And then he moved out of the shadows toward her, and her breath vanished.

"Oh, no," she whispered, dropping her arms from Dan. "Not

you, not you…" She waved one helpless hand. "How did you even get here?"

"I failed to catch you in time at the Golden Cross and came straight here." He stood before her larger than life and ten times as handsome and dear and wonderful, and she had no idea how to bear his presence.

"Why is it," he said softly, "that whenever you say goodbye to me, it is only by letter? Letters stained with tears?"

Of course he would have seen that, damn him, but did he have to bring it up when she was held together only by the weakest thread? She forced herself to meet his gaze. "Because I don't have the courage to say it in person."

And his eyes, wary and veiled, suddenly melted. He took her hand and raised it to his lips, and the blood sang in her veins.

"Oh, don't, please don't," she choked out. "Your Grace—"

"Come, let us sit down and talk. You should hear what we have been discussing."

Somehow, she sat beside Vera, leaning into her hug. It was just one more task to deal with before she fell apart in her own little bedchamber. On her other side, making everything twice as difficult, the duke folded his long person into the next chair, and again she forced herself to meet his gaze.

"I am not your cousin," she said bluntly. "I think you know that."

"I know that," he agreed steadily.

She drew in her breath. "Vera is your cousin."

"So I understand."

It didn't seem to have quite the cataclysmic effect she had imagined. "You knew that, too?"

"I began to suspect. Dunne is very good at tracing people, and the building did seem to be important."

"Anyway, no offense to His Grace," Vera said cheekily, "but who wants to be a nob?"

"Vera," Luke said warningly.

"Well, we've had all that! His Grace can give us a wedding

present if he wants, and throw any work he likes your way, but I'm not going to live with his family, and I don't want any public acknowledgments. My dad is going to give me away, and I'm going to marry *you*."

"Jimmie," Sal said, low, and her husband looked at her, both pained and angry. Perhaps she couldn't bear it, for she looked instead at Uncle Bill. "I'm sorry, Bill. It was a hard secret to keep, especially from you and Mary. And I shouldn't have lied about Kitty's birth name and set you all off on the wrong track."

"No, you probably shouldn't," Uncle Bill agreed heavily. "But I've already told Jimmie I understand why you did."

"The thing is, Mrs. Harris," the duke said, "you are very good at keeping secrets. And since it's what everyone seems to want, I'm more than happy to leave it that way. Though I do congratulate you on your daughter's character and will do anything either she or you wish in order to help her." He glanced from Sal back to Kitty. "From the world's point of view, nothing has changed. For all anyone knows to the contrary, Kitty, you are my blood relation. The great Ludovic Dunne has said so. No one will look down their noses at my choice of bride, and no one will ostracize you, cut you, or otherwise make your life unpleasant."

She stared at him, a wicked surge of hope mingling with disbelief. "You would live a lie? *You?*"

He shrugged. "Actually, I would do anything to live with you. But the lie will not be between us. It was one we told inadvertently in good faith, and if the world loves you as my betrothed already, I see no reason to tell them anything else."

His eyes, suddenly, unforgivably, were teasing. "But if you really want to, we can tell everyone you are the illegitimate daughter of one Maggie and, probably, her violent paramour Alf Smith, the same Alf Smith who is about to be executed or perhaps merely transported. Society, being what it is, will only laugh at me, and I find I don't really care. But it will be *very* unkind to you. You will be lonely, uninvited, the butt of cruel jokes, and treated as a social leper. It is not fair, but it is the way of the so-called *polite world*, and until we can change it, I think we can be pragmatic enough to be happy."

"If only for the children's sakes," Vera said irrepressibly.

Kitty gazed wildly from one to the other, and then at her uncle and cousins and at Luke and the Harrises. "You have all decided this, haven't you? Even before I got here. That I should lie and pretend for a coronet!"

Vera leaned closer and whispered in her ear, "For the man you love."

With a sound very like a sob, Kitty sprang to her feet. "You don't understand! It's *spoiled*! *I* am spoiled!" And she bolted for the door, rushing past surprised guests and throwing herself down the stairs, grabbing her cloak as she went.

She stormed out with some vague intention of going back to the cottage, to her own, familiar bedchamber, and curling up into a ball, alone with the realization that nothing could ever be the same. But by the time she realized she had forgotten the lantern, she was facing the dark path to the lily pond.

She halted, breathing deeply, and a voice behind her said, "I thought you would come this way."

Johnny. *The duke.* She closed her eyes. How much more strength would she need?

She felt movement beside her, heard the striking of flint, and then a light glowed on the ground, showing her Johnny's beloved figure crouched over the lantern. In profile, his face was handsome and tranquil, and yet she knew, somehow, that he was not calm at all. There was a slight tightness to his jaw, to his lips, that betrayed discomfort at the least. He closed the lantern and swung it up.

Only then did he look at her. "Shall we talk?"

And perhaps because he asked rather than insisted, she was helpless to refuse. He offered her his arm, and she took it. Did she imagine the faint relaxation of his muscles, the relieved twitch of his lips?

"Oh, what is there to say, Johnny?" she whispered.

"Everything," he said, moving forward up the path, "if you still call me by my name."

"It has become a habit in my head. Look, I thank you—God knows I thank you—for trying to salvage our plans and for being prepared to sacrifice your honor in such a way, but I cannot lie, live a lie in order to let you marry a nobody from the Seven Dials gutters."

He nodded as though taking in her points. "First, any sacrifice would be in letting you go, and my honor, like everything else, is wrapped up in you. We have already dealt with the lie part—really, it's just a game to get around the foolish rules of society that we had no hand in making but have some chance, perhaps, of changing. Which brings us to you, my nobody from the Seven Dials gutters."

"Are you making fun of me?" she asked in a small voice that she hated because really, she wanted to scream at the world, shout them down, shout Johnny down for his foolishness.

"God, no. I'm making fun of society's judgments. You are an exemplary young woman, kind and hard-working. You look after your family and help with the family business. You have been sheltered and cared for as much, if in a slightly different way from, my own sisters. You are pure, innocent, and sunny by nature. Now, me… My nature may be me mostly amiable, or at least sanguine, but I am far from pure and innocent. From a mischievous child, I grew into a youth who thwarted his family and happily embarrassed them over his frequent scandals. I fought duels, raked my way across Oxford and London without a care for my responsibilities or how my behavior might reflect on my family. But the truth is, I got away with everything because I was a nobleman, the heir to a duke."

"There is more to you than that," she said quietly.

"Yes. As there is more to you than the young woman I described. Or the child from the gutters who never did anything wrong. But society—the society I was born into and where we must live if we are to be together—will not forgive you for your birth. Although you could not help that any more than I could help mine."

He lit the way up the steps to the lily pond, and her mouth fell open. The area around the pond was lined with what looked like silk cushions and blankets.

"What...how did these things get here?" she asked, astonished.

"They're from my coach," he said apologetically. "I thought I would find you here when I first arrived, and since it's sheltered by overhanging trees from the rain and the worst of the winds, I thought we might as well be comfortable as we talked."

She waved one hand in a helpless gesture of dismissal. "Talking changes nothing. Life is not a fairytale after all, and what we know now *spoils* what we had."

"How? Do you love me less?"

"Of course not."

"You cannot believe I love you less?"

She gazed up at him, her heart beating hard at the boldness of what she was about to say. "You left me last night. You could not bring yourself to take me in the end because whatever you say now, I *am* spoiled in your eyes. I could not live with your contempt, however secret you made it."

His jaw actually dropped. "*That* is what you think?"

She dragged her gaze free of the growing intensity of his.

He said, "So I followed you here to Maida, worried sick for your safety, for...what?"

"Kindness," she whispered. "Your sense of what is right. But *this* would not be right. Not anymore."

Her hand had fallen from his arm when they had turned to face each other, but he reached out slowly and took it back. Stepping closer, he drew her hand up and placed it on the back of his neck.

"Look at me, Kitty."

Knowing it was a mistake, she looked anyway.

"Never in my life," he said deliberately, "have I pursued a

woman from *kindness*. I followed you because I love you and want to marry you. I let you go last night for all sorts of honorable reasons, none of which were to do with your birth. But if you knew the effort it took to drag myself away, let alone go to sleep with such raging arousal, you would pity me, not run from me."

He released her hand, and for some reason, she let it lie at his nape where he had left it. One arm slipped loosely about her waist. He cupped her cheek. "I'm no revolutionary. But your birth matters not one jot, not to you and me."

"But it *does*, Johnny! You must see…"

"Call me a coxcomb," he interrupted softly. "But I think you liked me long before I mentioned Cousin Margaret to you."

"You know I did."

"And as I recall, I kissed you before I realized you were the woman I was looking for. Attraction was always there between us and grew quickly into something much more, something we have no right to ignore, for our own sakes, for each other's. What right do I have to cause your unnecessary suffering? *What right do you have to cause mine?*"

She stared at him, the somehow novel idea that she could cause him pain echoing around her mind like a cry in the darkness. The duke was just a man.

Just a man…

A desperately beloved man who even now lowered his head and took her mouth.

$$ \cdot\!\!\!\!-\!\!\!\!\gg\!\!\!\text{(e.9)}\!\!\!\ll\!\!\!\!-\!\!\!\!\cdot $$

CHAPTER TWENTY-FOUR

THERE WAS NOTHING she could do about it, nothing she wanted to do. Helpless in her wondrous new discovery, under the onslaught of his warm, silken mouth, she could only hang in his arms, absorbing his love and the sweet pleasure of his kiss.

Until, with a sob, she grasped his hair between her fingers and kissed him back with all her hurt and anguish and passion. And sweet, desperate happiness. The kiss became another, deeper, and with his coat and her cloak thrust aside, she plastered herself to his body in a purely instinctive need to be closer to him.

His hips moved, and his legs, walking her backward in a luscious full-body caress. He swung her off his feet, lowering her to the ground in one arm while the other was busy about something she could neither see nor care about when she was so absorbed in kissing him.

She landed on cushions and blankets by the side of the pond. By the time she realized he was unfastening her cloak, his greatcoat was gone.

"What are you doing?" she murmured hazily against his lips.

"Seducing you," he whispered, "since it's the only way to convince you that I love you beyond anything the world could ever throw at us. And because I want to so badly that I will explode before I can lay my hands on a special license."

A gurgle of laughter escaped her, immediately lost in another deep, sensual kiss that she could feel right down to her toes. He tugged blankets over them, making their space cozy and warm despite the cold. There was little moonlight, but the glow of the lantern showed her his beloved face, his throat, and shoulders as he tugged off his cravat and wriggled out of his coat and waistcoat and shirt.

With eager, wondering hands, she explored the breadth of his shoulders, the hard muscle moving beneath smooth skin as he freed her from her gown, kissing each new area of skin he uncovered, his mouth open and hot, worshipping, unbelievably arousing.

The massive heat from his body seemed to have invaded hers as he caressed her naked breasts and curled his tongue around her nipple. She gasped, arching into him, and as if he had been waiting for just this moment, he tugged her gown and underclothes over her hips and free of her. She pushed at the waist of his pantaloons, wanting only more of his skin against hers.

In moments, the hot ridge of his naked arousal pressed against her stomach, and his hands, his wonderful, tender hands, smoothed over her hips and thighs, moving slowly, teasingly inward to what had become the raging core of her desire.

His breathing was ragged. There was more than a hint of desperation in his clouded, hungry eyes. Perhaps it was reflected in hers, for at his first touch between her thighs, she moaned and pushed into his fingers. He caressed, and her whole body shook in wonder, and then he was within her, huge and shocking.

Staring down into her eyes, he gave her a moment to get used to it, then gently rocked. The world began to spin off its axis once more, and she clung to him, her only anchor as they became one sweet, achingly joyous whole.

JOHNNY WAS AN experienced man. He was used to giving and receiving uninhibited pleasure. But this, with Kitty, was different and *new*. She had no idea how to please a man or herself until he showed her, and yet her immediate enjoyment of his caresses, her desire to touch him, to pleasure him, too, moved him as no other woman ever had, intensifying his arousal and his joy beyond anything he had ever known.

Love, it seemed, was the ultimate pleasure, in the physical as every other aspect of life.

And she took the hurt along with the bliss, trusting and passionate and...*Kitty*.

They lay together on his bundle of carriage cushions beneath the blankets, her tangle of hair trailing across his chest.

"Now, will you marry me?" he asked, running her hair through his fingers.

She nodded once, smiling, then propped her chin up on his chest. "Was I being foolish?"

"No more than I with my over-complicated notions of my own honor over your needs. Tomorrow, I'll see about the special license."

"Will I come back with you to the townhouse?"

"That would be improper," he said with mock primness. "You would have no chaperone since Aline has been persuaded to stay at the embassy, showing off her unpregnant state until word gets around that she is definitely not carrying any possible Hagerin heir."

"And then she'll be safe?"

"I believe so. Why don't you stay with your uncle, and we can be married here quietly before I take you home to Dearham Abbey as my bride? Perhaps, in the spring, we could go on a wedding journey to France and Italy and Greece. Maybe even Constantinople since we have friends there."

"We do?"

"Lord and Lady Wenning who, you might say, were responsible for our first meeting."

She smiled and kissed his chest. "You don't even remember that."

"Actually, I do. I was drawn to you, you know, but you were too respectable for me to trifle with."

"And now I'm not?" she teased.

He grinned. "Not after what you have just done. And no one married to Johnny Dearham could be considered entirely respectable, but I suppose we will just have to change minds."

"Starting with my uncle's. What if someone comes up here looking for us?" She didn't move, though, and neither did he, except to roll her and lay his head on her breasts.

"I don't think your family is that daft," he said.

In the end, it was the cold that drove him, reluctantly, to sit and gather their clothes. They dressed each other, and he pinned up her hair, and then, leaving the cushions and blankets under the tree, he put his arm around her waist, and they walked together toward their new life.

EPILOGUE

T HREE DAYS LATER, the Duke of Dearham's light traveling coach ate up the miles to Dearham Abbey, just a little too quickly for Kitty. Despite her husband's assurance that they had the whole family's support, she could not quite believe they would welcome her return as the duchess without serious misgivings, at the very least.

So, she chattered about other things, about Renwick's Hotel, which had opened to the public two days ago, and where she and Johnny had spent their wedding night, in tasteful if luxurious comfort. Of course, the thought of her deliciously wanton wedding night still made her blush, so she said hastily, "I was glad to see Toby working there. I believe Uncle Bill will finally whip him into shape."

"Well, he has no room for slackers," Johnny agreed. "But I think the hotel will do very well with the richer travelers. Especially with the poorer using the other entrance so that they don't offend the wealthy."

"No, but the poorer traveler will still be happy to be under the same roof as nobility."

Johnny moved and covered her hand, which was nervously folding the material of her gown into tiny, unnecessary pleats. "Kitty. Stop worrying. In any case, they'll be gone soon, and we'll have the whole place to ourselves for weeks. Look, there's the

Abbey."

She hung onto his hand as they bounced along the hard, frosty road well into Dearham land and then turned up the gracious drive to the house. Probably to distract her or give her courage or both, he bent and kissed her. So by the time the carriage pulled up at the front of the house, she was pleasantly dazed.

Footmen hurried down the steps from the house, closely followed by Martha and Lord Calvert with the children. By the time the carriage door was opened, and the steps let down, the dowager herself had appeared in the portico, escorted by Lord Peter.

As Johnny handed Kitty down, she saw that everyone, even the dowager, was smiling. Martha ran to her, laughing. "Welcome home, Your Grace!"

"Oh, my, that's me," Kitty said with awe, hugging Martha back.

Everyone was embracing Johnny or slapping him on the back. Peter and Calvert kissed Kitty's cheek, and the children clung to her hands, dragging her up the steps to where her mother-in-law gravely waited.

Kitty's heart thudded as she curtseyed. "I'm so sorry, ma'am," she blurted.

And the dowager's lips twitched into a genuinely amused smile. "For what, my dear? Finally taming my son? On the contrary, we are in your debt." She drew Kitty to her, kissing her cheek, then turned and walked her into the house, where the entire staff and Great-Aunt Augusta seemed to have assembled.

Johnny was beside her once more. Peter shouted, "Three cheers for the duke and duchess!"

The cheering almost deafened her. She couldn't stop smiling as Johnny led her between the applauding servants, across the hall, and up the staircase.

"You see?" Johnny whispered in her ear. "Everything is fine."

And she realized at last that everything was. More than fine. It was joyful.

About Mary Lancaster

Mary Lancaster lives in Scotland with her husband, three mostly grown-up kids and a small, crazy dog.

Her first literary love was historical fiction, a genre which she relishes mixing up with romance and adventure in her own writing. Her most recent books are light, fun Regency romances written for Dragonblade Publishing: *The Imperial Season* series set at the Congress of Vienna; and the popular *Blackhaven Brides* series, which is set in a fashionable English spa town frequented by the great and the bad of Regency society.

Connect with Mary on-line – she loves to hear from readers:

Email Mary:
Mary@MaryLancaster.com

Website:
www.MaryLancaster.com

Newsletter sign-up:
http://eepurl.com/b4Xoif

Facebook:
facebook.com/mary.lancaster.1656

Facebook Author Page:
facebook.com/MaryLancasterNovelist

Twitter:
@MaryLancNovels

Amazon Author Page:
amazon.com/Mary-Lancaster/e/B00DJ5IACI

Bookbub:
bookbub.com/profile/mary-lancaster